The Golden Book of
365 STORIES

The Golden Book of
365 STORIES

A STORY FOR EVERY DAY OF THE YEAR

By Kathryn Jackson · Pictures by Richard Scarry

GOLDEN PRESS · NEW YORK

Western Publishing Company, Inc.

Racine, Wisconsin

Thirty-second Printing, 1981
GOLDEN®, A GOLDEN BOOK® and GOLDEN PRESS® are trademarks of
Western Publishing Company, Inc.

I resolve

One Little Pig

JANUARY 1

Said one little pig, on New Year's Day,
"Though I've always liked having my own way—
Right now, with the year all span-brand new,
I resolve that I'll try a new way, too!"

He wrote on a paper, "I'll just stop pushing,
And, when folks say 'quiet!' I'll start shushing.
I'll share my apples with friends I make—
And I may even, might even, share my cake!"

He wrote on a paper, and did it, too.
And he did make friends, yes, one or two—
And he did make three and even more—
Why, in one, two, three, his friends were four:

A very small pig that hates a push,
A very old pig that loves a shush,
A policeman pig, who's an apple eater,
And his mother, who has a new eggbeater

For beating up eggs, for baking cake.
"Umhummm," she says. "That's just what I'll make
For one little pig who's as good as gold,
With the New Year already nine hours old!"

Mr. Lion's Northern Winter

JANUARY 2

MR. LION decided that he simply could not stand another hot, African summer. So he ordered a ticket to northern parts, and off he drove to the airport.

"Watch out for those terrible northern winters," his friends advised as they saw him off. "Take care you don't freeze as hard as stone!"

So as soon as his plane arrived in New York, Mr. Lion took an apartment with a huge fireplace, and put in an enormous supply of hickory logs.

Then Mr. Lion began to enjoy life.

He went on picnics and swimming parties with his new neighbors, and played tennis with them in the park. And one day, they all took a boat trip around Manhattan Island, and saw all the sights, even the Statue of Liberty.

Never had he enjoyed a summer so much.

It was over all too soon, and Mr. Lion prepared for winter. He built an enormous fire, and settled down by it with all his favorite books.

Since his apartment was steam-heated besides, the heat was soon terrific.

"Worse than an African summer!" cried poor Mr. Lion, fanning himself. "Still, one doesn't fancy freezing as hard as stone!"

And when his new friends stopped by to take him ice-skating, it was all they could do to get him to put his nose outside!

But once he was out, Mr. Lion had the surprise of his life. Even little babies were out having fun in the beautiful white snow.

"Oh wait!" he cried. "I must write to my African friends, and tell them how wrong they were!"

He scribbled on a post card: "Having wonderful time. Will write when I can."

Then away he went, skating, skiing, and tobogganing all through the long, not-too-cold winter.

But unfortunately, the post card Mr. Lion had sent was one of the Public Library, with a great stone lion on each side of the steps.

"Horrors!" cried his African friends. "Poor old lion *has* frozen—just as we expected. You see? There he sits—hard as stone—with some other poor chap! He says he will write when he can, but it's easy to see that he'll never thaw out again!"

And though they felt very sad for Mr. Lion, they couldn't help feeling just a little pleased, too, to think they had been so right all along!

You Never Know

JANUARY 3

ALL WEEK Jerry had been coasting down the hill on his new Christmas sled. And now he was tired of coasting.

"I wish I'd asked for skates for Christmas instead of a sled," he told his mother. "But I guess you never do know before Christmas what you'll want most after—"

"Well, Billy asked for skates," smiled his mother. "Maybe he'll lend you his for a bit."

Jerry was sure that anyone lucky enough to have skates wouldn't lend them to anyone—not even his best friend. But he took his sled and went down to the pond to watch the skaters, anyway. Round and round went his friend Billy. But oddly enough, Billy seemed to be watching the boys and girls coasting down the hill. And he didn't even smile till he caught sight of Jerry.

Then he came hurrying over.

"Hi, Jerry!" he called. "Why aren't you coasting?"

"I'm a little tired of coasting," said Jerry. "I'm kind of wishing I could skate."

"Are you really?" cried Billy. "That's wonderful—'cause I'm kind of wishing I could go coasting. Want to trade for a while?"

In two winks, the trade was made and Jerry was out on the pond. Skating was lots of fun, even though he did wobble, and Jerry liked it.

But when he saw how much fun Billy was having on the hill, and remembered how glad Billy had been to trade, Jerry decided that his new sled was a pretty fine present after all.

Winter Morning

JANUARY 4

Little squirrel,
Out there on the cold tree branch,
Do you want to come in?
Do you want to come in and see me?
In a minute

When the house gets warm
I will get out of bed,
And put my slippers on.
I will go downstairs
And open the door,
So you can come in and see me.

The Sneezy Bear

JANUARY 5

ONCE there was a little polar bear who began to have a cold. But he didn't want to stay indoors. So he said his cold didn't amount to anything. And he said that he had a good, warm snowsuit, anyway. And away he went, skipping through the deep snow, and fishing in the icy water.

That was pretty cold for a little bear with a cold. Pretty soon, he was sniffling and sneezing. The other bears, and the walrus children and reindeer, ran away from him, saying, "We don't want to play with you, 'cause you're catching!"

And a doctor, on his way back to the trading boat, took one look at the little bear and said, "You'd better get home with a hot-water bottle!"

The little bear just laughed at that good advice. But suddenly, his laugh turned into a cough and his eyes began to water. And his legs felt so queer and weak that he sat right down in the cold, deep snow—wishing he could go home, but not even able to get up.

And oh, how that little bear sneezed!

"Look at that!" cried all the father Eskimos "This sneezy little bear will start a regular epidemic unless we hurry up and do something about him!"

So they quickly sent their little Eskimos home, and they cut big blocks of ice, and they hurried up and built an ice igloo all around the little bear. Right over his top, sneezes and all.

A very kind lady Eskimo passed him in a hot-water bottle, a hot lemonade, and two double blankets in a cheerful red-and-white plaid.

All fixed up like that, the little bear began to feel better at once. In three days he was feeling fine. And in six days he was ready to go out again.

But it was days and days and days before he had anyone to play with. In the first place, all the other little bears, and the walrus children and reindeer and little Eskimos, had caught bad colds from the sneezy little bear's sneezes.

And in the second place, they were all pretty mad about it.

So, when at last they were well again, and the sneezy bear had managed to make friends with them again, he was a far wiser little bear.

He was such a wise little bear that, from that day to this, whenever he begins to get a cold, he stays indoors from the very beginning. And when he stops sneezing, and can go out again, all his friends are waiting to play with him— and very glad to see him, too.

The Strange Pitcher

JANUARY 6

ONCE there was a little boy who had a grandmother that lived in Italy. She wrote and said that she was sending him a present, and the little boy wondered what it would be.

But when the present came, it was a strange pitcher. It was made of pottery, with odd-looking leaves on it, the colors of fruit, and fruit that was the color of leaves.

And the little boy didn't like it.

"I don't like it," he told his mother.

"Oh, I do," his mother said. "See how nicely it goes with our dishes!"

So she put it on the table at every meal.

In the morning, it was full of orange juice for the little boy to pour for the whole family.

At noon, the strange pitcher was filled with milk for him to serve. And at night it had chocolate milk in it, or lemonade. Day after day, the little boy poured good-tasting things from the pitcher, and by and by, it didn't look strange any more.

One day, the little boy wrote to his grandmother in Italy and told her that.

At the end of his letter, he said, "Thank you very much for my beautiful pitcher. I like it very much."

And so he did.

The little boy thought that his own pitcher from Italy was the most beautiful pitcher in the whole world.

Ups and Downs

JANUARY 7

Out coasting, going up is hard—
It's more fun going down.

But when you skate, it's nicer up—
And when you're down—you frown!

Linnie's Galoshes

JANUARY 8

LINNIE could not put her own galoshes on. Her brother and sister helped her whenever mother was too busy, so she just went on and on not knowing how to put them on.

And then, one day when she woke up from her nap, it was snowing. Linnie could see her brother and sister out coasting on the snowy hill. And she hurried to get dressed so she could go, too. After she was all bundled up, she ran downstairs.

"Mommie!" she called. "Please help me put my galoshes on!"

But Linnie's mother didn't answer. She was out.

For a moment Linnie thought she might have to cry. But she decided she was in too much of a hurry for that. Then she thought she might go out without her galoshes. But who wants to get cold, wet feet, and maybe a runny nose besides?

Linnie didn't. So she sat down, and she pulled and she tugged until she managed to get both her galoshes on. Then, very slowly and carefully she zipped them up. That was very hard work!

Just as she finished, the telephone rang. It was Linnie's mother, next door making cookies with her neighbor. "Linnie," she said, "I know you must want to go sledding with the others—but I'm right in the middle of baking, so you'll have to wait till I can run over and help you with your galoshes—"

"No, I won't, Mommie," laughed Linnie. "No, I won't at all—because I put them on all by myself, and they're on!"

And then wasn't Linnie's mother surprised!

Cautious Mr. Cardinal

JANUARY 9

MRS. CARDINAL was eager to try the new feeding platform in the bare beechnut tree. But not Mr. Cardinal!

"How do we know it's safe?" he kept asking.

"We don't," his wife replied. "But we do know it's not safe to starve! Come on!"

"Not yet," said Mr. Cardinal. "Wait a bit—"

Just then two big bluejays flew up to the platform and began eating greedily. Along came sparrows, a catbird, and a big brown thrasher. A woodpecker landed beside them, and cried "Suet!" in a happy voice.

"Everything will be gone," wailed Mrs. Cardinal. "We won't even get a taste!"

But still Mr. Cardinal kept saying, "Wait!"

At last the other birds finished eating and flew off, looking fat and well pleased with themselves. Then Mr. Cardinal moved cautiously up the tree, tilting his head and hopping from branch to branch.

When he finally did land on the platform, and beckoned Mrs. Cardinal to join him, she went soaring up, happy to be in the middle of such a feast at last.

Mr. Cardinal, finding that nothing dangerous happened, was even happier than his wife.

And happiest of all was a little boy, inside his window watching the two red birds.

"Why, Daddy and I only put our new feeding platform up last night," he whispered to himself. "And already two hard-to-coax cardinals are out there having their breakfast!"

Grandma's Coal Stove

JANUARY 10

When Grandma comes to visit us,
She always says, "Land sakes!
I wish I had a stove like yours
For baking pies and cakes—
Why, you only turn a handle,
You don't even strike a light,
And you never have to test it,
'Cause you know the heat is right!"

But at her house in the winter,
When it's snowy everywhere,
I think her stove is nicer—
It's so cozy sitting there
Close beside it in the morning,
Watching all the coals glow red,
That I hope she never trades it
For a stove like ours instead.

Michael's Surprise

JANUARY 11

IN THE summer, all the children on the hill (except Michael, who was too small) helped in their mothers' gardens.

They were proud gardeners. And whenever one of them helped grow a specially fine flower, he was sure to come calling to all the others, "Come see what's blooming in my garden!"

But now it was winter. All the gardens were sleeping under the deep, cold snow.

So when Michael came to everyone's house, calling, "Come see what's blooming in my garden!" the children almost laughed.

"Nothing's blooming now, Michael!" they said.

But he looked so solemn, and so excited, that they followed him anyway. Up the snowy path they went, closer and closer to his house, where big icicles hung from the eaves. When they got to a sunny spot near the steps, Michael stopped them, and pointed to the snowy ground.

And there, growing out of the snow, in a cluster of shining green leaves—was a most beautiful white flower.

"Oh, Michael!" the children cried. "What is it, Michael?"

"It's a Christmas Rose," he said proudly. "I saw it in a catalogue, and Mommy ordered it. But I planted it in the fall almost all by myself —so maybe I'm going to be a gardener, too!"

The other children, still in a ring around the Christmas Rose, said, "Why, Michael, you're a gardener right now!"

Hurry Up!

JANUARY 12

*Let's put on our caps
And our snug snowsuits,*

*And our fuzzy mittens,
And big warm boots,*

*Let's open the door
And run outside—*

*'Cause the yard's all icy,
And we can slide!*

The Sleepy Fireman

JANUARY 13

THERE was once a sleepy fireman, who loved being a fireman, and was especially brave and willing. But at night, when the fire alarm rang, he was always last to wake up—and last man of all on the big hook-and-ladder.

Once he almost missed getting on altogether.

"That kind of thing will never do!" he told himself the next night, as he paced up and down. That sleepy fireman was even considering not going to bed at all, when a cold little wind blew up the hole for sliding down the sliding pole. And when it did, the sleepy fireman remembered that he could not sleep when he was cold.

"Not one single wink!" he cried happily. Then, quickly tying his blankets to those on the next cot, he hopped into bed. Deep in the night, the fire alarm rang.

What a noise! Up leaped every fireman except the sleepy fireman. They threw back their blankets, and back went his blankets, too. Br-r-r-r! That sleepy fireman was so cold that he awoke at once, dressed in a flash, slid down the pole—and was first man of all on the hook-and-ladder.

And since he was so wide awake, besides being so brave and willing, it did look as if it wouldn't be long until he'd be promoted to the splendid position of Fire Chief!

Checkers

JANUARY 14

*My cousin taught me how to play
Checkers, just the other day.
He had the red ones, and I had black,
And when I jumped his,
He jumped mine back.
He took so many that when we'd done,
He had all of mine, and so he won.
I think that when we play today,
We'll do it just the other way—
He can have black ones,
And I'll have red,
And maybe I'll win this time, instead.*

Snow, Snow, Snow!

JANUARY 15

"Snow, snow, snow!" grumbled Henny, busily sweeping her front porch. "I do wish winter would be over!"

"Do you, Henny?" asked her friend Jack Rabbit. "Do you specially like it to be spring-time, then?"

"Oh, yes I do!" Henny agreed. "Although—when April is showery and everything gets muddy, I begin wishing it would hurry up and be summer—"

"I see," said Jack Rabbit, with a twinkle in his eye. "How 'bout summer, Henny? Does it suit you perfectly?"

"Summer," sighed Henny. "Oh yes, summer's lovely. Only it does get terribly hot and

dusty in August, and by then I'm always ready for autumn, I can tell you."

"Well then, Henny," chuckled Jack Rabbit, "then I guess autumn must be your favorite season of all?"

"I expect so," Henny said. "Autumn's nice—except that when I have to keep raking leaves, leaves, leaves—I get to wishing that winter would come along."

"Winter!" cried Jack Rabbit, flopping down on the steps and laughing right out loud. "Henny, oh Henny! You just wished the whole year around—and right back to winter!"

Henny blinked with surprise, and then she laughed, too.

"Why, so I did!" she said. "Oh, Jack Rabbit, wouldn't it be awful if it did go by that fast?"

And happily saying, "Snow, snow, beautiful snow!" Henny skipped down the steps to help Jack Rabbit make a big snowman in her sparkling white front yard.

All Kinds of Legs

JANUARY 16

ONE DAY, a young giraffe went for a walk on his long, long legs—and a young elephant went for a walk on his round, stumpy legs—and a little tiger went along on his sleek, striped legs—and a little monkey joined them on his thin, gray legs with feet like hands.

They all walked through the jungle and across the plains to a big, cool river they all knew about. They all took big, cool drinks. Then they all stood on the bank chattering about whether to stay there for a while or start back home.

And suddenly, up out of the river came an enormous, angry old hippopotamus, furious because all that chatter had waked him up from his mid-day nap.

Toward the bank he came, on his great, shiny, stamping-with-fury legs—and away went the young giraffe, the young elephant, the little tiger and the little gray monkey. Back home they went, some faster, some slower—but all just as fast as they could go on their all-kinds-of legs—and they all got home, safe and sound, and just exactly on time for lunch.

The Weather Bunnies

JANUARY 17

"What is it going to do today?
Rain or snow?" the bunnies say.
They look at the sky, all woolly gray,

And watch the way the wind is blowing—
And they suddenly know—
'Cause it's suddenly snowing!

The Beanbag Tiger

JANUARY 18

THE beanbag tiger was lost. Not that he hadn't often been lost before. Why, that funny tiger was so full of beans and nonsense that Tommy never knew where to look for him.

Once he had been up on a shelf, higher than Tommy could reach. Another time, he had been under Tommy's bed, flat on his face and looking most forlorn. Still another time, Tommy had taken the top off his red caboose and looked inside, and found the beanbag tiger there.

But he wasn't in any of those places this time.

He wasn't on the toy shelves, either. Or in the toy box.

Tommy tried growling, which is a good way to call a lost tiger—and he tried whistling, which is a cheerful way to look for anything that's lost. But hunt, search, growl and whistle, not a lump or a stripe of the beanbag tiger could he find.

And then at last, just when Tommy was sure his tiger was lost and gone forever—he happened to look out his window into the bare oak tree. And there, hanging over a low branch, and waving one paw to say, "Come and get me —I thought *you* were lost!" was the tiger.

Yes, there he was, not lost at all and just as full of beans and nonsense as ever—waiting to be found so he could hurry up and get lost all over again!

Winter Wish

I think there's nothing quite so nice
As going skating on the ice.
When we go skating round and round,
Our voices have the clearest sound,
And all our caps and jackets look
As bright as pictures in a book
Against the rim of glistening snow.
But much too soon—it's time to go.

When I grow up, I'll skate all night
Under the moon's bright, frosty light,
And when it's morning, I'll just say,
"It's early—so I'll skate all day!"

The Angel Chimes

JANUARY 20

ONE long, dark, blustery winter day, when spring seemed too far ahead, and Christmas seemed too far behind, Jenny found the angel chimes in the desk drawer.

She polished the brass pieces till they were shiny, and put them all together. She found the candles that fit them, too—the little white

Jenny carefully carried one pot. Her mother carefully carried another, and they put one pot on each side of the angel chimes.

"Now let's see how it will look at supper time!" cried Jenny. So her mother lighted the little white candles, and the shining angels moved slowly around, ringing the bell. The

candles that make the pinwheel part go round when they are lighted—and put them in place.

Then Jenny set the table for supper, with the angel chimes in the center, and called her mother to come and see.

"All it needs now is some flowers," Jenny's mother smiled, nodding toward the window where the white African violets were blooming in their white pots.

lights made the brass sparkle. It made the white violets look even whiter, too.

"It looks just as pretty as spring," said Jenny's mother.

"It looks as merry as Christmas, too," laughed Jenny, because suddenly, the long, dark, blustery winter day didn't seem too long and dark any more. It seemed cozy and bright, and very close to supper time, at that.

The Timid Monkey

JANUARY 21

as ever, while the timid monkey stayed at home, shaking his head sadly and putting everything back where it belonged.

A TIMID monkey and his easy-going friend were going on a hiking trip.

"We must be sure to bring everything we may need," said he, packing away. "Warm clothes in case it's cold, cool ones in case it's hot —pots and pans in case we find something to cook, food in case we don't—cups for drinking from streams, water in case there are no streams —guns in case we see enemies, shields in case they see us—"

"My, oh me!" said his friend. "You certainly think of everything, don't you?"

"I take no chances," replied the timid monkey, tucking in blankets for sleeping—and books and cards and a lamp in case of not sleeping, and a whole carton full of ham sandwiches.

Then he tried to pick up one big bundle, and his easy-going friend tried to pick up the other. But those bundles were much too big and clumsy for either one to lift.

"Pshaw!" cried the timid monkey. "We just can't go then!"

"You can't," grinned his friend, reaching for a gun and one ham sandwich. "You can't, but I can—because I shall make do with what I find as I go along!"

And away he went, carefree and easy-going

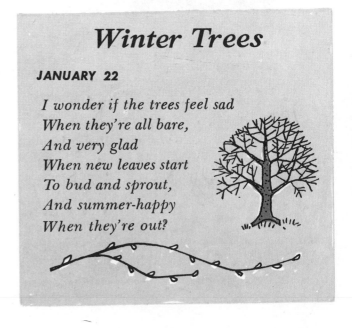

Winter Trees

JANUARY 22

*I wonder if the trees feel sad
When they're all bare,
And very glad
When new leaves start
To bud and sprout,
And summer-happy
When they're out?*

20

The City Rabbit's Vacation

JANUARY 23

"COME to the country, cousin!" said the country rabbit on the telephone. "How tired you must be of the slushy city streets and the cold stone buildings!"

"I am, and thanks for thinking of me!" cried his cousin.

With his skates and skis, he took the first train out to the country. How beautiful it looked, with fir trees poking up out of the snow, and a shining ice pond down in the hollow!

The city rabbit had a wonderful time skating and skiing with his cousin all day long. In the evenings, he loved sitting close to the fire, playing checkers—and popping corn to eat before they went to bed.

"Well, sir," yawned his cousin one evening. "Now that you've seen a country winter—I just bet you'll never want to go back to the city again!"

And much to his own surprise, the city rabbit replied, "Oh, I don't know about that—"

Because, suddenly and deep inside, he missed the hustle-bustle, and all the bright lights, and his city friends, and his own snug bed high up in a tall building—and even the slush that squished so pleasantly when he went out walking.

So, when his vacation was over and he stood on the train calling, "Good-by, and thank you, and come see me—" the city rabbit was just as happy to be going back home, as he had been to be going away.

Shush!

JANUARY 24

IT WAS quiet in the house. Shush! The mother was sleeping, taking a nap. Shush! The baby was sleeping, taking its nap, too. Drip, drip, drip! The water was dripping into the dishpan full of lunch dishes.

"Do you suppose we could?" whispered Katie.

"I suppose we *could!*" whispered Peter.

And swish, swish, swish! Katie washed all those dishes shining and clean. Peter dried them all, shining and dry. Then Peter put a chair at the cupboard, and opened the doors. Katie handed up the dishes, and Peter put them all away in the right places. But just as he reached for the last one—the big sandwich plate—it slipped out of his hands, and out of Katie's hands.

Crash! What a terrible crash! It woke the baby from its nap. The baby began to cry. It woke the mother from her nap. She picked up the baby, and down the stairs she came. Into the kitchen she came. But she didn't say, "Oh dear, my sandwich plate!" And she didn't say, "Why can't you let things be?"

She said, "Why, Peter and Katie! You did all the lunch dishes for a surprise!"

Then she put the baby in the high chair, and hugged her bigger children, and swept up the sandwich plate—and took out the cookie plate, and sugar, and eggs and flour, and all the good things she needed for making round, crisp, sugar cookies.

Timkitten's Mittens

JANUARY 25

TIMKITTEN was forever losing his mittens.

And his grandmother didn't mind at all. She dearly loved to knit mittens, and she just sat down, smiling happily, and made a new mitten to take the place of whichever one he had lost.

But Timkitten's mother and father did mind.

They kept telling him that he must learn to be more careful, but it did no good. So at last they told Timkitten that if ever again he came home with one mitten missing, he would not be allowed to go to the magic show. This was a dreadful thought!

Timkitten had been saving his pennies for months so he could go to that wonderful magic show, put on by a quite wonderful black cat with a top hat.

So he said he'd be very careful.

And he meant to be very careful.

But the next morning in school, when he was taking off his outdoor clothes, he found that he couldn't find one mitten.

Luckily, Timkitten knew how to write, and he had his saved-up pennies in his pocket. So he wrote a sign that said: "One cent reward for lost mitten, if returned to Timkitten."

He pinned it on the hall bulletin board and hoped for the best. But the best turned out to

be pretty bad. Because, at recess time, twenty-five of his school mates turned up with lost mittens—all of which belonged to Timkitten!

When he had finished paying rewards, he had not one cent of his saved-up pennies left—and he had mittens enough for thirteen kittens.

Poor Timkitten! He went home for lunch with his arms full of mittens, and his eyes full of tears.

"Never mind," said his grandmother. "We'll think of some way to fix things up—"

And by afternoon she had. Her plan sounded fine to Timkitten. His mother and

father agreed that it was a good idea, too. So Timkitten washed and dried all those mittens, and sorted them into pairs. The next day, he took them back to school. This time he pinned up a sign that said: "Beautiful second-hand mittens for sale. Apply to Timkitten."

During recess, the other kittens looked at the mittens, and just loved them. And since Timkitten was selling them for twenty-five cents a pair (really a bargain), their mothers gave them the money at lunch time.

Timkitten's troubles were over! He had money enough to go to the magic show, and to take his grandmother and mother and father, too. It was superb, and much better than the year before. And everyone had a hot chocolate after.

What's more, after all the to-do, Timkitten never again lost a single mitten, which pleased his mother and father enormously.

It didn't spoil things for his grandmother, either. Because all the mothers of the kittens in school wanted more of her beautiful mittens for next year. She was delighted to knit brand new ones for fifty cents a pair. And so she was kept busy knitting mittens all the year round.

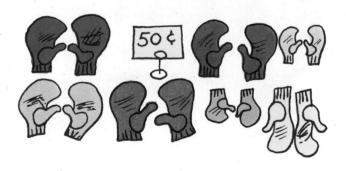

A Lucky Break

JANUARY 26

ALL winter long, the animals had been longing to go skating on the lake behind the zoo. At last the chimpanzee managed to slip the keys out of the zoo-keeper's pocket, and that night there was a merry skating party, indeed.

Only the elephants declined to try the ice.

"It would never hold us up," they sighed.

"Nonsense!" cried the hippopotamus. "Just watch me!"

In a moment, he was gaily skimming along in the moonlight.

With a thundering crack, the ice gave way, and everyone scrambled ashore.

Naturally, everyone was angry.

"It will be a long time before you're invited anywhere again!" scolded the chimpanzee, as he went about locking up the cages.

The poor hippo really did feel an outcast!

But meantime, the keeper had noticed that his keys were missing. He came rushing down to the zoo, prepared to put the culprits on a diet of bread and water. To his surprise, he found all the animals in their cages looking sound asleep, and his keys lying in the path as if he'd dropped them there.

"How careless of me," he cried. "I'm the one who'll have to be put on bread and water!"

Then he went back home and to bed.

"Only think," whispered the chimpanzee. "If he'd come any sooner, he'd have caught us!"

"What a narrow escape!" cried the other animals, all but the hippo who only said, "Ahem!" His friends were quick to agree.

"Yes, old fellow," they said. "It was you who saved us. How wise you were to crack the ice!"

And that made the poor old hippo feel so happy that he hated to admit it had all been an accident.

So he said, "Well, somebody had to do something!" and lumbered about looking wise and important for at least a week after.

The Wonderful Magician

JANUARY 27

THE wonderful magician was a big black cat who did the most wonderful things. When he bowed and doffed his tall silk hat, a white rabbit hopped out of it, and two white doves flew out, and a silver ball bounced out.

The ball bounced and danced in the air, never touching the ground at all. It bounced on the magician's tail and on his nose—and when he said "abracadabra," it broke into two halves, and out floated big, silken handkerchiefs in beautiful Easter egg colors. But when the magician tried to put them back in again, there were too many to fit!

So he tossed them up in the air, where they floated like colored clouds, light and soft overhead. Then the magician waved his wand and said "abracadabra," and they disappeared, and the rabbit and the doves disappeared, and *he* disappeared. And nothing was left on the stage except the great black velvet curtain on its silver rail.

Wonderful things he did, that wonderful magician.

The audience clapped and clapped. And they heard the magician's fine, deep voice say, "Thank you, ladies and gentlemen." But they didn't see him again.

He didn't appear and bow, because that wonderful magician really had disappeared—and he never came back until the next performance of his wonderful magic show.

Snow Tracks

JANUARY 28

Who went here?
A shy brown deer.

Who went there?
A sleepy old bear,
And a hoppity hare.

And who went here?
"I did," says a mouse.

"But you can't catch me—
'Cause I'm in my house!"

The Sad Little Clown

JANUARY 29

*The sad little clown
Just couldn't smile.*

*His friends knew why,
And after a while—*

*They fixed his trouble,
And in one-two-three—*

*That glad little clown
Could smile merrily!*

The Polite Little Boy

JANUARY 30

ONCE there was a polite little boy, but he didn't eat very much. He wouldn't taste beans, because he thought they looked too beany. Or carrots, because he thought they looked too carroty. And as for pudding, he thought it looked much too shaky to ever taste.

That little boy had a polite "No, thank you," for so many things, that all he really did eat day after day, was peanut butter sandwiches.

But one day, the little boy was invited to his friend's house for lunch, and he went. And there, everyone helped himself to the good things on the table.

"You help yourself, too," said his friend's mother. "Just take whatever you like."

Now the little boy didn't know what to do.

He couldn't take what he liked, because there was no peanut butter. He couldn't take nothing at all, because he had come for lunch. He couldn't even say a polite "No, thank you," because he was supposed to help himself.

So he took a smidgeon of everything there was, even beans and carrots. Very—slowly—he tasted a tiny taste of everything he had taken. And most surprisingly—

That little boy found that beans didn't taste too beany, and carrots didn't taste too carroty. In fact, everything on his plate tasted so good and right that it was gone in one-two-three.

And even after helping himself all over again, that little boy found that he had a big, eager, "Yes, thank you!" when his friend's mother asked if he wouldn't help himself to one more dish of the fine, shaky pudding he had never tasted before.

Wise Little Mice

JANUARY 31

*When little mice sit reading books,
It seems their mother never looks
To see if it is time for bed—
She sits and reads her book, instead.
But when they play noisy charades,
Or have exciting big parades,
It seems no time until, in pairs,
She sends them marching up the stairs
With orders to go straight to bed—
Tonight, they're reading books instead.*

The Careful Grocer

FEBRUARY 1

THERE was once a careful grocer who wished he could keep store and deliver groceries, too. But he couldn't do both.

So he hired a helper to drive his truck for him.

"Couldn't we take turns?" the helper asked.

But the grocer said, "Goodness no! Just think of the mistakes a person could make in keeping store!"

So day after day, they both went on doing the same old thing. Until once when the helper came in with a wrenched wrist, all done up in a big bandage.

"You certainly can't drive the truck today," said the grocer. "I'll do that, and you keep store. Only be sure you don't make any mistakes—"

And while he was saying that, he put Mrs. Smith's cookies in Mrs. Jones's order box!

Then away he drove in his red truck, having the time of his life.

"Oh dear," he thought when he stopped at Smith's. "I wish this weren't my last stop!"

And of course it wasn't. Because when Mrs. Smith found no cookies in her box, her little boy burst into tears.

"Never mind," said the grocer. "We'll go find them!"

With the little Smith boy beside him, he drove back from house to house. And when at last they found them at Mrs. Jones's house, they both felt like real detectives.

So the grocer took the happy little Smith boy home.

Then he went back to his store, where everything seemed to be going like clock-work. Things looked *so* well-kept that he said, "What do you say we do take turns with our work from now on?"

"I say capital!" cried his helper, clapping his hands together. "And look! My wrist is all well again!"

"Good!" the grocer said. "Then tomorrow's your turn to drive the truck, and I'll keep store."

Just to get a head start, they both began making up tomorrow's orders—each one trying to decide which was more fun, keeping store, or delivering groceries in the fine red truck.

Two Little Groundhogs

FEBRUARY 2

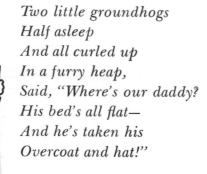

Two little groundhogs
Half asleep
And all curled up
In a furry heap,
Said, "Where's our daddy?
His bed's all flat—
And he's taken his
Overcoat and hat!"

"He's gone upstairs,"
Their mother said,
"To see how long
We can stay in bed—
If he sees his shadow
We'll stay right here,
Why, Springtime
Is very near—"

But shadow or no,
They never heard
What their daddy said,
No, never a word—
For, all curled up
In a furry heap,
Those two little groundhogs
Were sound *asleep!*

Tommy Turtle's Troubles

FEBRUARY 3

TOMMY TURTLE was such a slow-poke that even in the early fall, it was all his friends could do to get him to school on time. And as fall wore on, and the days grew colder, Tommy got slower and slower and slower.

One day it snowed, and Tommy got no farther than his doorstep. There he sat, all bundled up, and not even trying to get to school on time.

"Come on, Tommy!" called his friends. "You'll get kept in, and have no time to play in the snow—"

"I know," sighed Tommy. "And it's terrible awful. But my legs just don't want to go anywhere today."

All Tommy's friends looked at each other. Then, all together, they picked him up and carried him to school.

All Kinds of Hats

FEBRUARY 4

On Monday, Jimmy's an Engineer,
On Tuesday, he's Fireman Jim,
On Wednesday, a Pirate so bad and bold
That hanging's too good for him!

"That was fine," mumbled Tommy. "Maybe you'd better carry me every day—"

But just then, their teacher caught sight of him.

"Tommy Turtle!" she cried. "You're here too soon. Don't you know that little turtles are supposed to sleep all winter—and not come to school till it's spring?"

Tommy didn't say a word. He was already asleep and snoring. But all his friends looked at each other and giggled.

"It looks like Tommy did know," they said. "But we didn't!"

They soon had Tommy back home in bed.

And they ran all the way back to school, just in time for the last bell, and very glad that Tommy Turtle's troubles were over—at least until spring!

On Thursday, he launches his rocket ship
And zooms off into space,
On Friday, he may be an Indian Chief
With a savage, painted face,
Or a Big League pitcher on the mound—
Or maybe he's up to bat.
On Saturday, Jimmy is Cowboy Jim
In a ten-gallon cowboy hat,
Waylaid by a band of enemies
And shooting them left and right—
But on Sunday, Jimmy is only James,
And he's glad
    when it's Sunday night!

Finders Keepers

FEBRUARY 5

1. Poor Davey! On his way home from the pond, he lost one ice skate in the deep, white snow.

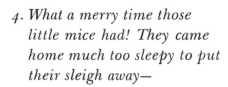

2. "Hello!" cried the little mice that night. "Here's a wonderful sleigh! Let's go for a ride!"

3. With two big mice for their high-stepping horses, in they all piled, one on top of another.

4. What a merry time those little mice had! They came home much too sleepy to put their sleigh away—

5. —so in the morning, close to a little mouse door in the back steps—Davey found his lost ice skate again!

Aunt Kangaroo's Handy Pocket

FEBRUARY 6

EVERY Sunday, when Aunt Kangaroo took her nieces and nephews for a walk, she rushed them so that they never had time to look around.

How those little kangaroos wished she would slow down!

"Well, here we are, Aunt Kangaroo," they said one fine Sunday. "All ready for our walk!"

"Good!" smiled their aunt, pleased to see that for once they had brought everything they might possibly need. They had sweaters, umbrellas, rubbers, napping pillows and blankets, a little lunch each—even a rubber raft.

All loaded down, the little kangaroos set out. As usual, Aunt Kangaroo was soon well ahead, hopping big, swift hops, and calling back, "Hurry up, come along, don't dawdle!"

But today the little kangaroos didn't hurry.

"We can't with all this to carry," they called.

"True," said Aunt Kangaroo. And she took their sweaters, umbrellas and rubbers, and tucked them in her handy pocket.

With that pocketful, she couldn't hop nearly so fast!

So the little kangaroos, trying not to giggle, asked her to please put their napping things in her pocket, too.

Then, paws over their grins, they asked her to just tuck in their lunches and the rubber raft.

Aunt Kangaroo most kindly did. And by now, her pocket was so crammed full that she just loped along, slowly enough for the little kangaroos to see all the sights.

For once in her life, Aunt Kangaroo had time to look around, too. And she enjoyed it so much that she was soon far behind the little kangaroos.

"Hurry up, Auntie!" they called. "Hurry up!"

"Why?" asked Aunt Kangaroo. "What's all the hurry? When you go on a walk, you want to see everything there is to see, don't you?"

"Yes," giggled the little kangaroos. "Yes, we do!"

And Aunt Kangaroo, her handy pocket full of things they didn't really need, just could not understand what those little kangaroos were giggling about.

Bouncy Bunny's Party

FEBRUARY 7

WHEN Bouncy Bunny was all alone in his little house, he liked to think up great things to do.

Things like putting on a play at school, and everybody clapping for him. Or playing on the bunnies' baseball team and catching a fast ball.

Best of all, Bouncy Bunny liked to think of having a big, exciting party with everyone having fun at his house. And one day he decided that he really would.

"I'll string up paper lanterns, and have balloons, and games, and all kinds of good things to eat," he thought.

"And I'll invite all my friends for Saturday night!"

And string up paper lanterns he did, a whole dozen. How beautiful they would be when they were lighted!

And balloons he had, all blown up and tied in clusters so everyone could choose his favorite color.

Bouncy Bunny certainly had plenty of good things to eat, after mixing and tasting and baking all week. As for games, he had planned the most wonderful ones, because he was so good at thinking things up.

But in all the excitement of getting ready for his party, he almost forgot to invite his friends.

Just in the nick of time, just as he was about to light the lanterns—Bouncy Bunny remembered he had forgotten.

So, with his heart going pitter-pat, he ran to the house of each of his friends.

"Come on!" he panted. "I'm having a party, and you're all invited. But please hurry up— before it's over!"

"Hurrah!" cried his friends. "We're coming!" And they skipped along with Bouncy Bunny, who fairly bounced with pride as he opened his own front door.

His friends could hardly believe their eyes when they saw all his lovely party fuss. And what a time those bunnies had, eating under the glowing lanterns, and choosing exactly the right balloons, and playing all the dandy games that Bouncy Bunny had planned!

They stayed and stayed. And when they said it was the best party ever—and that they were very glad they had been invited, Bouncy Bunny blushed as pink as a rose, and said they couldn't possibly be half as glad as he!

I'll Be Me

FEBRUARY 8

Yesterday, I was wishing that
Instead of me, I could be my cat.
I could go wherever I liked to go
In my furry suit
Just right for snow,
Without any boots to be putting on,
And no one to bother where I'd gone.
If I took the notion, I even might
Go out for a walk in the middle of night!
But today I decided I'd rather be
Instead of my cat, just simply me,
'Cause I'm learning to skate
And I couldn't do that
In a thousand years
If I were my cat.

The Partners

FEBRUARY 9

POOR Mr. Rhinoceros couldn't see very well.

"Everything looks blurry," said he, standing knee-deep in the river, and still as a stone, "and, oh dear, wouldn't it be nice to know how things really look!"

And just as he said that, he heard someone else say, "Oh dear!" It was a very small hare, sitting on the bank looking very blurry, and saying, "Oh dear, if only I could get across the river to nibble the tender leaves I see growing there!"

"Goodness!" thought Mr. Rhinoceros. "Imagine being able to see clear across!"

Merry February

FEBRUARY 10

Some darkish days in February
We all get sort of we-don't-care-y
And coast downhill without our sleds,
And pile big snow heaps on our heads,
And, though we know it isn't nice,
We even slide across the ice
On our slippery snowpants' seat
Instead of on our rubbery feet.
After a while, of course, we get
As cold as ice, and very wet,
And then, as quietly as mice,
We go indoors. It's very nice
To have a crispy cookie treat,
And warm our chilly hands and feet,
And watch our snowclothes steaming dry.
We just can't think, although we try,
Why we were feeling we-don't-care-y
In cozy, merry February!

With that, he waded to the edge and bowed to the small hare. "I can easily ferry you across the river, my little friend," said he, "if you will tell me how things look when we get there—"

"Agreed!" cried the hare, jumping up and down for joy.

So Mr. Rhinoceros took him aboard, and he was soon on the other side of the river, nibbling away. When he had eaten his fill, he hopped back on his friend's broad back, and told him exactly how everything had looked.

And from that day to this, neither Mr. Rhinoceros, the ferryboat, nor his friend the bright-eyed hare, have ever had to mutter, "oh dear!" ever again.

The Birthday Snowman

FEBRUARY 11

THIS year, Kim was going to buy his mother's birthday present himself. He had saved up half a dollar, and he was going to get her a handkerchief in a box with a ribbon around it.

"That's what ladies like," he told himself, skipping down the snowy path with the half-dollar in his hand. But suddenly, Kim slipped on the ice. Down he fell, and up went the half-dollar. And hunt and search as he did, Kim could not find it.

Poor Kim, with no present at all to give his mother at suppertime! Suddenly he had an idea.

"I can make a snowman," he thought. "Maybe she'd like that!"

He began rolling a big snowman right away. But when the snowman was finished, out near the kitchen window where his mother could laugh at it while she was cooking, he wasn't a bit sure that it was a good present.

"It isn't the kind in a box with a ribbon around it," he told himself. "And that's what ladies really like—"

But just as Kim thought that, he saw something shining in the snowman's middle. It looked like a piece of ice or a shiny button.

But it wasn't. It was a shiny piece of money— Kim's own half-dollar that he had lost!

He pried it out of the snowman and ran down to the store as quickly as he could. He bought a pretty handkerchief in a box, and the store lady put a ribbon around it.

"Here's one of my presents for you, Mommy," Kim said at suppertime. "The other one's outside the kitchen window."

Kim's mother liked her handkerchief so much that she had to hug Kim three times. But when she saw her snowman present, she seemed to like it even better.

"Why Kim!" she said. "Why Kim! He's the nicest snowman I ever had!"

Mr. Lincoln

FEBRUARY 12

Mr. Lincoln was a tall man,
A lean man, a long man,
A grave man, a kind man,
A wise and very strong man.

He loved his great country,
And knew it had to be
A land where everyone could grow
In brotherhood, and free.

And even when it meant a war
Between his countrymen,
With bowed head and grave face,
He took his writing pen—

That tall man, that lean man,
That strong man and wise,
And signed his name to freedom,
With tears in his eyes.

Hello!

FEBRUARY 13

Every day I try to catch
A chipmunk for a pet,
I think he'd like to be one—
Though he isn't certain yet.
But he did look very friendly,
And not afraid at all,
When he peeped at me
This morning, from his
House out in the wall.

Mrs. Bear's Valentine

FEBRUARY 14

MR. BEAR was very wise. He planned his Valentine surprise for Mrs. Bear on New Year's Day. He wanted something sweet and gay, and he thought of something! Looking smug, he said, "I'll get a big hug from that good Mrs. Bear of mine, when she sees her Valentine!"

Next day, he went to the five-and-ten. He bought a nice, white bowl, and then a bag of pebbles—white and tiny—and round and brown and sort of shiny, he bought some bulbs —yes, one, two, three. He planted them all secretly, and watered them, and hid them well deep in his closet. "I can tell when it is time to take them out," he whispered. "They'll begin to sprout!"

They did. He put them in the sun. Now Mr. Bear thought it was fun to keep his room all neat and clean, so his surprise would not be seen by Mrs. Bear. Two weeks in the sun, and two weeks more, and on the very day before St. Valentine's, up in his room—the bulbs burst into starry bloom!

"Oh, what a beautiful surprise!" cried Mrs. Bear, with shiny eyes, when she saw her Valentine. "Now, Mr. Bear, you come see mine—"

She'd made him pancakes, stacked up high.

"Oh good!" cried Mr. Bear. "Oh my! Come on, sit down, have some of mine!"

So, side by side, and feeling fine—they both ate up his Valentine.

Pigeons

FEBRUARY 15
Pigeons seem to like it
Living in the town;
They like it on the park paths,
Strutting up and down;

They like to rest on ledges,
And roost around the steeple—
But best of all, they seem to like
Being close to people.

The Bridge to Nowhere

FEBRUARY 16

AWAY out in the quiet middle of nowhere, a little stone bridge crossed over a narrow, salty inlet.

A few cars and trucks went over the little bridge, and a few small boats went under it, going putt-putt-putt. But most of the time there was nothing to see except a saucy seagull or two, back from faraway places.

"Still here?" they called. "Still cheerfully going nowhere and seeing nothing, little stick-in-the-mud?"

"Still here," said the little bridge. "Not that I wouldn't like to see a bit of the world. But I can't—anyway, I like being cheerful."

And cheerful he certainly was. The cars and trucks hummed over the little bridge so happily that more and more drivers began coming that way, instead of using the big, crowded bridge near the city.

After a time, there was so much traffic on the little stone bridge that a gas-station man built a gas station just beyond it. A lunch wagon for hungry truck drivers came next, and store keepers put up their stores. Then a real estate man built houses for all those men and their families.

So at last there was a cheerful, busy town close to the little bridge, and the people named it Bridgeton.

Now when the seagulls call, "Still here, little bridge? Still going nowhere?" the little bridge laughs, "Still here. Why go anywhere, when the whole, exciting world comes to me?"

And the saucy seagulls circle over him in great surprise, without one single saucy word to say.

Mountain Climbers

FEBRUARY 17

We piled a pillow mountain up,
And I climbed to the top.
But then I slipped——
I wish we'd fixed
A softer place to stop!

Who Nibbles the Moon?

FEBRUARY 18

Who nibbles the moon?
Who takes a bite
Out of its roundness
Night by night,
Till nothing's left
But a crust—and then
Who bakes the moon
All over again,
And hangs it up
All round and bright,
And ready for someone
To nibble and bite?

Mumps and Measles

FEBRUARY 19

RICKY had measles, and he didn't like it much.

He had to stay in the house for two whole weeks, with no scratching even though he itched—and no looking at books though he liked to look at books.

And Peggy had mumps.

She had a lump on one cheek, and then a lump on the other. And while she could read and draw, and eat lots of ice cream, she didn't think a week indoors with mumps was much fun, either.

And then Ricky and Peggy heard that Peter, who was just getting over the measles, had come down with mumps.

"Poor Peter!" said Ricky. "I'm glad I just have measles!"

"Poor, poor Peter!" said Peggy. "I'm glad I have nothing but a couple of mumps!"

Things didn't seem bad at their houses, after all.

But they certainly did seem bad at Peter's house!

"I'm the unluckiest boy in the whole world," he wailed.

"I wouldn't say that, Pete," said his doctor. "Almost everyone gets measles, and almost everyone gets mumps. This way—you'll get them both over with at once."

While Peter was thinking about that, the doctor closed his bag and said to his mother, "Ice cream will taste good to this chap. You can give him all he wants—"

And then Peter smiled a big, happy lopsided smile, because things at his house didn't seem bad at all.

The Squabbling Squirrels

FEBRUARY 20

THREE little squirrels, furry and fat, came scampering merrily down the tree.

"Mommy said we could!" they chattered. "She said we could sleep all night in our tree-house we're going to make!"

And skipping along, they agreed that their house must be rainproof. And big enough for all three (bushy tails and all), and plenty of acorns to nibble.

But that was the last time they did agree.

Because two of those little squirrels were squabblers. And in a minute, they were at it again.

"Here's a good tree for our house!" cried one.

"No!" said the other "This one's better!"

They squabbled over that till it made the third little squirrel's ears hurt. So he said, "Just like always!" and went off by himself.

Just after that, blip! blip! two big acorns came falling down, and landed on the squabblers' heads.

"You blipped me!" cried one.

"No, you blipped me!" cried the other. And tweak, pummel and punch, they were having a regular tussle.

So it went. They went right on squabbling till it was almost night. Then, with no tree-house to sleep out in, the two little squirrels started sadly home.

But halfway there, a little voice called to them.

"Look up here," it said. "Look at me!" And there was their brother, in a dandy tree-house he had made.

"Ohhh! You're going to sleep out all night," they wailed. "And we can't!"

"Yes, you can," called their brother. "Plenty of room for all three of us, bushy tails and all. Just get some acorns for us to nibble—and come on up!"

In a whisk and a flash, those two little squirrels had their cheeks full of acorns. So up the tree they scampered, furry and fat, and too merry to care a jot who was first through the tree-house door.

But some animals are extra-hungry on the long, cold winter nights. The shy, quick rabbit leaps across the snow, looking for roots or young branches to nibble. The sly, slim weasel slinks out, hoping to catch an unwary rabbit. The crafty, swift red fox trots along the frozen stream, hoping to catch a weasel for his breakfast.

And in the morning, when the barnyard animals stir in their sleep, and the people yawn and stretch in their beds, and the hungry morning birds hop in the snow looking for crumbs—the prints of the hungry night creatures have marked it before them.

Winter Nights

FEBRUARY 21

WINTER nights, long and dark and still, are a good time for sleeping.

The sheep and cows go early to the big red barn. The hens cluck drowsily at sunset, fluffing their feathers for warmth. The barn cat curls up in the hay, too sleepy to chase the little mice in the walls, or to scold the bats and the old owl dozing high up under the snowy roof.

People go to bed early too, after the long winter evenings. And boys and girls sleep in their snug beds while outside the silent snow drifts down, for a morning surprise.

Yes, winter is a good time for sleeping.

Some animals think it such a good time, that they sleep from frost until spring. This is the way of the bear, and the woodchuck. And squirrels and chipmunks sleep in winter more than they are awake.

Hip, Hip, Hurrah!

FEBRUARY 22

When I grow up, I'll be President—
I'm pretty sure of that—
And I'll ride a horse, like George Washington,
And I'll wear a tricorn hat.
I won't make speeches, like presidents now,
I'll just make a proclamation
That every year, when my birthday comes,
All over the whole, wide nation,
There'll be parades—with fifes and drums,
And flags that toss and fly—
But instead of cherry, we'll all make merry
With our favorite kind of pie.

Trains

FEBRUARY 23

Which is nicer—
I don't know—
To go on a train,
Or to see people go?

Which is better,
To be inside,
Waving and going
For a ride—

Or to be outside,
And waving back,
And watching the train
Speed down the track?

Which is nicer?
I think I know,
It's nicer to watch
Except—when you go!

The Too-Long Train Ride

FEBRUARY 24

ONCE there was a little boy going for a long train ride. He rode and he rode, and the train went on and on, over miles and miles of bare, white, sandy desert. Nothing moved anywhere. Not so much as a gopher or a small rabbit. Not so much as a single bird. And after a while, the little boy felt sure there was nothing moving anywhere.

He wanted to ask his daddy if there would really be Indians when they got out west. But his daddy was sleeping.

He wanted to ask his mother to ask his daddy—but his mother was fast asleep, too. So the little boy looked out the window again. And now the train was traveling up the mountains. Up and up the bare, rocky mountains it went. When it was very high—the little boy found himself looking down into a deep, white canyon. At the mouth of the canyon, far, far below—there stood a little wild horse. Anyone could tell it was wild, anyone at all, from the way it shook its head and raced out of sight, frightened by the faraway train.

"A little wild horse!" whispered the little boy. "If there're still wild horses—why, I guess there're still real Indians, too!"

And he leaned back in his seat, that little boy—and rode and rode, and the train went on and on and on, only now the ride didn't seem too long any more.

Winter Mealtimes

FEBRUARY 25

Squirrels eat hoarded acorns,
Rabbits dig for roots—
We shop for our groceries,
Wearing rubber boots—

Birds find theirs like magic,
They don't even know—
I'm the one that leaves it
For them, in the snow!

Here Comes Buzzy!

FEBRUARY 26

"Look out!" honked the cars on the highway. "Put on your brakes, 'cause here comes Buzzy!"

Scr-e-e-ch! They all jerked to a stop, to keep from skidding in case he decided to buzz them. And of course he did. Down he came, that little show-off airplane—so close that some of the older cars were shaking for hours after.

"Look out!" groaned the tall buildings, wishing they could duck. "Here comes Buzzy!"

And here he did come, missing one, but zooming off with its flag waving from his tailpiece.

"Never mind," said the other buildings consolingly. "One of these days, that Buzzy will get his come-uppance!"

"Not I," laughed Buzzy. "I'm too smart!"

And he went right on buzzing steeples and towers, houses and barns, and even herds of cows—who never should be hurried or worried. And then one day, Buzzy saw a little handcar rolling along the railroad tracks, heading for a dark tunnel in the mountainside.

"I'll give him a buzz!" thought Buzzy.

And down he swooped, so busy planning to go very close without crashing—that he never saw the locomotive rushing out of the tunnel!

"Lo-o-o-ok o-o-out!" it whistled, when it saw Buzzy about to cross. "O-o-o-out of my way!"

Buzzy tried—but it was too late. Just as he thought he was safe, the big locomotive rushed past, clipping a piece off his tail.

Poor Buzzy. The next thing he knew, he was in the repair shop, feeling very sick and queer.

It was two whole weeks before he was all fixed up and ready to go flying again. When he did go, everyone was most surprised to see him. And after a bit, they were glad, too.

Because, while Buzzy still did lots of daring tricks (why not? He was a stunt plane, after all), he did them away up high in the air. And no one, not even the tallest tall building, had to say, "Look out! Here comes Buzzy!" ever again.

Miss Mouse in the Cupboard

FEBRUARY 27

Miss Mouse, in the cupboard,
Do you suppose that nobody saw you,
And nobody knows you are hiding there
In shivering fright, with quivering whiskers,
And eyes bead-bright, and hunched-up haunches,
And straining ears, eating our cookies—
And your own fears?
Miss Mouse in the cupboard,
Why do you think that we left them there,
With some milk to drink in a wee blue pitcher,
The size for a mouse,
Unless you were welcome in our house?

A Manner of Speaking

FEBRUARY 28

WHENEVER Bear and his friend Foxy had a bit of shopping to do, they seemed to meet at the crossroads.

"Hello!" Bear always said. "Where are you going, Foxy?"

"Uptown," said Foxy. "Where are you going?"

"Oh, I'm going downtown," Bear said. "Too bad we aren't both going the same way!"

So there they always parted, going into town by different roads. Both were such busy shoppers that they never met until one winter afternoon, just as the stores were closing. And then, both piled high with packages, they almost bumped head on!

"Why, Foxy!" cried Bear. "What in the world are you doing here? Come along and have supper with me."

"What are you doing here?" Foxy returned. "And I'd love to—only it's time for my dinner."

Again the friends shook paws. But just before they parted, Bear said, "Foxy, what do you eat for dinner?"

"Hamburgers, French fries and ice cream," said Foxy.

"Just what I eat for supper," laughed Bear. "So your dinner and my supper are the very same thing!"

"Why, so they are!" Foxy agreed. "And—and, Bear! Since we're both here in the middle of town—your downtown and my uptown must be the same, too!"

"They certainly must!" said Bear, slipping his paw through Foxy's, and heading for the nearest restaurant.

And ever since then, whenever he and his friend Foxy meet at the crossroads, they trot happily into town together.

February Twenty-Ninth

FEBRUARY 29

Today's my first real birthday,
But I'm not one—I'm four!
I guess there aren't many boys
Who always grow up more

Than their birthdays say
They have. It's fun, but sort of queer,
To have your birthday on a day
That comes just in leap year!

The Bear Next Door

MARCH 1

THERE was once a little boy who lived next door to a bear, and they played together every day.

They rode their bicycles together, and learned how to roller skate together, and as a special treat, they sometimes even stayed over-night at each other's houses.

The little bear never stopped talking about the fun he had at the little boy's house, and the little boy told about the bear's house morning, noon and night.

"At Bear's house," he said at breakfast, "we don't bother with napkins, and please and thank you, and all that—"

"At Bear's house," he said at bedtime, "we go fishing in the middle of night whenever we want—"

And every time his bath was ready, the little boy said, "At Bear's house, it's *never* time to take a bath."

"Well!" said his mother at last, "Perhaps you'd better go and live at Bear's house, and *be* a bear!"

So she helped him pack his bag, and opened the door for him.

But once the door closed, the little boy didn't rush next door as he usually did. He went very slowly down the walk—and halfway down, whom did he meet but the little bear!

"Hello," he said, "where are you going?"

"I'm—I'm going to your house to be a boy," gulped the little bear. "Where are you going?"

"To your house, to be a bear," the little boy said. "But, oh dear, I'd much rather go back home and just be me!"

"I'd rather just be me, too," cried the little bear, and home he ran, just as fast as he could run.

The little boy hurried home, too. He tiptoed through the hall and peeped into the living room.

"They—they have a little bear over at Bear's house," he said, in a very small voice. "So do you think you could use me for a little boy again?"

"Of course I do," said his mother. "I certainly do!"

So pretty soon, the little boy was in his own bed, all tucked in and fast asleep, and dreaming about all the fun he would have next day with his friend the bear next door.

The Beautiful Blue Car

MARCH 2

ALL week, hammer and bang, two little monkeys had been busy making themselves a car. They painted it a beautiful blue color. And the minute the paint was dry, they took turns riding and pushing their new car up and down the sidewalk.

That seemed lots of fun, until their cousin came along.

"Why don't you take your car up the hill?" he asked. "Then you can both ride down—with nobody pushing."

"What a good idea!" cried one little monkey, hopping out.

"Let's do it!" said the other, and up the steep hill they went, both pushing their new car.

At the top, both climbed in. Then down they started, going faster, and faster, and faster, and never noticing that they were headed straight for a tree until—

Crash! Into the tree they banged, and their car folded up like an accordion! Luckily, the little monkeys landed in the soft grass and weren't hurt at all.

"But our poor car!" they cried. "It's a wreck!"

And it certainly was! It took the little monkeys another whole week to straighten it out and paint it a beautiful blue again. Pretty soon, their cousin came along again.

"Hello," he said. "Why don't you—"

But that was as far as he got.

"Never mind!" cried both little monkeys at once. "If you want to play—you can take turns riding and pushing our nice, straightened-out blue car—which we like just exactly as it is!"

Three Little Lions

MARCH 3

Three little lions
In one big chair
Grin when the wind
Blows round their lair,
"That's a lion wind
Out there," they say.
"Maybe we can learn
To roar that way!"
And their mother says,
"Then run on outdoors,
For when March comes in
With such lion roars,
It's a quiet lamb
As time goes on—
So hurry, before
The lion's gone!"

The Speedy Little Zebra

"DADDY," said the little zebra, "Daddy, will you teach me how to run speedy and fast like you do?"

"Yes, I will," smiled his daddy, delighted to hear what a speedy runner he was. "I'll give you a lesson right now."

So out they went to the flat plains, a fine place to run.

"Now," said the daddy zebra, "first you—well, you know how to walk, don't you? Running fast is like walking fast, only faster—"

"Like this?" asked the little zebra, trotting off.

"No, no!" called his daddy. "Faster, faster!"

So the little zebra tried going still faster.

"How's that?" he asked.

"Still not fast enough," his daddy said. "The secret is to *think* about running fast—faster than anybody in the world."

"All right," said the little zebra. "Will you run with me?"

His daddy said, "Sure, yes," and away they raced across the flat grassy plains. Now the little zebra thought hard about running fast. He thought even harder about running faster than anybody in the whole world. And all at once, he looked and saw that he was running almost as fast as his daddy!

"One more hard think," he told himself, "and I'll be running *just* as fast!"

But just then, his daddy stopped running.

"That's the end of today's lesson," he said.

"Oh," said the little zebra. "Oh, Daddy, why?"

"No sense in running ourselves ragged, you know," the daddy zebra explained. And he didn't add that, for a while at least, he wanted to stay the speediest runner in the family.

A Pet for Mrs. Fieldmouse

MARCH 5

LITTLE Mrs. Fieldmouse wanted a pet for her birthday.

"And a pet she shall have," said Mr. Fieldmouse. "The only question is—what kind?"

"Where is it?" cried Mr. Fieldmouse.

"Oh, I don't actually *have* it," his friend said. "But I read in the encyclopedia that in the Orient (whatever that is), crickets in small cages are often kept as pets—"

"A cricket!" Mr. Fieldmouse cried. "Why, of course! The very thing!"

So together, the two friends hurried out to the country. It was growing quite dark by the time they had made a sturdy little cage of braided meadow grass. They turned over a good hundred stones before they found a cricket small and cheery enough to suit them.

"Why, I don't know of *any* kind small enough!" cried his friend Mr. Housemouse.

And Mr. Fieldmouse, who had never thought of that, certainly did now! He thought about it day and night. But on the very day before her birthday, he still had not thought up a pet for Mrs. Fieldmouse.

So, ears drooping and tail dragging, he set out to get her a different present. Poor Mr. Fieldmouse was feeling very sad about that, when suddenly, he heard Mr. Housemouse pattering after him.

"I have the very pet!" he was calling.

But at last it was in the cage.

"A beautiful present!" said Mr. Fieldmouse. As it was now past midnight, and already his wife's birthday, he invited Mr. Housemouse to come straight along to her party.

So along they went, singing, "Happy Birthday," while the cricket chirped his merriest. And since little Mrs. Fieldmouse heard them long before she saw them—and guessed that they were bringing her the present she wanted most—she had her cake on the table and the candles lighted, just as the two friends came skipping up to the door.

Mirrors Are Funny

MARCH 6

Mirrors are funny—
When I look in mine,
I always see someone who's looking just fine.
Though people insist that my shoes are undone,
And instead of two mittens, I only have one,
That my hair isn't combed,
And my face isn't clean,
That's not like the someone I always have seen!
They say, "Stand up straight!"
And, "Stop frowning like that!"
And, "Here, let me brush the dry mud from your hat!"
And, "If you could see yourself, I'll tell you, Miss—
You surely would try to do better than this!
Go look in the mirror!"
I do. And in mine
I always see someone who's looking just fine.

Do you think, if I tiptoe when I go upstairs,
And look in the mirror when it's unawares—
I'll see what they see—when I didn't prepare
To look in the mirror up over the stair?

It's an Ill Wind

MARCH 7

"Ooh, but I hate wind!" sighed Granny Goose, all huddled in her house. "It sounds so lonely that it makes me feel lonely, too."

Then whipp, whupp, whirr! an envelope blew against her window, and little as she liked to brave the wind, out she went to get it.

"My oh my!" she said. "It's an invitation to lunch at Henny's house. What a lovely surprise for me on such a lonely, windy day!"

Henny was so surprised to see her! "When my note blew away," she cried, "I recalled how you hate wind—and thought it useless to write another!"

"Me hate wind?" said Granny Goose, happily sitting down. "Well, maybe I did once—but not after the good surprise it blew my way today!"

Not for Sale

MARCH 8

I wanted a kitten
But try and try,
I couldn't find any
At all to buy.
Not at the grocer's,
Or hop, hop, hop,
Not at the baker's
Or pet man's shop.
When I did see some,
(I did at last)
At the washing woman's
As we went past,
I asked, "How much?"
And she said, "Why,
Nobody has money
Enough to buy
A kitten, you know!"
And one, two, three,
She gave me a kitten,
She gave it to me!

The Cowboy Shirt

MARCH 9

LARRY was a little boy who wanted a cowboy shirt more than anything anyone could buy anywhere in town.

He said so, too. Every Wednesday, when he and his mother went downtown, he asked if there was a cowboy shirt on the shopping list.

But his mother always said no. She always said, "After we've bought your shoes (or haircut, or underwear) all our money will be spent."

And at last, on a new-pajamas Wednesday, Larry had given up hoping that a cowboy shirt would ever get on the list. He followed his mother into the store, and up to the pajama counter. He looked at all the pajamas Mr. Prentiss put on the counter. But especially, Larry looked at a beautiful cowboy shirt that must have been put there by mistake. He looked at it, and he touched the cowhead and the lariat on the collar.

And suddenly, Larry's mother said, "Well, Mr. Prentiss, Larry seems to like the cowboy pajamas best of all, so we'll take two pairs."

Cowboy pajamas! Oh my! When the package was wrapped, Larry carried it, and very tightly, too. And all the way home he thought that maybe he could wear the shirt in the daytime, and the shirt and pants at night—and so be a cowboy all day and all night, too.

Which, as it happened, was the very way things turned out!

Poor Old Foxy

MARCH 10

SNIFF, sniff, sniff! came Foxy, closer and closer to the old packing box where three fat little pigs were hiding.

"Don't breathe!" whispered one little pig.

"Don't whisper!" whispered another. "Don't make a sound!"

But the third little pig just had to sneeze. And try as he did to hold it back—out it came in a most tremendous:

A-A-A-A-A-ACHOOOOOOOOO!

What a sneeze it was!

It made old Foxy jump so high and hard that he landed head over heels in a patch of prickly-burrs.

While he was trying to get right side up, and trying to get out without too many prickly-burrs—the little pigs crept out of the box and ran all the way home.

Once they were safely inside, the third little pig blew his nose, and smiled a big smile.

Then suddenly, the second little pig sneezed a-a-a-achoo!

And the first little pig sneezed a-a-a-a-achooo!

And then all three little pigs burst out laughing just to think how high old Foxy had jumped—and how high he would have jumped, if all three had had to sneeze back there in the packing box and had held back and held back, until all three sneezes had come exploding out in one enormous, tremendous, terrific:

A-A-A-A-A-A-A-A-A-ACHOOOOOOOOOO!

Froggie's Voyage

MARCH 11

Froggie made a little boat,
He made a paddle, too.
"Come on," he said to Mousie,
"There's lots of room for you!"
But furry little Mousie said,
"The water's much too chilly—
If we fell in, how cold we'd be!
Why Froggie, you're just silly."
"Who's going to fall in, anyway?"
Cried Froggie with a grin.
Then suddenly, while showing off,
He tipped—and tumbled in!
One hop, and he was out again
He dried in two hops more—
But Mousie (who's not waterproof)
Was glad she'd stayed on shore.

That made him very sad, indeed, until presently, strolling through the jungle, he saw a little monkey asking its mother the very questions he wanted to ask.

The mother monkey answered while her little monkey listened and learned the answers. The little giraffe listened and learned the answers, too—though of course he still wanted to know lots of other things.

"I don't have to ask," he thought, "I don't have to ask at all, as long as I listen!" And now he kept turning his soft little ears this way and that, as he strolled along, so he wouldn't miss a single thing.

And he learned a lot—and the more he knew, the more he learned by listening, too—that smart little, wise little, growing-up giraffe!

Under a Leaf

MARCH 13

Under a leaf, left from last fall,
You may find anything at all:
An army of ants, busy building a town,
A green little toad pulsing up and down,
A big, black beetle, cleaning house;
A new little snake, or an old little mouse
Sound asleep in his grassy bed.
You may see a lizard, quick and red,
Go darting out when you turn it over,
Or the pale green shoots of this year's clover,
Or dozens of spiders, hatching from eggs,
And running off on their wispy legs,
Or even a turtle in his shell
Maybe under the leaf.
You never can tell
What's under a leaf that fell last fall—
You may find anything there at all.

The Growing–Up Giraffe

MARCH 12

A LITTLE giraffe strolled at his mother's side, with his soft, brown eyes full of questions.

"What makes the sky so high and blue?" he wondered. "And why are rainbows and what is dew? And what is water, and why are bees, and why do leaves grow up high on trees?"

But he could not ask even one question, for no giraffe, big or little, has any voice for asking.

Spider Fuzzy-Leg

MARCH 14

Spinning spider
Fuzzy-leg,
Tummy round
As spider egg—
With his beady
Spider eye,
Suddenly, he
Sees a fly.

Spinning stops,
He waits, instead,
Till his sticky
Spider thread
Traps the busy
Buzzing fly,
Greedy Spider,
Spider-sly!

The Goats' House

MARCH 15

AT THE top of a rocky hill, two homeless young goats found a small board house—weathered and empty—just as they had heard.

The young he-goat was delighted, and ready to move in at once. But his sister found fault with everything.

"There's no fireplace," she said. "And just look at that big hole in the roof! Besides, this rocky land is too rocky for growing any kind of garden!"

"One thing at a time," said the he-goat. "Now, first of all, we'll need a fireplace—"

And he started at once to work, digging up rocks and rolling them into the house. His sister just watched, looking rather sour, but before very long he had built a fine stone fireplace, with a chimney to let smoke out.

"Well, that's some better," his sister said. "Especially the way you made the chimney fill up the hole in the roof. But what good is a house, when the land around is so rocky that we'll never grow anything to eat?"

"Won't we?" asked the young he-goat. "Let's just go out and take a look—"

So out they went, and when his sister looked at the land, she almost forgot herself and smiled.

"Why!" she cried. "There are no rocks—every last rock seems to be gone!"

"Of course they're gone," said the young he-goat. "Because I used every last rock to make our fireplace and chimney."

And this time his sister really did smile.

"Come on," she said. "Let's go get some seeds, so I can make us a garden!"

So away they went, to buy a hoe, a rake, and some seeds, with the little she-goat looking as if she had no fault to find with anything, any more.

Bunnies in Spring

MARCH 16

Three little bunnies
In a row,
Noses in sunshine
And tails in snow.

Three little bunnies
Hop three hops—
Nibbling curled-up
Sweet fern tops.

Three little bunnies
Make a ring,
Hippity-hopping
Because it's Spring.

Shane O'Deirg's New Shoes

MARCH 17

WHENEVER Shane O'Deirg needed new shoes, his grandfather brought them from Dublin town. And a wonder it was, the way they fit—snug as a glove and neat as a pin—with Shane never there to try them on.

"How do you do it, Grandfather?" Shane always asked. "How do you get them to fit so well, every single time?"

"Ah, there's nothing to that, lad," his grandfather said, "Not when you've once caught a leprechaun, and seen the way *he* goes about it. One look he takes at your bare, brown foot, while you hold him fast. Then he feels your foot all over with his wee, brown hands, to learn the shape of it—

'Let me go, now,' he begs, 'and I'll have you a pair of beautiful new boots by morning!'

'Aye, do that, wee man,' you reply. 'And I'll leave you a piece of gold for your trouble—'

Then you open your hand (for once he's promised, a leprechaun's good as his word) and whisht! off he goes. All the long night, if you listen, you can hear him tap-tap-tapping away at his work. And in the morning, sure enough, there are your new boots waiting—neat as a pin and snug as a glove—though you'd never once tried them on. A wonder it is, the way they do it—or did it, back in the old days when I was a lad, and the wee folk were everywhere—"

"A wonder indeed!" Shane O'Deirg always sighed, wishing leprechauns were still about.

But when he looked again at his own new shoes—so snug and trim and neat—he thought that the leprechauns were no greater wonder than his own grandfather, who bought his shoes in far-off Dublin town.

The New Salesman

BILLY had to sell ten boxes of seeds to help buy a new slide for the schoolyard. That meant at least ten doorbells to ring. And when Billy started out, he had a strange and shy feeling inside himself.

"Maybe Mother will buy them," he thought, ready to turn back. "Or I could, with my spending money."

But Billy knew his mother didn't want all those seeds. He knew he liked to spend his money on things he wanted, too. So he walked bravely up to the house next door, and rang the bell. When Mrs. Jones opened it, Billy thought she didn't seem one bit like his good friend Mrs. Jones. She seemed like a stranger, who certainly didn't want to buy any seeds.

Just the same, he said, "Hello, Mrs. Jones. Will you buy some seeds to help us get a new slide for our school?"

And then Mrs. Jones smiled exactly like Mrs. Jones.

"Why, yes I will, Billy," she said. "I was going downtown for some, but this is much handier."

She bought them, just like that! And Billy, with money in his pocket, and only nine boxes to sell, hurried off to ring the next door-bell— where Mrs. Brown was probably just wishing for some nice, fresh seeds for her garden.

The Big Red Wagon

JOAN AND TOBY had had a big red wagon. It had been a handy wagon to pull rocks in, and to carry toys in. It had been a dandy wagon to take rides in, too. But now it was lost.

Toby looked out in back where the rocks were. The wagon wasn't there.

Joan looked out on the porch where the toys were. But the wagon wasn't there.

Joan and Toby both looked down in the cellar where the bikes were kept.

But no, the big red wagon wasn't there, either.

Nobody seemed to know where it was. Not even the twins next door, who sometimes borrowed it to ride up and down. Not even mother, who had kept saying, "If you don't put your wagon in the cellar at night, it's sure to get lost!"

"And now it *is* lost," sobbed Joan.

But just when she was saying that, a little boy was coming up the hill. He was a little boy who did know where the big red wagon was.

Because it had rolled down the hill, and into his yard. And he had found it there when he went out to play. And right now, it was right in back of him, because he was pulling the big red wagon up the hill—

And straight back into Joan and Toby's yard.

The Hungry Policeman

MARCH 20

OFFICER O'HALLORAN was a big, fine figure of a policeman, and always hungry. He walked his beat, up and down Market Street, keeping a sharp eye on things and getting hungrier and hungrier. He passed Tony's Fruit Store, with its outside stand heaped with luscious fruits, and licked his lips.

"Have a banana, Officer O'Halloran?" grinned Tony.

But Officer O'Halloran shook his head and said no, thank you, he never ate on duty. Then he went past the delicatessen, full of cheeses, cold meats, potato chips and pickles. And when Max, the proprietor offered him a whole bologna, he closed his eyes and shook his head. So it went, all day long. Past the candy store, the bakery, the peanut man, the chestnut man and the jelly-apple man went poor Officer O'Halloran, saying, "No, thank you, not on duty," and getting hungrier and hungrier. At last his day ended, and he fairly ran home, up the stairs, and into the kitchen.

"You must be hungry, man!" cried his wife, who was dishing up corned beef and everything. "Sit and sup!"

"Not while I'm on duty," groaned poor Officer O'Halloran, purely out of habit. Then he opened his eyes, threw his cap in the air, and cried, "But I'm *not* on duty now, am I?"

And he sat down and ate the most enormous meal you ever saw, that big, hungry, fine figure of a policeman. As his wife said, 'twas always a pleasure to cook for him.

SPRING

Henny's Surprise

MARCH 21

ALL AROUND the year, Henny was proud of the eggs she laid. But with the first day of spring, Henny thought of Easter. Plain white eggs didn't suit her at all.

"I'm going to lay beautiful, all-colored ones like the Easter Bunny brings," she said.

And off she ran to the meadow, to a secret nest she had built. There Henny tried and tried to lay pink, blue, yellow, and purple eggs.

But all she ever got were white ones. And to make things worse, the other hens kept bobbing past to ask how things were going.

"How are the eggs, Henny?" they asked. "How many colors do you have now?"

Henny didn't say a word. She just sat on her nest to hide the eggs, and smiled wisely, and hoped that some magic would turn her eggs pink, blue, yellow, and purple by Eastertime.

But nothing did, even with Easter almost there—all six eggs were as white as ever. And here came all the other hens, eager to see them.

"Oh me!" gulped Henny. "I'll just have to tell them I didn't lay colored eggs, after all."

And just as she said that—crack! went one of the eggs under her warm feathers.

Crack! Another opened, too.

Crack, crack, crack, crack! All six white eggs hatched. So, by the time the other hens got to Henny's nest—what did they see but six fuzzy little chicks.

My, weren't those other hens surprised!

And my, oh my, wasn't Henny surprised, and pleased! And proud! So proud, that when the other hens said, "What darling chicks, Henny! Did they really come out of colored eggs?" she said proudly:

"No, out of just plain, fine white eggs."

And ever after that, fine white eggs suited Henny perfectly, all around the year—and at Eastertime, too.

The Hopkins' Compromise

MARCH 22

1. Spring—and everything was looking so bright and new. "Let's paint our house," said Mr. Hopkin. "Blue is a bright, new color!"

2. "Red is brighter and newer," Mrs. Hopkin cried. And the little Hopkins liked yellow best for a color.

3. "Well, well," said Mr. Hopkin. "Let's compromise!" So he poured blue, red and yellow paint into one pail—

4. And everyone stirred, and everyone dipped, and everyone painted — and their house turned out a rich brown.

5. "Blue, red *and* yellow is a delicious color," they all agreed, admiring their house, which looked as tasty as a chocolate Easter egg.

The Runaway Wind

MARCH 23

The runaway wind came by today
Calling, "Come on, let's run away!"
He pulled my coat, and tugged my hair,
And promised to take me everywhere.

I wanted to go till I asked him when
He thought we'd be back home again,
And he whooped with whirly, wicked glee,
"Oh, never again, if you come with me!"
So I said, "Well then, I guess I'll stay,"
And let him go on his runaway way
All by himself, today.

Mrs. Mouse's Rainy-Day Things

MARCH 24

MRS. MOUSE ran upstairs, looking for her umbrella. And Mr. Mouse ran downstairs, looking for Mrs. Mouse's overshoes.

"She should have a hanky, too," said one little mouse, opening the bureau drawers.

"—and her waterproof raincoat!" called his twin, searching everywhere for it.

Then Mrs. Mouse called from the attic, "Oh dear, my umbrella's not here!"

And Mr. Mouse grumbled, "No overshoes in this whole cellar. Where in the world can they be?"

And the two little mice said, "We can't find her hankies or raincoat, either! Now Mommie

won't be able to go to the store, and we won't have anything good for our supper!"

The whole mouse family was almost in tears, when suddenly the rain stopped, and the sun came out.

Away went Mrs. Mouse, acorn basket over her arm, skipping merrily around the puddles. And while she was gone, Mr. Mouse and the twins searched until they found her umbrella and overshoes, her hankies and her raincoat.

"How clever you are!" cried Mrs. Mouse, when she came home. "Now please put them all safely away for a rainy day."

"Yes indeedy!" said Mr. Mouse and the two little mice.

But all three were so very eager to see what Mrs. Mouse had brought in her basket that they never could quite remember exactly where it was that they had put Mrs. Mouse's rainy-day things.

The Sun and I

MARCH 25

When just above the mountain,
The sun pops up its head,
I know it's time for me to be
Hopping out of bed.

And when it's at its highest,
Right overhead, at noon,
I go and wash my hands for lunch,
Which will be ready soon.
Then after, while I'm playing,
The sun slips down, until—
It blinks, "It's time for supper!"
And half-hides behind the hill.

At last, all of it's hidden,
And the sky's a big, dark cup,
And I wish the time were morning—
And the sun and I were up.

Dr. Upping
and Dr. Downing

MARCH 26

Dr. Upping and Dr. Downing never even spoke to each other.

And all because Dr. Downing, who took good care of everybody's teeth, claimed that no one should ever eat lollipops.

While Dr. Upping, who took good care of everybody's everything except teeth, thought the world of them.

"Nothing's so cheering as a lollipop!" he always said, offering one to each patient at the end of a visit.

The boys and girls certainly agreed with him.

But when Dr. Downing heard them unwrapping cellophane on the way downstairs, and then saw them skipping down the street eating their lollipops, he was furious.

"Dr. Upping," he shouted up the speaking tube at last. "This lollipop business has *got* to stop!"

That made Dr. Upping furious, too.

He zipped down the stairs as if he were on an escalator, knocked furiously on Dr. Downing's door, and shouted, "Let's talk reasonably about lollipops!"

"Lollipops," fumed Dr. Downing, "are bad for people's teeth."

"Now look here!" Dr. Upping replied. "Lollipops may not be good for people's teeth, but they do make people happy. And happy people are healthy. And healthy people keep their teeth healthy by brushing them after meals and after lollipops—"

Then, purely from habit, Dr. Upping held out a lollipop, and said, "Care for one?" Purely from surprise, Dr. Downing took it, and popped it into his mouth.

It happened to be wild cherry, which tasted so good that it made Dr. Downing's eyes begin to twinkle.

"You know, Dr. Upping," he said after a bit. "I believe you're right. A lollipop may well be a good thing now and then."

He put out his hand, and Dr. Upping shook it heartily.

And then, as it was nearly time for office hours, Dr. Upping went happily upstairs, and Dr. Downing, humming away, went back into his own office.

The Wonderful Pushcart

MARCH 27

A strange little man comes to our town,
He pushes his pushcart up and down
And calls, "Come buy, come buy what I'm
    selling!"
But what it'll be, there's no way of telling—
It may be nuts with loose, soft shells,
Or wonderful, tinkling glass wind-bells,
Or folded-up lanterns, or paper things
That turn into fans or birds with wings,
Or queer-looking hats to wear on your head;
Or it may be kites to make, instead,
Or paper flowers in bright bouquets
That pop out of shells, and on other days
It may be rice cakes, still oven-hot—

But whatever you thought it was—it's not!
So we save our pennies, and wait for his cry,
"Come buy what I'm selling! Come buy!"

Nero

MARCH 28

Nero's the oddest kind of cat—
He won't play with string
Or things like that,
He doesn't chase mice,
Or sit on laps,
Or go out prowling,
Or take cat naps.
He never meows.
He won't even purr.
He just likes to sit,
Like a king in fur,
Watching to see that we all do
Exactly the things he wants us to.

Steam Shovel

MARCH 29

I know what I'll do when I get big,
I'll run a steam shovel.
Dig, dig, dig,
I'll make the shovel go up and down,
Making a mountain, high and brown,
Making a hole so deep and wide
That a whole new house will fit inside.
I'll dig and dig until it's night,
And then I'll very carefully light
Some danger lanterns, and put them around,
So people won't fall
In my hole in the ground.

Busy, Busy Beavers

LITTLE BEAVER sat all by his lone on the river bank. And oh, how he wished somebody would notice him.

"Busy, busy beavers," he chanted softly. "Too busy to take a little beaver swimming, or get him something good to eat, or tell him a story even—"

But it did no good. All the big beavers were so busy building a dam, that they didn't even hear him.

So Little Beaver tried chanting louder, and still louder.

But still it did no good. Those big beavers went right on pushing logs into place, and carrying twigs and mud, and chinking the spaces between the logs. Not one of them, not even Little Beaver's own mother and daddy, so much as looked at him!

And that made him feel so lonely, and so cross, that before he quite knew what he was going to do—he had jumped up and fairly shouted:

"One thing I know! When I grow up I'll be a fishy old fish, or a squirrelly old squirrel, or even a skunky old skunk! But I won't be a busy old beaver—too busy to have any fun!"

The big beavers heard him this time, all right. All of them, except his grandpa, dropped what they were doing and stared right at him. And his daddy stared so sternly that Little Beaver was pretty sure he was in for a good paddling with his daddy's paddling tail.

Oh my, all that Little Beaver wished now, was that the big beavers would be busy again. Too busy to even notice that there was a little beaver around!

But there he was, everybody staring at him, when suddenly his grandpa called to him.

"Look here, Little Beaver," he said. "I need some help patting the mud into these chinks. So come on over, and I'll show you what I mean—"

"I'm coming, Gramp!" called Little Beaver. "Here I come!"

Then splish! he dived into the water. Swish! he swam to his gramp's side. In two minutes, Little Beaver was so busy patting in mud with his flat little tail that all the big beavers stopped staring, and smiled.

And Little Beaver, having a dandy time pat-pat-patting away as busily as any beaver, was very glad he'd learned how to use his little patting tail—before his daddy had made up his mind to use his big paddling one!

Smoky's Come-Uppance

MARCH 31

WHENEVER Rags saw Smoky, the big, swaggering cat next door, he felt ashamed of himself.

"If only I could chase him up a tree!" he told himself. "After all, dogs are supposed to chase cats."

But whenever Rags tried, Smoky swaggered up to him looking so big and bad that, before the poor puppy knew what was happening, he was the one being chased.

It was the same with the other puppies. Not one of them was a match for that big gray Smoky.

"Not one of us," thought Rags one day. "But—but I just bet *all* of us could take him down a peg!"

He ran to tell the other puppies. And laughing inside, but barking loud, fierce barks, they all slipped through the gate and rushed straight at Smoky. What a noise they made! The big cat didn't swagger this time. He didn't even look to see who was coming. He just streaked up the nearest tree.

"We did it!" barked Rags. "We did it at last!"

"We certainly did!" gulped the other puppies, because Smoky was up so high that no ladder in the neighborhood could reach him. At last clang, clang, clang! the fire engine came to get the big cat down from his high perch. Rags and the other puppies, and all the dogs and children crowded around to watch the exciting rescue. But the firemen weren't pleased.

"Fire engines are for putting out fires," they said, when Smoky was safe. "And there's a rule against dogs running around loose."

So the next day, all the dogs were kept in their own yards. But they didn't mind. Neither did the other puppies. And neither did Rags, because Smoky was staying close to his own house, too—and he wasn't swaggering at all.

April Fooling

APRIL 1

It sleeted a little,
It snowed some, too,
And rained for a bit;
Then the sky got blue
With a rainbow curving
Up over the hill,
And the sun felt hot,
But the wind felt chill.
"Oh," cried a Mouse,
"Will you please tell me
What time of year
This can ever be—
Winter or summer
Or spring or fall?"
He was all mixed up,
Couldn't tell at all—
And just because
He never knew
That April likes
April-fooling, too.

The Jolly Baker

APRIL 2

THERE was once a jolly baker who baked the most delicious things all week long.

"I wish I could bake on Sunday, too," he told his friend the greengrocer.

"Why don't you, then?" asked his friend.

"It would be a waste," the baker said. "Everything would be a day old by Monday."

"It wouldn't if it were all eaten up on Sunday, would it?" asked the greengrocer.

"Why no, it wouldn't!" the baker cried. He rushed into his kitchens, and baked to his heart's content.

Along about teatime, he lighted his shop, and set up a big table with heaped-up plates of little cakes, and an enormous pot of his best China tea. Then he stood at his door, welcoming his friends as they came strolling up.

"My, oh my!" they cried, happily sniffing the air. "Can we buy your delicious baked things on Sundays now, too?"

"Indeed you can't," said the jolly baker. "Sunday is just the day for a tea party! Come along in—and help yourselves!"

The Wrong Side of Bed

MR. BEAR was a good-natured bear, except for when he first got up. Then he grouched at Mrs. Bear, grumped at the little bears, and even growled at himself.

Later on, he was always sorry about it, too.

"I'm sorry I grouched," he told Mrs. Bear.

"I'm sorry I grumped," he told the little bears.

"Oh, that's all right," they always said. And one day, Mrs. Bear added, "I guess you just got out of the wrong side of bed."

"How could that be?" thought Mr. Bear. "All my life I've gotten out of the same side—"

It really was a puzzle. By noon, it came to Mr. Bear that he always had been grouchy in the morning, too. And at night, just as he was dropping off to sleep, Mr. Bear thought he knew just what was causing the trouble.

So the next morning, when Mrs. Bear called him, Mr. Bear did not get out of his own side of bed. Instead, he rolled a walloping big roll over to the other side. And he landed on the floor—bedclothes and all—with such a thump that Mrs. Bear and the little bears were sure he must be in a specially bad humor.

But Mr. Bear came downstairs smiling from ear to ear.

"My goodness," cried his wife, "you're smiling!"

"I know it," grinned Mr. Bear. "And all because I figured out that the wrong side of bed is the right side for me—"

Mrs. Bear had trouble understanding that, and the little bears didn't even try. It was quite enough for them that, from that day on, Mr. Bear was a good-natured bear all day long.

Four Little Cats

APRIL 4

Four little cats
Sat down and cried,
"It's raining rain
All over outside!

We can't play hide,
We can't play race,
All we can play
Is rain-in-the-face!"

Then all at once,
And not looking sour,
They all exclaimed,
"It was just a shower!"

And four little cats
Ran out to play
In the dewy blue
Of an April day!

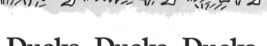

Ducks, Ducks, Ducks

APRIL 5

THREE little ducklings, all in a row, set out for a walk one bright spring day. Never having been anywhere, and never having seen anyone except ducks, ducks, ducks—they thought that ducks were the only people in the world.

So when they met a trim hen that said, "Cluck!"

And an old turkey gobbler who said, "Gobble-gobble!"

And a fat young pig saying, "Oink-oink-oink!" those three little ducklings could hardly believe their eyes *or* ears.

Back to the pond they waddled, all in a row,

Sayings

Grown-ups have sayings
That, plain to be seen,
Mean something much different
From what they should mean.

If you're telling them something,
And they start "Well-welling,"
It means they're not hearing
One word of your telling.

And "Sometime," means "No time,"
And "Maybe," means "No,"
So I think when I'm grown up,
Wherever I go—

And whoever asks me,
I'll say, "I just guess!"
To whatever they ask me—
Because that means, "Yes!"

If you ask them for something,
Like a new kind of pet,
And they say, "Well, we'll see—"
We just don't. They forget.

If you ask to be read to,
And wait almost forever,
It's 'cause "After-a-while,"
Very often means, "Never."

and giggling till their little tummies ached.

"Oh, Mother!" they cried. "We met the funniest ducks you ever did see! One was a red duck, with a little, sharp bill, and do you know what it said? It said 'Cluck!' "

"That was no duck," said their mother. "It was a hen."

"Hen," said the ducklings thoughtfully. "Well, anyway—then we saw an even funnier duck. Big and brownish, with a fan for a tail, and it said, 'Gobble-gobble—' "

"That was a turkey," the mother duck said.

"Turkey," repeated the little ducklings.

"But then, oh then, we saw the funniest duck of all! It had no feathers and no wings, and too many legs, and a curly little fishworm tail—and it said, 'Oink-oink-oink!' "

"And it wasn't a duck, either," their mother explained. "It was a pig, saying what a pig says."

With that, she waded into the water and went paddling off. And her three little ducklings, all in a row, paddled after her, saying, "Pig-turkey-hen," over and over—and chuckling to think how many folks there were in the world, besides ducks, ducks, ducks.

69

The Bunny Gardener

APRIL 7

THE LITTLE tan bunny never did get enough to eat. And all because, whenever he found a fine, green and growing garden, and tiptoed in—somebody shooed him right out again.

"Mean old gardeners!" he sobbed, hopping away. "If I had a garden, I wouldn't shoo hungry people out of it!"

"Why don't you have one, then?" asked a hungry crow.

"I will!" said the bunny. "Why, I just will!"

So he dug and raked and planted and watered and weeded his own little garden. And first thing each morning, out he hopped to see if his plants were growing big enough to eat.

At last one morning, they were. But right in the middle of them sat the hungry crow, and a hungry hen and woodchuck, gobbling away, before the bunny had had so much as a taste.

"Shoo!" he shouted angrily. "Get out of my garden!"

The hen and woodchuck backed away. But the crow gobbled faster and said, "You said that if you had a garden—you wouldn't shoo hungry people out of it!"

"So I did," the bunny admitted. "But that was before I knew that gardens are lots of work. Shoo now, Crow!"

And he made such a fierce face that the crow really did stop eating, and asked, "Wh-what if I help you work? I can plant seeds where things get eaten up—"

"I can water the plants for you!" called the woodchuck.

"I can weed out all the weeds!" offered the hen.

"In that case," said the bunny gardener, with a happy smile, "I won't have to shoo hungry people out of my garden, because in that case—it will be our garden—"

Then down he sat, with his new helpers around him. And all four of them nibbled and chewed and gobbled away, until they felt fat and full and fine enough to start on their gardening work.

The Busy Gardener

APRIL 8

"Stop bothering us!" said the cutting worms,
And the beetle bugs, and the sleepy moles.
"It's much too early in Spring for you
To dig up our houses the way you do!"

"If I'm a bother—I beg your pardon,"
The gardener said. "But I'm digging a garden.
A garden without any stones or stumps,
Of good, soft earth without any lumps—
A garden where carrot seeds will grow,
And little green peas in a viney row,

Mr. Bunny's Egg Hunt

Poor Mr. Bunny!

He looked and looked in the dim moonlight, and still he could not find any place to start his egg hunt for the last little boy on his Easter list.

The grass was clipped too short for hiding anything, the bushes had no low branches left on them, and all the trees had little fences around them that meant, "Keep out."

"Well," he told himself, "I'll just have to leave this basket, eggs and all, in the living

And tasty herbs, and crisp wax beans,
And radishes, too, and salad greens—
So that's how it is. I'm digging a garden,
And if it annoys you—I beg your pardon."

"No trouble at all!" cried the cutting worms,
And the beetle bugs, and the hungry moles.
"We're in your way, sir! We'll all be going—
But we'll all be back
                    when you get things
                                    growing!"

room. It's a nice, pretty basket, and it will be very nice and all right—"

And hop, hop, hop, he started toward the front door with his key for opening any lock. But as he went, whisk! the moon went down, and pop! the sun peeped up. And then Mr. Bunny saw something he hadn't seen before. All over the lawn, here, there, and everywhere —were crocuses, white and yellow and blue ones looking like Easter eggs set on end.

"Looking *exactly* like Easter eggs set on end!" laughed Mr. Bunny. And hop, hop, hippity-hop, round and round he went, hiding Easter eggs. He put them here, there, and everywhere —looking exactly like crocuses popping up in the grass.

Then he left the last basket in the living room, with its chocolate bunny, and its chocolate egg, its lots of jelly beans, and a big, glistening sugary egg to look into—but with plenty of room for Easter eggs, too.

"As anyone would be sure to see," smiled Mr. Bunny, hopping into his little pink, sugary truck.

And away he drove, yawning and ready for bed. just as the last little boy in the last house was yawning and smiling—and all ready to wake up.

Surprise

APRIL 10

Out in the barn
In a nest of hay,
Six warm eggs
Are tucked away.
With five little pecks,
And five little picks,
Five crack open
And five little chicks
Hop out—all yellow,
With wobbly legs.
Then peck and pick,
The last of the eggs
Cracks open, too—
And what do you think?
Out comes a chick
As black as ink!

Spring Peepers

APRIL 11

I have a secret
That nobody knows.
In the little woods
Where nobody goes,
There's a secret song
That grows and grows
As I tiptoe down
To the brook's cool glade,
Where, in the summer,
We go to wade.
But when I get there,
Most suddenly—
The song stops still,
And I never can see
Who does the singing!
Not that I mind—
I like secrets best,
When they're hard
To find.

All Kinds of Houses

APRIL 12

WHAT a beautiful Spring day!

All the little animals came hurrying out to play.

Little Bear tumbled out of his cave house. Little Rabbit hopped out of his burrow. Little Squirrel scurried out of his tree house, and Frisk, the little dog, came frisking out of his doghouse.

Little Turtle came out to play, too. And all day long, while the little animals played together, he bumbled along in his shell, which *is* his house. Little Turtle was always the slowest. He was "it" so often that sometimes the others just had to laugh at him (behind their paws, of course), but little Turtle didn't mind.

When the sun went down, all the others had to go home, back to cave house or burrow, stone house, tree house, or doghouse. They all had their supper indoors, and went to bed indoors.

But not little Turtle. He gobbled a fat bug and a tasty fly, and took a drink at a nearby pool. Then he pulled his head and tail and his four little legs into his shell (which *is* his house) and slept outdoors, under the stars—just like a great explorer.

A Day for Growing

APRIL 13

ONE April Saturday, it began to rain.

It rained so hard that it drummed on the roof, and beat on the window panes.

Jock watched that rain come sweeping down.

He watched it come down more slowly, changing from a sweep of rain into a splattery dripping and dropping.

Then Jock wanted to go out in the rain. So he put on his boots, which were fine and big. But when he put on his raincoat—it was much too small. It was too short in the sleeves, and reached only to his knees, and wouldn't buckle across the front at all.

"I grew too big for it in the winter!" he told his mother.

"You certainly did!" his mother laughed, turning him around to the mirror.

That little old skimpy raincoat looked so funny that Jock had to laugh, too—until suddenly, the doorbell rang.

"It's probably Skip coming to get me!" he said. "Only I can't go out with no raincoat. I can't go anywhere!"

By that time, Jock's mother had answered the door. Back she came with a store package in her hands.

"It's for you," she told Jock. "The delivery man brought it just in time."

Jock opened the package as fast as he could. In it, there was a new raincoat and hat—the yellow slicker kind—plenty big enough for him, and for growing besides.

So he took off his little, last-year's raincoat, and put on his big, new one for this year. And out he went into the fine, wet rain that was making everything outdoors grow bigger and bigger, too.

Treasure

APRIL 14

Yesterday,
For the very first time,
I lost a tooth—
And I found a dime
Under my pillow
(Just as they said)
This morning, when
I woke up in bed.

A dime for a tooth!
Think how rich I'll be
When I lose them all!
Why, just look at me—

With dozens of teeth
In two long rows,
And when one comes out—
Another one grows!

Topsy Turvy

APRIL 15

THERE was a little girl who could get things topsy-turvy in no time at all. Why, she and her mother spent so much time picking up, that they never did have time for a walk before lunch, or a story before supper.

And the little girl didn't like that at all.

Neither did her mother.

"Why, Topsy Turvy," she said one day, "I just don't see how one little girl can make such a muss!"

"I don't, either," sighed the little girl.

But the next day, she watched to see. And what she saw was—that she kept taking out more and more and more and MORE things to play with.

"Maybe," she thought, "maybe if I put one back, before I take another one out—it will be different."

And that was what she did. Every single time she reached for a new toy, she put away the one she was tired of, first. By picking-up time, that little girl could hardly believe her eyes.

Her mother was even more surprised.

"Why, Topsy Turvy!" she cried. "How did you *ever* get everything picked up so quickly?"

"It's a secret," said the little girl, whispering in her mother's ear. She whispered something else, too.

And her mother smiled, "Of course I don't have to call you Topsy Turvy! I'll call you your own name—Ann."

She did, too. She called her little girl Ann when they went for walks, and when they read stories. Because ever since then, there's nothing topsy-turvy in that whole house—not even Ann.

Tag-Along Lamb

APRIL 16

"LOOK here, little Tag-Along," said Mother Sheep one morning, "you're getting too big to follow me around like a baby lamb. You should be skipping and playing on your own. So go along now, and have a good time—"

"All right," said her little lamb. "Here I go!"

With a proud skip-hop, he frolicked off. Then thud! that little tag-along stopped in his tracks. Because with no one to follow, he didn't know where in the world to go.

By now his mother was well out of sight. But a rough, black colt was racing by, so he followed it across the sunny meadow. He followed a frisky calf down the rolling pasture hill. Then, seeing the farmer and his hay wagon going past, the little tag-along lamb followed them.

Down the lane he went, out to the road, nibbling wisps of new-mown hay. They tasted so good that when the farmer caught sight of him, and called, "Hyah! Go along home!" the little

Indian Sign

LITTLE Red Fox went tiptoeing through the woods with his two fox brothers.

"Where are we going?" asked one. "Down to see the little tree with a yellow bird singing on its top?"

"Nope," said Little Red Fox. "You took us there yesterday, and this is going to be lots more exciting than that."

"Where are we going, then?" asked his other brother. "Down to see the old red stump with a little red snake on it, eating up red ants?"

"Nope," said Little Red Fox. "You took us there day before yesterday—and this is going to be plenty lots more exciting."

Now Little Red Fox's brothers could hardly wait one more minute to see where he was taking them. And they didn't have to, either. Because in half a minute, he stopped and showed them a row of birch trees, all bent one way.

"Ho hum," said one of his brothers. "This isn't much of an exciting thing to see."

"Ho hum," agreed the other. "No, it isn't."

"Isn't it?" whispered Little Red Fox. "Well, it just happens that Indians bend trees that way to make a trail. And these trees weren't bent last fall—so Indians must have—"

"Indians!" cried his brothers. "They've probably set out fox traps!"

Then away they ran. And they looked so excited and frightened that Little Red Fox (who knew perfectly well that a winter ice-storm had bent those trees) started running, too—and was the first one home.

lamb turned his back, and pretended he couldn't hear a thing.

But just then, along came the farmer's little boy, riding his bicycle home for lunch. He saw the trouble and said, "I'll take care of this for you, Daddy."

He nudged little Tag-Along around with his front wheel, and started him trotting. And, ringing his bicycle bell to keep the lamb trotting, he rode at his heels until they both turned in at the farm gate.

"There!" said the farmer's little boy. "I'm getting to be a real big help around here!"

"And I'm getting to be a real big lamb," thought the little tag-along lamb. "Why, I'm so big that people are beginning to follow me!"

Then away he went, to find his mother and tell her all about it. And this time, he went along with a proud skip-hop, not needing to follow anybody at all.

The Lost Brown

APRIL 18

WHENEVER the Browns went grocery shopping, Mrs. Brown said, "Now remember, if any of you get lost—stay right where you are until the rest of us come and find you."

She tried her best to keep her five little Browns together, too, by counting noses now and then, and by having them walk two-by-two.

But one day, Billy Brown stopped at the cookie counter. It took him a long time to decide what kind he liked best of all. And when at last he looked for the other Browns—he couldn't see one of them.

"They're lost!" thought Billy. And that made him feel frightened, until he remembered about lost Browns staying put till they were found.

"All *I* have to do is find them!" he told himself.

And up and down the aisles he went, past canned food, food in jars, meats, vegetables, frozen foods, baked things, and things for scouring and cleaning—but not one single Brown did he see.

"They're not lost in the store," he gulped. "So maybe I'd better look outside in the parking lot."

That was a big job for a boy Billy's size. There would be plenty of cars in the lot. Some of them might be moving, too. Billy wondered if he could get to the Browns' car all by himself.

Then, just as he got to the store door—he wasn't all by himself any more. Mrs. Brown and four little Browns came running up and crowded around him.

"We couldn't find you anywhere!" they cried.

"I couldn't find you anywhere, either," said Billy.

"Of course not," said Mrs. Brown. "All of us were rushing around—and just missing each other, no doubt. Now if ever you get lost again, Billy, please do as I say—and stay put until we find you."

Billy blinked. He was all ready to say, "I see! It's the one who's all alone that's lost!" But before he could, Mrs. Brown said, "Here, Billy, you can push the grocery cart, and walk two-and-two with me—"

So Billy didn't say a word. He just went along with the other Browns (all two-by-two), and he steered the cart straight for the cookie counter —to show his mother the kind of cookies he had decided were the very best of all.

The Park

APRIL 19

If I owned the park,
If the park were mine,
I'd never put up a single sign
That said, "Don't pick flowers!"
Or, "Don't climb trees,"
Or, "Please don't feed
The animals, please!"
I'd just put up one that said, "Hello!
Please go wherever you'd like to go,
And do whatever you'd want to do—
If the park were yours,
And the animals, too."

Lucky Mrs. Hen!

APRIL 20

"WHAT an April!" sighed Mrs. Sheep, looking out at the rain. "I should be cutting my grass, but how can I?"

"There never *was* such an April," mooed Mrs. Cow. "Here it is, time to plant my garden, and all I can do is sit inside and worry about it!"

"Last year this time we went on a picnic," squealed the little pigs. "Remember how sunshiney it was, and how good everything tasted out there in the woods?"

And Mr. and Mrs. Goat just sat at their window, with long faces, saying, "Rain, rain, go away—"

But little Mrs. Hen put on her apron and cleaned her house. When every corner was spick and span, she did her baking, clucking happily to herself. Then she made doughnuts. And that day, just as she was sprinkling them with sugar, the rain stopped and pop! out came the sun!

"Just in time," clucked Mrs. Hen. "I'll wash windows."

She did. And she cut her grass and planted her garden.

Then since the day was so beautiful, Mrs. Hen packed a picnic basket. She stopped to see if her neighbors could come along. But none of them could. Not one!

"All this bright sunshine makes it plain to see that my house must be cleaned," sighed Mrs. Sheep.

"Yes, indeed," groaned the others. "And after that, there's all the outside work to do. *We* can't go gallivanting off whenever we take the notion—"

They did sound snippy. But lucky little Mrs. Hen hardly even noticed. She waved good-by, and without a care in the world, went hurrying off to have her picnic in the beautiful, sunshiney, springtime woods.

Spring Bouquet

APRIL 21

I picked a yellow one
That was a daffodil,

I picked a white one,
That I call johnnyquil,

I picked a blue one
With little hanging bells,
Spilling out the lovely way
A hyacinth smells.

I picked a rosy primrose,
With yellow at the edge—

And a jack-in-the-pulpit,
From underneath the hedge.

I left all the rest of them
To grow outside,
But I needed a few of them,
You know—inside.

The Strange Case of Mr. Camel

CRANKY Mr. Camel came rushing out of his darkish house, fairly stomping with rage.

"Look here, everybody!" he shouted. "While I've been in bed with a cold—sniffling and coughing, and not able to eat a bite for days—somebody has been stealing my hump!"

"Why, nobody'd do that, Mr. Camel," said Mrs. Elephant. "There must be some mistake—"

"Mistake, eh?" snorted Mr. Camel, turning around so every one could see how little was left of his hump. "It's robbery—and I'm going to call the police!"

"That's hardly necessary," said Mrs. Elephant, "Especially since we have no police. Besides, if we all meet at my house, over a good lunch, we can surely find some clues ourselves."

"I doubt it," grumbled Mr. Camel. But suddenly realizing that he was very hungry, he trooped along in with the rest, and was soon sulkily eating away.

He only snorted when Mr. Zebra asked if he had looked under his bed for his hump. He glared when timid Mrs. Giraffe asked if he was sure he had *had* a hump. And when Mr. Rhinoceros (looking most mysterious) asked where he'd last seen his hump, Mr. Camel threw down his napkin.

"Right on top of my back, of course," he cried. "Right where it always was—right there—"

He turned around to point at the exact spot. And there, right where it should have been—and looking quite as big and humpy as ever—was Mr. Camel's lost hump!

"Who put it there?" shouted Mr. Camel. "Who put it back while I wasn't looking?"

"Nobody did," said Mr. Rhinoceros. "Because I *was* looking. And I observed that the more you ate, the bigger your hump grew—"

"Oh my!" cried Mr. Camel. "Oh yes, of course. I—I just forgot that that's what my hump is for—for storing extra food. So when I wasn't eating, there *was* no extra, and my hump just melted away—sort of—"

And he did look so sheepish that Mrs. Elephant gave him an extra large helping of date pudding.

"That should keep it from happening again today," she smiled.

"It should indeed," agreed Mr. Camel, and for once in his life, he didn't look cranky at all.

Too Many Brothers

APRIL 23

MANY a time during the year, Ting Ling thought to himself that he had too many brothers.

And why not? When he wanted a new bamboo fishing pole, his father shook his head and said it was now Second Brother's turn to be given one.

When Ting Ling wished for a new winter suit, his mother shook her head and said there was only enough cloth and padding to make one for Third Brother, who was in rags.

If there was but one bowl of rice left over, or one lichee, or one bite of sweet, white mooncake, and Ting Ling's mouth was watering for it—whisk! and Fourth, Fifth, Sixth or Seventh Brother had gobbled it first.

And when there was a round, golden orange in the little Chinese house, with seven brothers, Ting Ling never got more than one-eighth of it. No wonder he often wished he were his friend Loo Wan, who had more of everything—except brothers!

But as the year rolled around, it brought the Festival of Kites, when every Chinese man and boy flies a kite to honor his ancestors. Then Loo Wan and his father stood on the hill, flying but two kites. And the Ling family stood flying all of theirs.

Ting Ling counted their kites, gliding and dipping in the air like a whole school of strange and wonderful fish.

"Nine," he whispered proudly. "More kites than any family in the whole village—" Then he looked down at his little brothers, one by one, and smiled a smile as wise as any ancestor's. Because that day—that one day, anyway—Ting Ling was sure that not one of his many brothers was too many, after all.

Come with Me

APRIL 24

Come with me—
Oh, come and see!
There are blossoms now
On the beechnut tree,
And though the oak tree
Is dark and bare,
A pair of robins
Are nesting there;

And any minute
The willows mean
To burst out in leaf—
Their tips are green
With the coming ones,
Oh, come with me—
It's spring again,
And there's lots to see!

New Neighbors

APRIL 25

WHEN the big house next door was empty, Polly kept wondering who would come to live there.

One day, an old lady looked at it, and came out shaking her head. "I love that big kitchen," she told the real estate man, "because I love to bake—but the rest of the house is far too big for me."

A stout man looked at the house next door, too. He told the real-estate man that he liked the big, dry basement because he had lots of pets. But otherwise, he said, he had no need for such a big house.

Then a pretty lady looked at the house. "I like everything about it," she said. "Except that —even with our three children—we certainly don't need seven big bedrooms!"

That house seemed to be just too big for anyone.

But just when Polly was sure no one ever would come to live next door, the real-estate man took down the *For Sale* sign. And a few days later, a moving van came rolling up. Polly watched the men unload, and tried to guess who was moving in.

The moving men took out a rocking chair that might belong to an old lady who loved to bake. They carried out armloads of things that could belong to a stout man who liked pets; a cat's sleeping basket, a dog's eating bowl, an enormous fishbowl, and three bird cages.

And then they began to unload beds. A grandmother's poster bed, a mother's-and-daddy's bed, a pair of bunk beds, a crib, and three beds just like the one Polly slept in herself.

All at once, Polly knew who was coming to live next door.

"It just has to be a family with a grandma," she told herself. "A family with a grandma who loves to bake, *and* a daddy with lots of pets, *and* a mother with so many children that they do need all seven big bedrooms!"

And oh my, how Polly wished they would all hurry up and come to live in the big house that was exactly right for them!

Mr. Sugarplum's Rainy Day

APRIL 26

MR. SUGARPLUM did not like rain.

He said it was a dark, wet, splattery bother. And on rainy days, he sat scowling in his easy chair, his feet tucked under his five cozy, furry cats.

The only time he brightened up was at mealtime. Then Mr. Sugarplum went to his kitchen, and made a big kettle of soup.

"Nothing nicer than good, hot soup on a rainy day," he told his cats, who smilingly agreed.

But one rainy day at mealtime, a very rainy day at that, Mr. Sugarplum found nothing at all to put in his big soup kettle.

"Not so much as a carrot top!" he cried. "Someone will have to go to the store!"

His cats made it clear that they weren't going. All five disappeared under the easy chair, with never a whisker showing. So Mr. Sugarplum, bundled into all the rainy-day clothes he could find, and scowling most dismally, set out himself.

Never a glance did he waste on the shining, rain-washed town, or the swift little streams at the curb full of paper sailboats, or at the park —all clean and green and fresh.

"Dark, wet, splattery bother!" he scowled. But when he got to the grocery store, Mr. Sugarplum's scowl turned into a grin.

"What beautiful vegetables!" he cried. "What full peapods, what crisp carrots! What round, red tomatoes, juicy okra, succulent mushrooms—and what golden, bursting ears of corn! I've never seen such an array!"

"They are extra-fine," nodded the grocer, filling Mr. Sugarplum's basket to the top. "And all, of course, because we've had our share of fine, rainy days!"

"Is that so?" marveled Mr. Sugarplum. "Is that really so? And only think—I never knew!"

On his way home, Mr. Sugarplum splashed in the puddles, and admired all the fine, rainy-day sights. He even made a little boat out of his grocery list, and sailed it at the curb.

His cats were amazed when he came home, all dripping wet but fairly beaming.

"Nothing nicer than good, hot soup on a rainy day," he remarked as he put his big soup kettle on the stove. Then, peeping into his market basket, Mr. Sugarplum amazed his amazed cats still more, by adding, "In fact, I don't know of anything much nicer than rain, on a fine, wet, rainy day."

Inside—Me

APRIL 27

Outside, rain on the windowpane,
Dripping sheep in the muddy lane—

Slickery cows that shine and munch
Wet green grass for their picnic lunch,

Outside, birds in the wet, black trees,
And the dampish garden-smelling breeze,

And rushing streams to sail a ship in,
And splattery puddles to splash and slip in;

Outside, everything wet and free,
And inside—high and dry—just me!

Poor Tired Bunny!

APRIL 28

1. "Bunny, will you get me the machine oil?"
   "I'm too tired."

2. "Just hand me the screwdriver, please Bunny?"
   "I can't, I'm too tired."

3. "How about giving me a hand with this
   bicycle pump, Bunny?"
   "Oh, I'm *much* too tired."

4. "There now, the bike's all fixed and ready
   to try out!"
   "I'll try it out!"

5. "No thanks, poor tired Bunny! You're too
   tired to bother—"

The Springtime Bunny

APRIL 29

A LITTLE bunny was born in the spring, and loved the spring, and thought springtime was all there was. But one day spring was over. It was summer, and the little bunny did not like that at all.

"Oh, oh, oh!" he cried sadly, "All the good, tasty, brand-new little things of springtime are gone!"

And he would not hop and skip through the beautiful, bright summer with the other bunnies. He would not romp and race through fall with them, bouncing in the leaves and hiding behind the big, moon-round pumpkins. And when winter came, with its snow and blow and tinkling ice, he crept deep down into his burrow—and there he stayed, staying sad and wishing for spring, and it all gone.

But one day, when winter ended, and a springtime smell curled down into his burrow, the little bunny came creeping up. All full of wonder, and with his nose twinkling, he crept slowly up—and what do you think? Spring was back.

"Spring is back!" he cried joyfully. "It came back!"

"Of course," laughed a wise old bunny, passing by. "It always comes back, every year—over and over and over!"

"Over, and over, and over!" whispered the little bunny, so happy that he just had to hop. And so he did, he hopped through spring, summer, fall and winter—having just as much fun as the other bunnies, although he still did love springtime best, and does to this very day.

Tenants

APRIL 30

*A trim little wren,
In her prim little way,
Looked in our wren house
Yesterday.*

*She twittered and called
To her trim little spouse,
And he looked, too,
In our new wren house.*

*They talked it over
And flew away.
But they both came back
Again today—*

*They're in there now
And they're building a nest,
So they must have liked
Our wren house best!*

Henny's May Basket

MAY 1

VERY early on May Day morning, Henny ran to her small front door. She opened it eagerly, and peeped out. But her doorstep was just as bare as if it weren't May Day at all.

"Nobody made a May Basket for me!" she said sadly.

Still, it was very early, so Henny fixed herself some breakfast, peeping out the door between jobs. She ate her breakfast, running to the door between bites. And she even washed her dishes, between trips to the door.

But even then there was no May Basket on her doorstep.

"Well," said Henny at last, "since nobody made a basket for me—I'll just make one for myself."

She took a small basket, and hurried out into the morning to search for Mayflowers. That was fun to do. And when her basket was filled, it was so pretty that Henny fairly skipped back toward home.

But as she was passing her friend Bunny's

house, she looked at his door—and there was no May Basket there, either.

"Poor Bunny will be so disappointed!" she thought.

Then Henny smiled and whispered, "No, he won't, either!"

Up his path she went, very quietly. She hung her own May Basket up on Bunny's latch. And she tiptoed away, so pleased to think how happy and surprised Bunny would be, that she quite forgot she had no basket of her own.

"May Day is nice," Henny clucked happily. "I love May Day!"

And that was long before she came to her own little blue door, and found the pretty May Basket that Bunny had made, and left hanging there for her.

The Saturday Pony

PETER was a little boy who wanted a pony.

Long before his birthday was coming, he asked for one for his birthday present.

But his mother and daddy shook their heads.

"Ponies are for people who live in the country, Peter," they said. "You can't have one in a city apartment!"

Then they both asked Peter to think up some different presents, and he did. Instead of a pony, he asked for cowboy boots and a cowboy hat. He asked for a book about a pony, and a picture of a pony to hang up in his room.

But of course a pony was still what he wanted most of all.

That was the way it was with Peter.

When his birthday came, he tried on his fine, new cowboy hat and boots. He hung his pony picture on the wall opposite his bed. And he asked his daddy to read his pony story.

"Later on, Peter," smiled his daddy. "Right now it's time for breakfast—and then I thought you and I might go to the park for a while—"

Peter liked that. He loved to go to the park. It was big and green, and there was a zoo in it besides. But this time, his daddy didn't take him to the zoo. Instead, he led Peter along a different path, and around a curve, and—right straight to a pony ring, with six ponies in it!

Over the gate, a big sign said, PONY RIDE—10 CENTS.

And before Peter could ask for a ride, his daddy smiled his biggest smile. "Just found out about this pony ring, Peter," he said. "And I thought we could come here every Saturday and have a ride. That is—if you'd like that for a surprise present?"

"I would, Daddy!" gulped Peter. "Oh, Daddy, I would!"

But, strangely enough, Peter didn't take his first ride that very minute. First, he climbed on the fence and watched all six ponies very carefully. Because first of all, Peter wanted to be quite sure which one of them he wanted to choose for his own Saturday pony.

Too-Little Bear

Little bear's mother was going to bake bread. "May I help?" asked little bear.

"Oh no, little bear," his mother said. "I'll be very, very busy baking. And you're so small that you might burn your nose or paws."

"Oh," wailed little bear, sitting on the front steps in a sad little heap, "I'm too little for anything!"

But just then, out came his big daddy bear.

"I wouldn't say that, little bear," he said. "I'm going to the store, and you're exactly the size to go pick-a-back on my shoulders."

So little bear dried his eyes, and away they went.

They bought butter for the bread, lemons for the fish, mayonnaise for the salad, and a whole gallon jug full of honey, besides.

"Well sir," said little bear's daddy when they got home, "I never could have carried all that without little bear's help!"

That made little bear feel fine, quite as big as any little bear needs to be—and plenty big enough to eat as much of their good supper as anyone in that whole, big bear family.

MAY 3

LITTLE bear was the smallest. He was smaller than his sister, much smaller than his brother, much, much smaller than his mother, and much, much, much smaller than his big daddy.

And lots of times, little bear was left out of things. One day, he seemed left out of everything!

His sister was going to pick salad greens, and when he asked to go, she said, "Oh no, little bear, I'll be busy picking greens, and you're so small that you might get lost."

His brother was going fishing.

Little bear asked to go along, but his brother said, "Oh no! I'll be very busy fishing, and you might fall into the pond."

To the Barber's Shop

MAY 4

Once a month
With a hop, hop, hop,
Off I go to the
Barber's shop.

Once a month
With a snip, snip, snip,
He cuts my hair
And home I skip.

Five Little Kings

MAY 5

One day, on a trip to Samarkand,
Five little kings grew weary of sand,
And they all complained of bumps and pains
From tripping over each other's trains.

Said one, "Your Majesties, friends, and brothers,
I think we'd each better hold each other's—"
"What a splendid plan!" cried the other four.
"Why didn't we think of that before!"

So off they started. Each bearing a train,
They went round and round in an endless chain,
Looking pleased as punch—despite the sand.
But they never *did* get to Samarkand!

Isn't it Strange?

MAY 6

1. *Isn't it strange, how long it takes,*
   When a cake's in the oven,
   Before it bakes?

2. *Isn't it odd, when the icing's mixed,*
   How long it takes till
   The cake's all fixed—

3. *So you can have the bowl, and a spoon*
   For scraping it with?
   And isn't it soon—

4. *As quick as a wink, it seems to me,*
   Till the bowl's as empty
   As it can be!

The Little House

MAY 7

DOWN by the roots of the big oak tree, there's a little house that was made by me. It's made of sticks, all laid criss-cross—with tiny windows.

The roof is moss.

There's a door in front, and a fence and gate, and a clump of violets, blooming late, makes a quite nice garden. I think it will grow.

And besides, I think—

And besides, I *know* that somebody lives there. I saw him go in, very quick and sly. I peeped in the window, and one bright eye was looking out—looking back at me! But I couldn't quite tell, and I couldn't quite see who it really was—who it really can be—that lives in the house that was made by me, down by the roots of the big oak tree.

Walking in the Woods

MAY 8

When we go walking in the woods,
And picking violets—three by three—
We whisper, 'cause there might be wolves
Or grizzly bears behind each tree.
There might be angry elephants,
Or lions looking for a fight,
Or striped tigers lurking there

In all the striped forest light.
There might be wolves—
There could be wolves—
There might be anything at all—
But all there ever really was,
Was one wild rabbit.
It was small.

Miss Mousie's Surprise

MAY 9

"Just plain fur isn't nearly fine enough for such fine spring weather!" cried Miss Mousie one day. "I must have a whole outfit of beautiful new spring clothes."

And away she went, to shop in all the stores in town.

But none of them, not even the one with a dolls' department, had anything nearly small enough to fit Miss Mousie.

Poor Miss Mousie! She was so disappointed that she started home with brimming eyes. But just as the first tear was dripping down her cheek—what did she see but a little girl, sitting under a tree and crying as if her heart would break.

"Oh, oh, oh!" sobbed the little girl. "Here I've made all these beautiful new spring clothes for my smallest doll—and they're all much too small to fit her!"

At that, Miss Mousie caught sight of the clothes. They really were beautiful—even the little panties were edged with lace—and when Miss Mousie tried them on, they fitted as if they were made for her.

"Look at me!" she cried. "I'm Miss Mousie— and I've come to have tea with you!"

Now the little girl looked up. When she saw Miss Mousie looking every inch a fine lady, she dried her eyes and smiled. "Why, Miss Mousie!" she said. "I'm glad to meet you, and tea will be ready in no time at all!"

And she ran to get her smallest doll dishes, so that she and Miss Mousie could have tea, under the tree, on that beautiful, bright spring day.

Mother Chipmunk's Day

MAY 10

ONE morning Mother Chipmunk went to wake her children. But oh my, all five little chipmunks were already up, and all five little beds were made!

So she hurried in to see that her children washed their faces and paws. But all five little washcloths had already been used, and all were hung up to dry.

"My, my!" the surprised mother chipmunk cried. She skipped down the stairs to get breakfast ready—and everything was already ready, piping hot on the stove. And there was a nosegay of primroses at her place.

Now, with Mother Chipmunk too surprised and delighted to say one word, out of the pantry ran five, smiling little chipmunks, with their paws out for hugging. Their mother hugged them all, and asked if they'd done all this themselves.

"All but the stove cooking," said the proud little chipmunks. "Daddy did that, so we wouldn't burn blisters on us."

"That's right," smiled their daddy, coming in. "I did that, because it wouldn't do to have blisters on Mother's Day, now would it?"

"No, it wouldn't," said Mother Chipmunk.

"No indeed," agreed her children. And not one of them even mentioned the blister on the inside of their daddy's paw. But, since they'd put salve on it, and since it had stopped hurting—it wasn't a thing Mother Chipmunk had to know right then, was it?

Hop, Hop, Hop

MAY 11

HOP, hop, hop, a very young grasshopper started out to find something tasty for breakfast.

"Which shall I have—some tasty grass, or a crisp bit of daisy stem?" he thought to himself. But close behind him hopped a greedy old frog, out looking for breakfast, too.

"A grasshopper will suit me fine," whispered the frog, all ready to snap. But a hungry white duck was waddling behind that old frog, thinking what a big breakfast he would be.

The duck opened his flat, yellow bill, but before he was quite close enough to gobble the frog—up crept a lean, hungry fox with a bag over his shoulder.

"Aha!" he whispered. "Roast duck for me!" He opened his bag, all ready to scoop the duck into it.

And just then—*Bang! Bang! Bang!* a hunter stepped out from behind a tree, and shot at the fox.

Luckily for Foxy, the hunter had aimed badly, and he missed.

So away went the fox, streaking deep into the woods.

Away went the duck, splashing into the pond.

Away went old frog, fast as he could hop, to hide deep down under a log he knew about.

Then hop, hop, hop, along went the young grasshopper, so busy wondering what had made that loud *Bang! Bang! Bang!* that he had tasty grass for his breakfast, and some daisy stem, too.

And home he hopped, fat and full and safe and sound, with nobody at all following along behind him.

Sing for Supper

MAY 12

The baker's busy baking bread,
The farmer's busy growing,

The fisherman is catching fish,
And rowing, rowing, rowing.

The cow is busy giving milk,
For butter, too, and cheese.

The ice-cream man is busiest—
So many kinds to freeze!

Engineer Eddie

MAY 13

EDDIE had an electric train that he could make run around and around its tracks. And a wooden train that would go over bridges and under tunnels —wherever he wanted it to go.

He even had an engineer's suit and cap. Eddie wore them whenever his daddy took him down to the station to watch the trains go by.

Big black freight engines chugged past, and electric engines went smoothly by, with quiet passenger cars behind them. Sometimes a great diesel would rush past, blowing its deep, blasting hoot that sounded scary, but exciting, too.

The engineers of all the engines always waved to Eddie.

And one day, when Daddy had parked close to the tracks, and Eddie was leaning out the window, a big diesel came to a stop right beside their car. Eddie didn't have to wave to the engineer this time. He was close enough to the diesel to say hello.

The engineer said hello, too. Then he pointed at Eddie, and said, "I know you're going to be an engineer when you grow up!"

And hooting the diesel's loud, exciting horn, he started it down the tracks again.

"Well, well," said Eddie's daddy. "Now how do you suppose he ever knew that?"

But Eddie didn't answer right then. He was busy watching the big streamliner disappear around the curve. And he was very busy thinking that when an engineer had been railroading long enough to run a great, speedy engine like that—he surely ought to know another railroad man when he saw him.

And Mother's busy cooking—
So we know what we'll do,

We'll set the table all ourselves,
That's being busy, too.

There! Everything is ready,
And pretty now, and neat,

And all the busy-ness is done,
So let's sit down and eat.

Knew-What-She-Knew

MAY 14

KNEW-WHAT-SHE-KNEW was a little yellow cat. She knew what she knew, and she liked what she knew, and she thought she knew all there was to know.

One day, her big mother cat offered to teach her how to climb a tree. Up, up into the thin, swaying branches she looked, that little cat, and she mewed:

"What do we do when we get all high up?"

"Why," smiled her mother. "Then down we climb again!"

"Up a tree and down again is the same as staying where you are!" said Knew-What-She-Knew.

And there she stayed, down with all the safe little things she knew—until along came a big black dog with a terrible bark. Then up the tree she went, slipping and sliding, but lucky enough to reach a high branch.

That little yellow cat was very glad when at last her mother cat found her, and showed her how to climb down! She ate her supper meekly, and went to bed without a word, because now Knew-What-She-Knew really did know quite a lot. She knew that she knew more than she had yesterday—but not nearly as much as she'd know tomorrow.

So, ho hum! she curled close to her big mother, and closed her round yellow eyes, and went to sleep.

The Very Nice Road Man

MAY 15

ONE morning, a man was fixing the road. Timmy watched him putting tar and broken stone in all the holes, and tamp-tamp-tamping it down.

"What a lot of holes in this road," he said. "My back's hurting now—what will it be by night?"

He said that out loud, not exactly to Timmy. But out loud, and when anyone asks a question, he must want an answer.

Timmy thought so, anyway.

"It will be a very sore back if you fix all those holes," he said. "But I have a new shovel, and I think I could fix the small ones."

"I see," said the man. "Well, you get that shovel, and we'll see how it works out."

"Yes, sir!" said Timmy. "Yes, sir!"

So presently Timmy was dipping his shovel in the tarry pail, and filling holes, and tamping them down. The road-fixing went so fast that it was half done when the whistle blew.

"Lunch time," said the man, going to his truck for his lunch pail. "You'd better trot home, sonny."

"I'm not sonny, sir," said Timmy. "I'm Timmy—and I think I could go and get my lunch pail, too."

"Okay, Timmy," said the man. "I'm Bill, and I'll wait and eat with you."

Timmy's mother put his lunch in a tin box, and Timmy and Bill sat on the curb, eating and talking about roads and holes, and driving trucks.

After lunch, they fixed more holes.

And when all the holes were fixed, they cleaned their tools in a pail of tool-cleaner. It took all the tar off Timmy's shoes, too.

"Good stuff you have there, Bill," said Timmy.

"Yes, it is, Timmy," said the man. He put his pails and his shovel and tamper in his truck, and hopped in and started the motor.

Timmy got out of the road, and watched him turn his big truck around.

"So long, Timmy," called the man as he drove down the fixed road. "See you when there's more holes!"

"Okay, Bill," called Timmy. "See you, Bill!"

Then he took his clean shovel and his empty lunch pail and went up the fixed road—thinking about the very nice road man, who was his good friend Bill, and feeling very glad he wouldn't have a very sore back tonight, after all.

Kites

MAY 16

Like sailing ships,
Our kites all fly
To and fro
Against the sky.
What foreign places
They might go,
Except that we
Down here below,
Stand on the
Shining harbor sands
And hold their anchors
In our hands!

"What kind of strategy?" the others asked.

"Borrow something of his," said Owl, slowly and impressively. "And forget to take it back."

Everyone was most impressed. So they went to borrow Gander's new station-wagon, which was his favorite possession.

"Help yourselves," said Gander, who really was good-hearted. "Mind you drive carefully, though."

"Oh, we will!" called the others.

Gander waited all day for his beautiful station-wagon to come back. He waited and waited, and by evening, he was in a terrible state.

"After all," he cried indignantly, "one's own things are one's own things! I'd best ride out and see what they think they're about!"

He ran to his garage to get his old bicycle. But when he rolled it out of its corner—there were Mrs. Hen's popcorn popper, Owl's candle-lantern, and Rabbit's pancake griddle, all tucked away and forgotten.

Gander stopped being angry, and looked very shame-faced, indeed. "High time I took those things back," he told himself.

And loading them all into his wheel-barrow, he hitched that to his bicycle and pedaled furiously off.

"Here comes Gander!" called Owl. Then he and all the others piled into the station-wagon, and drove out to the road.

"Just on our way back with it," they told Gander when he pedaled up. "Hope you weren't worrying?"

"Not at all," gulped Gander, quickly returning all the things he had borrowed. "Quite all right."

"That's that," grinned Owl, hugging his candle-lantern when Gander had gone. "I think our strategy worked."

And since Gander never again borrowed so much as a nail without returning it promptly, Owl was right, as usual.

Sauce for the Gander

MAY 17

GANDER had a bad way of borrowing things, and then forgetting to return them. He had Mrs. Hen's popcorn popper, Owl's candle-lantern, and Rabbit's pancake griddle.

"We'll have to use a bit of strategy on Gander—" said Owl.

Peep in the Basket

MAY 18

Peep in the basket,
What do you see?
Five little kittens—
And one is for me!

Five little kittens—
Which one shall I choose?
The gray one that's purring?
The white one that mews?

The all-over black one,
The black with white paws,
The tigery-striped one?
I can't choose because—

Each one, when I pet it,
Seems surely the best.
So—could you keep the basket—
And give me the rest?

A Hat for Jenny

MAY 19

SUMMER, winter, spring and fall, Jenny's hat was a round one. Sometimes it was brown, sometimes blue, sometimes straw-colored straw—but it was always round, with a big brim and streamers down the back.

And that was that. That was Jenny's hat.

Jenny did wish it had a flower, or a feather, or a *bit* more to it! But her mother always said, "There will be plenty of time for that," and bought her a new one just like the old ones.

And then, one day, Jenny's grown-up cousin was going to be a bride. She chose Jenny as her flower girl, and she chose everything that Jenny was to wear. Everything was beautiful. But the hat—a bonnet with flowers all around, and a tiny ruffle inside—was the most beautiful thing that Jenny had ever seen!

"It suits Jenny perfectly, doesn't it?" asked her cousin.

And her mother said, "Yes, it does. After the wedding, it will do nicely for parties and Sunday School."

As for Jenny, she patted the flowers, and wondered why her mother had ever said, "There will be plenty of time for that"—because she was sure that there never would be enough time for wearing that beautiful, beautiful hat!

Feeding the Ducks

MAY 20

When we go down beside the lake
We take the ducks some quite stale cake,
Or bread that's very hard to chew—
'Cause we don't like it,
But they do.

They gobble it, and thud, thud, thud!
Show off by walking in the mud,
And quacking proudly as they do,
'Cause we don't dare to—
And they know!

Spring Fever

MAY 21

"GRAMP," said Jimmy. "Gramp, will you play me a tune on your fiddle?"

"Not now, Jimmy," muttered Gramp, who was half asleep on the sunny porch. "I'm too sleepy with spring fever. You go along and take a walk, or something—"

Jimmy asked what spring fever was. But his grandfather only muttered and snored. So Jimmy did go for a walk. He walked all around the barnyard, thinking about spring fever. And he noticed a very strange thing.

All the old animals were drowsing, the old mother cat and the old mother pig, the goat, the sheep, the cow and the horse.

But their children weren't sleepy. All those new, young animals were frisking and frolicking in the spring morning as if they had suddenly gone wild.

Jimmy watched them. He sniffed the strange smell of new grass and new flowers and warm sunshine. And suddenly, he felt wild, too.

He went racing through the chicken yard, zig-zagging like a wild pony. He went tearing back to the house, whooping like a wild Indian.

"Gramp!" he cried, pounding up the steps, "I know what spring fever is now! It's something in the air—and it makes young folks feel lively, and old folks feel drowsy—doesn't it, Gramp?"

"Oho," said Gramp, opening his eyes and reaching for his fiddle. "Oho, is that so?"

Up he jumped, and he began playing "Oh, Susanna" so merrily, and dancing such a lively dance, that Jimmy had a hard time keeping up with him.

"Maybe I don't know what spring fever is, after all!" panted Jimmy at last.

"Maybe you sure enough don't," laughed Gramp, playing and dancing faster still. "Maybe nobody does—"

And Jimmy, prancing high and free in the wonderful-smelling springtime, thought he didn't really care what spring fever was—as long as he and Gramp were having so much fun just having it.

The Fox Friends

MAY 22

ONCE there were three little foxes who did everything together.

"Share and share alike," they murmured, curling up warmly in one snug, hollow log. "All for one, and one for all!" they agreed, as they ladled out stew from one big, steaming kettle. And even when it came to dogs—if a dog dared chase one little fox—he soon found himself chased by all three. But one day, the fox friends went fishing.

They sat on the bank with three poles, three lines, three hooks, and three fat worms—thinking of the delicious fish fry they would have.

Soon one little fox caught a sunfish. It was hardly a morsel, really. Then the second little fox caught a good-sized bluegill—just the size for the enormous appetite he had.

"My, oh my!" he cried, slyly tucking it under his arm, "I just remembered that it's my aunt's birthday, and I promised to help her blow out her birthday candles—"

He was just about to go trotting off by himself, when the third little fox caught a most beautiful big pickerel, enough for a feast for all three.

"Oh-er-oh well," stammered the fox with the bluegill, "perhaps her birthday isn't today, after all. And if it is, she's quite old enough to do her own blowing—that lazy old aunt of mine!"

And crying, "Share and share alike!" he rushed about, gathering firewood, and building a fire, while his friends—who knew perfectly well that he had no aunt—sat on the bank, laughing up their sleeves and not lifting so much as a paw to help him.

The Broken Moon

MAY 23

Last night I saw the strangest sight:
The moon, all big and round and white,
Was floating in the wet, black lake;
Then suddenly, I saw him break
Into a thousand shining scraps,
When somebody—
A frog, perhaps—
Jumped in the water for a swim.
Poor moon, that seemed the end of him!
But soon the lake was still, and then
The moon was back, all round again,
And big and bright and shiny, too—
Put back together, good as new!

Poor Mr. Robin

MAY 24

POOR Mr. Robin was most disappointed when he first saw the skinny, scrawny, noisy little babies that had hatched from Mrs. Robin's beautiful sky-blue eggs.

"Why, they're all mouth!" he gulped.

"Naturally," said Mrs. Robin. "They're hungry. Go and get them something to eat."

Away flew poor Mr. Robin, very crestfallen, to pick fat worms and crisp bugs in out-of-the-way places. Even so, he kept meeting friends who kept asking if the baby robins had hatched.

"Not yet," said Mr. Robin hastily. "Not quite yet!"

This went on for days and days. At last Mr. Squirrel, Mr. Chipmunk, and Mr. Bluejay all announced that their new babies had come, and invited Mr. Robin to come and take a peep. Mr. Robin did. And when he saw the skinny little squirrels, the scrawny little chipmunks, and the noisy little bluejays—he felt much better about his own babies.

"My babies have suddenly hatched, too!" he cried, puffing out his red chest. "Come and see!"

By this time, the baby robins were fat and lively, with downy feathers and round, bright eyes. Mr. Robin's friends all pronounced them the handsomest babies in the whole neighborhood. And Mr. Robin hopped about looking so proud a father that Mrs. Robin forgot she had ever been cross, and flew off to find their next meal herself.

All Kinds of Ships

MAY 25

Of all the ships that sail the bay:
Tankers, freighters, steamers,
And battleships, so swift that they
Go trailing foamy streamers—

And Coast Guard boats, and fishing boats,
And tugboats, pulling strings
Of barges, carrying sand or coal,
Or cars, or other things—

Swim Like a Frog

MAY 26

"TEACH me to swim," begged Bets. "Please teach me!"

"All right," said Mother. "Put your hands on the bottom and kick your feet like a frog—"

Bets tried that, and it was easy. Her frog-kicking feet pushed her forward, so she walked on her hands—which was almost like swimming. And she practiced and practiced.

"What do I do next?" she asked the day after.

"You paddle your hands like a frog, too," said Daddy.

Bets tried to do that, too. She tried again and again. But try as she did, she couldn't *quite* take both hands off the bottom at the same time.

"Go out a little deeper, Bets," Mother suggested. "Then try paddling your hands like a puppy running."

So Bets went out a little bit. She tried and tried to paddle like a puppy, and still she could

And holiday boats, with crowds aboard
And music playing, too,
And even fireboats, speeding past
And calling, Whooo-Whoo-Whoo—

I really think, of all of them,
I like the ferryboat best,
For when I ride it 'cross the bay,
I get to see the rest.

not get both her hands up off that nice, safe, sandy bottom.

And then, one day when Bets was trying, a rolling wave came in. It made the water so deep that she couldn't keep her hands down. It was so deep that Bets had to do something, so she did. Without knowing quite *how* she was doing it, her hands and feet were both going. Bets was swimming!

"You're doing it, Bets!" said Mother.

"You did it, Bets!" said Daddy, swinging her up out of the water and giving her a squeeze. "You can swim!"

"Yes, I can!" laughed Bets. "I really can—but not exactly like a frog, or a puppy, either. When I was swimming, it was much more like myself —staying up in the water!"

And she wriggled out of Daddy's hug, back into the water to swim like herself all over again.

Cock-a-Doodle-Do-Nothing

MAY 27

"COCK-A-DOODLE-DO!" crowed a gay little rooster, upon a sawhorse, calling to the sunrise.

"Much ado about nothing!" clucked the hens, busily laying eggs in their straw nests. "Cock-a-doodle-do-nothing, that's who he is— never laid an egg in his life!"

"Is that so?" the little rooster replied. "Well, it just happens that I could lay eggs if I chose. And if I laid eggs, they wouldn't be little old plain eggs like yours. They'd be big eggs, as big as the sun—and they'd be all colors, beautiful colors like my tail—red, green, purple, everything—"

He took a big breath, to brag some more, but before he could, one hen cackled, "Why don't you then? Why don't you, why, why, why?"

"Why?" asked the rooster. "Why, because I don't choose to, that's why. It would put your eggs to shame—make you feel all droopy and sad and sick. And it's my job to see that you all keep happy and chipper and well!"

The hens glanced at each other, not quite sure that the rooster was only bragging. But since none of them wanted to take a chance on being outdone, they went on with their egg-laying with the quietest of clucks.

And the gay little rooster flapped his wings and called cock-a-doodle-do to the sun, which was up on top of the mountain by now, and looking quite the biggest and most beautiful egg that anyone could think up.

Big, Bigger, Biggest

MAY 28

"Aha, little blowfish!" said a flounder. "I'm bigger than you, and I'll be much rounder when I've gobbled you up!"

And he did it, too. But a tuna said, "I'm bigger than you. I'm longer and stronger, and ready to sup—"

And the tuna gobbled the flounder up.

But a tarpon laughed, and leaped and cried, "I'm big enough to have you inside, with room for a jellyfish beside!"

So he gobbled the tuna—one, two, three! But a shark came along and cried with glee, "I'm big enough to eat *two* tarpon!"

And flip and swallow—the tarpon's gone!

The shark sailed off, and his grin was wide, as he flipped back on his right-up side.

"Big as one is," he said, "I figure that there's always sure to be someone bigger!"

Which was true enough—for presently, a boat sailed up, and one, two, three, the shark was caught, and the sea was bare. There wasn't a **big** fish anywhere. There were no fish swimming anywhere in it—except one little minnow, the size of a minute.

Poor Old Spider

MAY 29

Poor old spider. She had spun a web in the kitchen, and cook had whisked it down with a tea-towel. She had spun another in the corner of the parlor, and the parlor-maid had sniffed, "Cobwebs!" and brought it down with a feather duster.

The spider had tried a web in the nursery, the master bedroom, and the guest room. But nurse and master had each swept her web away—and the guest (an old lady in a nightcap) had screamed until the groom rushed in and swept that web down with a long handled broom.

"Oh me!" sighed the poor old spider. "I'm not wanted anywhere—" sadly, she followed the groom, hoping to get back a fly still caught in a wisp of web that clung to his broom. Across the yard she walked, and into the stables.

Buzz, buzz, buzz! There were flies everywhere. The horses were frantic, brushing their tails and stamping their feet to keep off the flies. In no time, the old gray spider had spun a new web, and caught three of the troublesome pests in it.

"What a clever trick!" cried the delighted horses. "Do make your home here, madam, and do spin more webs!"

"I shall indeed," smiled the happy spider, hardly knowing which pleased her more—the wealth of flies, or the bit of praise. And there she lives, contentedly spinning, to this very day.

Decoration Day

MAY 30

Just yesterday, the beach was bare;
Only the sand and sea were there,
And a seagull, high in the wild, gray air,
And the little sand-crabs, and me.

Today, with bright umbrellas out,
And happy crowds that laugh and shout,
And all this sunny sand and sea, I doubt
There ever was—just me!

Three Little Indians

MAY 31

One little,
Two little,
Three little Indians, away out in the West, had feather headbands, doeskin clothes, and all the beaded rest.

They had arrows that were straight and true, to go with their shooting bows. And they all went hunting in the woods, whenever they pleased or chose.

They had canoes to paddle (with three little paddles), and they rode their ponies without any saddles, and they all liked dancing, too.

Whoop!

Whoop!

Whoop! went those three little Indians, dancing round and round to the thump-athumpthump of the tom-tom drums, with their feet going pound, pound, pound.

Then around the fire with the other braves, they had pemmican and tea. And they went to bed (when they went to bed) in an Indian tipi.

As snug as bugs in their bearskin rugs, they sang the songs they knew—of the moon up high, and the stars in the sky, and the night winds blowing, too—till—

One little,
Two little,
Three little Indians, curled in a cozy heap, were as quiet as the quiet night—for they all were sound asleep.

The Homesick Mailman

ONCE there was a mailman who put letters in three hundred mailboxes every day. Whew! that was a lot of letters! And when his vacation came, he packed a knapsack, hopped on his speedy motor bike, and set out on a trip.

"I won't so much as lick a postage stamp till I get back," he said, whizzing past mailbox after mailbox.

For a time, that was fine.

But then the mailman began to get a strange and lonely feeling inside. The more mailboxes he passed—the worse he felt. And when he came to a post office that looked very like his own post office—whew! that mailman felt so strange and lonely that he almost turned around and went straight back home!

First, however, he nipped into the post office just to look around. He'd no more than sniffed the good, familiar smell, when he smiled and nipped out to buy three hundred colored scenic post cards. On them he wrote, "Having a wonderful time. Your friend, the mailman-on-vacation."

Then he bought three hundred of the post office's best stamps, and licked them, and felt *much* better.

And when he had mailed all the cards back home to all his friends on his route—whew! that mailman felt perfect!

"Won't they be surprised and glad to hear from me!" he chuckled, as he whizzed along, drinking a strawberry soda in a paper cup, and thoroughly enjoying all the sights he saw on his splendid vacation trip.

Mitty's Mistake

JUNE 2

"COME along!" said Mitty the cat, opening Polly's cage. "Come along, and get your things, 'cause we're going to the zoo!"

"What's the zoo?" asked Polly. But Mitty just smiled and said, "Hurry up!" So Polly hurried and Mitty hurried and they both hurried to the zoo.

They saw lions and tigers and giraffes, and an elephant as big as a house, almost—and bears, and a seal that barked like a dog and made Mitty jump. They saw a leopard that was black, and a leopard that had spots, and some funny monkeys. Then they saw a crow who said, "How do you do?" and invited Polly to lunch.

Polly looked at Mitty, and Mitty said, "Go right ahead!" and hurried home for her own lunch. But not a crumb did she get.

"I think you've had your lunch!" said her mistress, looking at Polly's empty cage.

"I did not!" cried poor Mitty, but it did no good. Not a bite of lunch did she get. And at supper time, it looked as if she'd get no supper, either. But presently, scritch-scratch, scritch-scratch! Polly was at the door asking to come in.

"Oh," said Mitty's mistress. "Oh, come in, Polly. And Mitty, I am sorry to have misjudged you!"

What a fine big supper Mitty had then! And since Polly confided that she was much fonder of Mitty than of the crow, the day ended quite as happily as it had begun.

Butterflies

JUNE 3

Over the white phlox
In the garden there,
Seven little butterflies
Are dancing in the air;
Clustered there like petals,
And white phlox white:
Will they all be flowers, too,
When they come down
And light?

The Ant Friends

JUNE 4

In the morning, Timmy was all by himself.

All his friends were in school. And all his grown-up friends were busy. They all called, "Hi there, Timmy!" as they came along. But after that, they went away again.

"Next year, I'll go to school," Timmy told himself.

But next year was awfully far away. Even after lunch, when his friends would be out, seemed much too far away. So Timmy poked around under the porch to see what he could find. He found everything that was always there; fireplace logs, dry leaves, and tin pail.

And then Timmy found something else. He saw one log with a splintered sort of valley in it. And up and down that valley marched a whole family of shiny black ants.

"Hello," said Timmy, crouching down. "I'm glad to see you."

The ants all nodded their heads, as if they were glad to see Timmy, too. So he watched them going up and down, carrying little bundles of food. Under the log they went, to put the bundles away. Out they came again, to get more bundles. They stepped out of each other's way. They helped each other carry big bundles. And they went up and down, and up and down, but they didn't go away.

Timmy didn't either. He was so busy watching that it seemed no time until his mother was calling, "Time for lunch, Timmy!" It wasn't morning any more. Soon all his friends would be coming to play with him.

"Good-by, ants," said Timmy, hopping up. "I'll see you in the morning—"

His ant friends nodded their heads, still marching busily up and down. And they didn't go away, because the next day, when Timmy came to see them—there they still were, waiting for him to come.

Finger Paints

JUNE 5

Finger paints are lots of fun,
And lots of colors, too—
Red, and yellow as the sun,
And green besides, and blue.

Squishy, squashy, on they go,
Like every-colored mud,
And with a swishy, swirly whirl,
A patting and a thud—

We make red seas, or yellow skies,
Whole worlds of green or blue—
Besides, our fingers get to be
Such lovely colors, too!

Six Little Drummers

JUNE 6

Six little drummers on parade
Told each other, "We might get paid
For drumming south and north and east—
If we do, we'll buy ourselves a feast!"
Boom! Boom! Boom!

But one little drummer broke his drum,
One little drummer bumped his thumb,
One little drummer lost the beat,
One little drummer felt the heat,
One little drummer tripped on a stone—
And one little drummer drummed alone:
Boom—Boom—Boom!

Then one big captain cried, "Harr-um!
I'll pay you well if you'll lose your drum!"
So one little drummer stopped, at least—
Till six little drummers had a feast!

Poor Mousie!

JUNE 7

Mousie, I just hate to see
All these bangs and bumps,
And bandages, and scratches, too,
And falling-downstairs lumps!

Once might be an accident,
Maybe even twice—
But it isn't an accident
When three times thrice

You slip on a roller skate
You've left on the stair,
And you get up sobbing—
To put it back there!

The New House

JUNE 8

JIMMY liked the new house. He liked his new room, which was bigger and nicer than his old one. He liked having a woods to play in, and a new garage. And he liked all his new neighbors, too. But for all the new neighbors, there wasn't one who was a little boy Jimmy's size—and Jimmy did not like that at all.

One day, when he was very busy not liking it, a big steam shovel came rumbling up the hill. It rumbled right into the vacant lot across the street and started to dig a big hole. Now Jimmy was so busy watching that he forgot everything else. He didn't even notice when a car came up the hill. He didn't even notice when someone got out of the car and stood beside him.

But he did notice when someone said, "See that big digger? It's digging the cellar for my new house!"

Jimmy did notice that. He looked to see who was talking, and it was a little boy just his own size!

"Good!" said Jimmy. "Your new house will be across from my new house—and we can play together every day."

"Yes," said the new little boy. "Yes, we can."

And the two stood side by side, watching the big steam shovel work—and thinking that moving was just about the best thing that one little boy, and then another little boy, could *ever* do!

Lost–and Found

JUNE 9

THE old farm horse was very proud of his fine straw hat. It kept the rain off his head, and the sun, too, and it gave him a splendid, dressy look besides.

But one day, the wind whisked it up and away, and out of sight. The old farm horse walked miles and miles looking for it. He was away for days and days and days, and at last, head down and tail drooping, he gave up the search and started home.

When he trotted into his own barnyard, the speckled hen was just hopping off her nest. She strutted up and down, teaching her newly-hatched chicks to scratch for their lunch. They ate so hungrily that the old farm horse found he had a big appetite, too.

"May I eat a bit of your hay?" he asked timidly.

"Help yourself," said the hen. "I shan't even need a nest now that my children have hatched."

So the old farm horse nibbled away, and when the last tasty wisp was gone—he saw that she had made her nest in his own fine straw hat!

With a happy neigh, he flipped it up in the air, caught it deftly on his head, and went racing all around the barnyard—looking pleased and delighted, and splendidly dressy besides.

The Rooster Struts

JUNE 10

The rooster struts,
The rooster crows,
And everywhere the rooster goes
The shy little hens side-step and bow,
"Make way for the rooster!
He's coming now,
With his wonderful tail
And his golden eye,
Make way for the rooster—
He's passing by!"

The rooster flaps,
The rooster blinks,
And it's very clear the rooster thinks
Each shy little hen wishes she were he!
But each little hen
Clucks happily
As she settles down
On her brooding nest—
For being a hen is
What she likes best!

What Would You Do?

JUNE 11

"If you had a penny, lad, what would you buy?"
"Since I haven't any penny, sir, I can but cry."

"If you had two cents, lad, what would you do?"
"As I haven't got two cents, sir, I can't tell you."

"If you had three cents, lad—what then, lad?"
"I haven't got three cents, sir, and I'm just sad."

"Lad, here's a penny, and two cents, too—
And three cents beside it—now what will you do?"

"I'll buy me a currant bun with sugar on top—
I'll buy me a white mouse to skip and to hop—
I'll buy me a kite, sir, to fly in the sky—
I'll thank you and thank you, and bid you good-by!"

The Little Gray Shadow

JUNE 12

A LITTLE gray shadow went hopping along the cabbage rows, so swiftly and lightly that it was hard to be sure that there was anything there.

"Hmmm!" said the farmer. "It may be no more than a cloud passing over the moon."

And he went along to bed.

"Hmmm!" said a thin little fox. "It may be no more than the shadow of a wish!" And he went to bed, too. But in the morning, when the farmer's shadow fell across the sunshiny rows—there were little bites bitten out of all his biggest cabbages! And when the shadow of the thin little fox fell across the path—he saw little footprints going goodness knew where!

That night, the farmer waited up, holding his gun.

The fox waited, too, ready with an open bag.

But that night, no little gray shadow hopped along the rows. Maybe it was because there was no moon. Or maybe it was because, deep in his secret house, a fat little rabbit was sound asleep—smiling and dreaming of the lovely, plump shadows that cabbages make on a quiet, moonlight night.

The Greedy Little Fox

JUNE 13

"I'M HUNGRY!" said a greedy little fox, licking his chops. "I have the biggest appetite I ever had!"

And off to the barnyard he trotted, to find a nice, big supper. He soon spied a nest full of fresh white eggs—just the kind for a big, tasty omelet.

But the little fox turned up his nose. "No omelet for me," he said. "I'm much too hungry for that!"

Along he went, until he saw a fat white hen (exactly the kind for a delicious stew with rice) scratching in the dust.

But not even such a fat hen suited that greedy little fox today.

"A mere morsel," he sniffed, and he trotted on down to the lake, where two great swans were gliding towards shore.

"Now there's something I like!" he whispered. "Two swans, roasted and with gravy, will be just the thing for supper!"

So he hid in the rushes, sly as sly, until the swans came up on the shore. Then out he leaped, looking very fierce, all ready to catch one in each paw.

But one little fox, fierce or no, is no match for two great swans! With flapping wings, and necks out-stretched, and a furious hissing, they chased him away from the lake—and up the hill, and back into the woods.

That little fox was so glad to be safely home that he hopped straight into bed, with no supper at all.

"I'm not even one bit hungry," he said. "And when I do get another appetite—which will be tomorrow—it will be just the size for an omelet of big, quiet white eggs!"

The Wonderful Birthday

JUNE 14

JILL always had a wonderful birthday, with lots of cards, and lots and lots of presents, and even a birthday party—and a big cake, with candles to blow out.

But to Jill, the very best part of her birthday was that there were beautiful red, white, and blue flags flying all over town. They fluttered in front of houses. They waved from the tops of buildings, and they floated above the big parade that marched down Main Street.

Jill was sure that her birthday was as important a day as Christmas, almost—or the Fourth of July! And on her fifth birthday, up on her daddy's shoulder watching the parade, Jill said so, right out loud.

"Nobody else has parades for their birthday, or flags everywhere—do they, Daddy?" she cried.

"Why, Jill!" said Daddy, sounding surprised.

"Don't you know about today? I'll tell you on the way home."

And so he did. Daddy told Jill that years ago, our country had had no flag. He told about George Washington wanting one—and about Betsy Ross, who had made the first beautiful red, white and blue flag.

"June fourteenth is the day it became our flag, Jill," he said. "So we call it Flag Day, and celebrate by flying the flags everywhere and by having a parade—"

Then Daddy looked sideways at Jill. He thought she might be disappointed that the flags weren't for her, after all.

But Jill looked even happier than before. Because she thought that having her birthday and the flag's birthday together was even more wonderful than having it all to herself.

The Funniest Clown

JUNE 15

ONCE there was a little circus, so merry and gay that it came to be known as The Greatest Little Show on Earth.

This made the circus man feel so proud that he wanted new posters, saying that in big, red letters.

"A fine idea," the poster-man said. "And how about a poster with a picture of your funniest clown, and saying THE FUNNIEST LITTLE CLOWN ON EARTH?"

"Capital!" agreed the circus man, rubbing his hands together. "Only, I don't know which one is funniest—"

But he meant to find out. So he told all the clowns, and he said, "In one week, we'll decide by watching how hard the audience laughs."

Now, when the circus man said that, every single clown wanted his own picture on the

poster. Every single one stopped helping the others be funny, and went off by himself to practice being funniest.

Before the week was over, none of them were even speaking to each other—and oddly enough, none of them could make the audience laugh hard at all!

The clowns were all terribly sad.

And the circus man was almost beside himself.

"The contest is off!" he announced at last. "We just won't have any clown poster at all."

But before he could telephone and tell the poster-man, things changed again. All the clowns stopped trying to be the funniest. All of them helped each other think up ways to keep the audience laughing and happy. All of them began to have fun together again.

And over-night, all those little clowns were even funnier than they had ever been before.

They made the audience laugh so hard and loud that the poster-man could hear it when the circus man telephoned him from the town drug store.

"Well, well!" he said. "I just guess you've found out which one of your clowns is the funniest!"

"On the contrary," said the circus man. "They're by far the funniest all being funny together. So please make the clown poster this way. Have all their pictures on it together, and make the big red letters say: ALL THE FUN-NIEST LITTLE CLOWNS ON EARTH."

And back to his gay little circus he went, eager to tell every one of his funny clowns all about that.

The Daytime Moon

JUNE 16

The moon has a surprising way
Of sometimes being up by day.
He looks as white as any cloud,
And though perhaps it makes him proud
(The same, I guess, as you or me)
To stay up late, so he can see
What people do when he's asleep,
He really doesn't seem to keep
Quite wide awake.
He seems so very pale and dim—
It must be just too late for him!

My Friend the Clock

JUNE 17

When I was small, I thought the clock
Said nothing but, "Tick-tock, tick-tock."
But when a person understands
About its numbers and its hands,
It tells us what to do all day;
The time to work, the time to play,
The time to come, the time to go,
And when to eat and sleep. I know
Its language now, and so you see,
It can tell all those things to me,
As it goes quietly, "Tick-tock,"
All through the day, my friend the clock.

The Circus Parade

JUNE 18

Here come the lions and elephants,
And the acrobats and all,
And the thinnest man,
And the smallest man,
And the man that's eight feet tall.
And the musical seals,
And the bears on wheels,
And the horses prancing by,
And the proud ringmaster with his whip,
And his hat that's shiny and high.
Here come the band and calliope,
And the strange, dark camels,
Three by three—

And a troup of clowns, doing somersaults,
And flips, and flops, and jigs,
With funny faces, and funny clothes,
And the funniest hats and wigs!
Here they come, and there they go—
And we're going where they went,
All through town, to the circus grounds,
And the show in the circus tent!

Miranda Remembers

On Circus Day, Joey always hurried out to the circus grounds to carry water for the elephants. That was a big job for a boy Joey's size, and a very good job, too. He made friends with the elephants, especially Miranda the queen, who had taken to him at once.

Besides that, when Joey finished carrying water, the elephant trainer always said, "See you next year, Joey," and gave him his pay—a ticket for the Big Show!

But one year, when Joey got there, the old elephant trainer was gone. "Sorry, son," said the new one, "I've already hired two water boys —didn't know about you—"

Joey was disappointed enough! And just then, the boys came by, swinging empty pails. They were big boys, much bigger than Joey. And they were mean boys, too.

"Out of our way, kid," said one, pushing Joey aside.

That made Joey very angry. But Miranda was twice as angry. She liked Joey, and she didn't like anyone who was mean. So Miranda flatly refused to drink the water those boys brought. Instead, she began to trumpet angrily.

Now, whatever Miranda did, the other elephants did, too. So before long, all the elephants were trumpeting, and not one of them would so much as touch their water.

"What's going on here?" asked their new trainer, hurrying up. "Miranda, what's wrong?"

Miranda stopped trumpeting. She waved her trunk at the big boys and snorted. Then she pointed at Joey, and made a soft, coaxing sound.

"So that's it!" said the trainer. "All right, boys, you'll have to look for another job. Joey, here, said he was the regular water boy—and it looks like Miranda remembers—"

So away went those big boys, not caring to argue with Miranda around. Joey hurried to carry water for the elephants. He had to be home in time for lunch, if he hoped to be back in time for the afternoon performance.

But even so, Joey found time to rub Miranda's big head the way she liked him to do. And he hugged her around one big leg, too— before he went running off to get his pay—his ticket to the Big Show.

Snowshoes the Second

JUNE 20

WHEN Snowshoes had been lost for a whole week, Stevie's family stopped looking for her.

But Stevie hadn't stopped looking for his dog.

"I just have to find her," he thought, going deeper into the woods. Maybe Snowshoes had lost her way chasing a rabbit. She might even be caught in a trap!

"Here, Snowshoes!" he kept calling, in a shaky voice. "Here, girl! Here, Snowshoes!"

And suddenly, up the path raced a flurry of tan fur, white feet, and wagging tail.

"Snowshoes!" cried Stevie. "Oh Snowshoes, you're back!"

Snowshoes wriggled and barked for joy. Stevie hugged her and stroked her, and even let her lick his face. And when at last he looked up, another boy was standing in the path watching him.

"Hi," the boy said. "I see you know my dog Tippy."

"Tippy!" cried Stevie. "She's my dog Snowshoes! She was lost for a week, and—oh! maybe you found her and took care of her?"

But the boy shook his head. "Nope," he said. "She's my dog that my Uncle Pete gave me. And I just got her back last week—after she was lost two whole months."

Then he called, "Here, Tip!" and Snowshoes ran to him.

"Here, Snowshoes!" called Stevie, and back she came.

"Golly!" said the other boy. "Golly. I guess she's Tippy *and* Snowshoes—and I don't know what to do!"

"I don't, either," Stevie said. "Come on, let's go ask my father—"

Stevie's father listened to the other boy's story. He saw the dog run to him when he called, "Here, Tip!"

"I'm sorry, Steve," he said. "But it's plain that Snowshoes was lost when she came to us. She was his dog first, so she's his dog now."

Stevie's eyes filled with tears. But he nodded his head and said, "Yes. I—I guess she is—"

The other boy didn't look very happy, either.

"Well, I guess we'd better go now," he said. "My name's Tom Elliot—and maybe I'll see you again."

A few days later, Tom did come to Stevie's house, too.

He didn't bring Snowshoes with him. But he did bring a fluffy little tan puppy, with four white feet, and a madly wagging tail.

"She's yours, Stevie," Tom said. "My Uncle Pete sent her to you for your own dog—"

And Stevie couldn't say a word. He just nodded and smiled, and hugged and hugged that funny, fat, wriggly little Snowshoes the Second.

SUMMER

Time A-Plenty

JUNE 21

Oh, there'll be lots
Of time today:
Time for a picnic,
And time to play,

Time for a boat race
Up stream and down,
Time to go shopping
And see the town;

Time for a story
And singing a song
When supper's over,
Today is long—

The longest day
In all the year,
The sun is highest,
And Summer's here.

The Wise Little Chipmunk

JUNE 22

DEEP down in his little stone house, a hungry little chipmunk sat playing his piano. And close by his doorstep lurked a sly and hungry weasel, ready to gobble him the moment he came out.

Now the little chipmunk knew this, and just to tease, he played "Pop goes the weasel," and sang it, too.

"There's a song worth singing!" cried the weasel, pretending to be greatly pleased. "Come out, little chipmunk, and we'll sing it together."

"After a bit and after lunch," said the wise little chipmunk. "Right now, I want to make a surprise for you."

At this, the sly old weasel forgot to be sly. Home he went, to lunch on left-overs—and the little chipmunk scurried out and had a fine meal. Then, with a matchbox, a match, and an old piano string, he made a small mandolin and left it on his doorstep.

The weasel was delighted. He picked it up, and was soon strumming and singing away—while the wise little chipmunk played and sang inside. And so fine did they sound, both together, that the weasel never again thought seriously of catching the little chipmunk for breakfast or lunch—or even for Sunday dinner.

It's Nice to Know

JUNE 23

It's nice to know, when I'm in bed,
That across the world
It's day instead—

And children there are having fun,
While it's their turn
To have the sun.

The Swing

JUNE 24

I have a swing in the apple tree.
I'll push you in it,
If you'll push me
For a ride up high
And higher still—
Across the valley
And up the hill,
Watching the branches
Sliding by
Green and shady
Against the sky,
Up toward a soft, white cloud, and then,
Down toward the sliding earth again.
I have a swing in the apple tree,
And I'll push you in it
If you'll push me.

Mullen Is Pretty

JUNE 25

OLD Mrs. Sheep and her family took fine care of their pasture. They kept the grass cropped short, as close to the ground as moss, and only the round, blue rocks and the tall mullen rose up on the hillside.

Secretly, Mrs. Sheep wished they could clip down the mullen, too. But it was much too fuzzy-tasting.

"Anyway, it's pretty," she assured herself. "Quite pretty. We'll just leave it there." And since all her family heartily agreed, she was very proud of the way the pasture looked.

But one day, a little donkey who was passing by noticed the mullen. He was a hungry little donkey, and he thought he could make a fine meal of those leaves, if only the sheep would let him.

So he said he didn't think the pasture looked one bit pretty.

"Those mullen spikes look untidy," he called. "If that pasture were mine, I'd soon have them out of the way!"

The Interesting Umbrella

JUNE 26

IT started to sprinkle, so Mr. Winkle (who always had lots of pocket money) hurried into a nearby, queer little store to buy an umbrella.

"What kind?" asked the clerk. "Dusty black or musty black, lady's or gentleman's—the kind for rain, or the kind for rain and other interesting things?"

Bursting with curiosity, Mr. Winkle chose the last.

At first he had trouble opening his new umbrella. But once it was opened, it spread way out—and it also began to rise up and up like a gas balloon, taking Mr. Winkle with it.

"Only think," he murmured, peeping into top floor offices where people were putting on their raincoats and rubbers. "*I* shall never have to wear either, ever again!"

With this, he rubbed the handle happily, and began at once to descend. But Mr. Winkle never did quite touch the wet pavement. He went floating just above it in a splendid, bouncey fashion, wondering what Mrs. Winkle would say when she started to chide him for having wet feet—and looked—and saw that they were quite magically as dry as toast!

"Come in and get them out of the way, then!" snapped old Mrs. Sheep, pushing open the gate.

"Just watch me!" the little donkey cried. In he raced. He took a big mouthful of the nearest plant, and one mouthful was much too much!

"Oooh, ach, ooof!" he spluttered, blowing it out. "Oof, what awful stuff! Worse than a mouthful of cotton and turkey feathers!"

He was ready to be off, but Mrs. Sheep wasn't letting him go so easily. "Go on, go on, eat it and get it out of the way!" she said.

"Nope," said the little donkey, backing away. "I've changed my mind. That mullen looks pretty in the pasture—it would be a *shame* to eat it!"

"That's what we think," smiled Mrs. Sheep, quite mollified.

The little donkey never did forget that fuzzy mouthful of mullen. So whenever he passed, he remarked on how pretty it looked. And old Mrs. Sheep smiled and nodded, and looked very pleased and proud, indeed.

The Traveler

JUNE 27

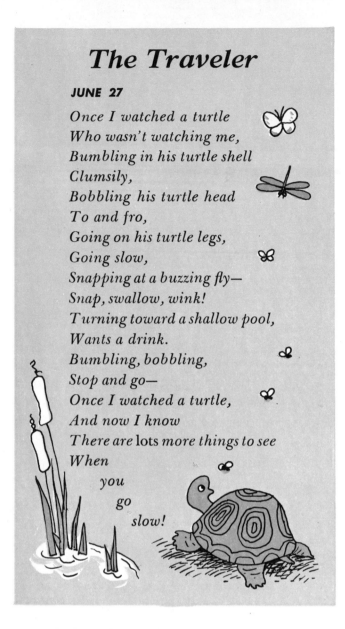

Once I watched a turtle
Who wasn't watching me,
Bumbling in his turtle shell
Clumsily,
Bobbling his turtle head
To and fro,
Going on his turtle legs,
Going slow,
Snapping at a buzzing fly—
Snap, swallow, wink!
Turning toward a shallow pool,
Wants a drink.
Bumbling, bobbling,
Stop and go—
Once I watched a turtle,
And now I know
There are lots *more things to see*
When
　　you
　　　go
　　　　slow!

In the Garden

JUNE 28

An ant has to walk almost an hour
To get to the top of a rosebush flower.

A grasshopper has to hop and hop
To get himself away up on the top.

Even a bee has to buzz and fly
To get up there—'cause it's pretty high.

But I can just stand there with my nose
Right on top of a big, red rose!

120

Old Tom

JUNE 29

IN his day, Old Tom had had many a fight with many a dog. Many a dog had gone yelping off with his big, barking face scratched. Many a dog had worn himself out, leaping at a tree in which sat the big Tom, who had merely smiled.

And many a dog hadn't dared come one step closer to the big Tom, with his back arched, his tail bristling, and his face like a fierce, snarling lion.

Today, the big old Tom was old. He was too tired to scratch, or to arch his old back and spit at the dogs. He was much too old and slow to climb a tree before a lithe, young dog could catch him.

But Old Tom didn't know that. He sat on the porch railing, growling low in his throat, "Just let one dog come anywhere near me! I'll soon show him that I'm one Old Tom who's not to be trifled with!"

Yes, there he sat, with his old tail waving, and his eyes no more than green slits, growling as fiercely as ever he did. And all the dogs, young and old, tiptoed by without troubling him at all. The old dogs remembered the old days too well, and the young dogs heard his fierce growling, and told themselves, "There's a big old Tom who's not to be trifled with!"

The Merry-Go-Round

JUNE 30

The others like to get right on
For a ride on the merry-go-round—
But I always like to wait a bit
In the whirly music sound,
Watching the horses going by,
'Cause it takes me time to decide
Which horse of all is the one I want
For the one I'm going to ride.
I like to watch the pranciest one
That goes away up high,
Then I like to find the quietest one,
And after I find him, why—
I like to go all by myself
Through the whirly music sound,
And climb on his back,
And hold on tight,
And go round and round and round.

Balloons, Balloons!

JULY 1

"BALLOONS! BALLOONS!" called the balloon man.

Up and down the streets he went, with his brightly colored balloons bobbing above his head, and their cool shadow bouncing under his feet.

"Balloons! Balloons!" he called, and out of all the houses came boys and girls to buy their favorite colors. Then red balloons, blue balloons, yellow, green and purple balloons went floating above their heads—away from the big bunch the balloon man carried.

Some balloons went bang! in a minute or two. Some went pop! in an hour or two. One floated up into a chestnut tree, and one went sailing across a fish pond.

But by nighttime, not one balloon was left in anybody's house. Except the balloon man's —he had lots.

After supper, he blew them up, and put them on sticks, and tied the sticks together. Then he tied the end of the string to his chair, and got ready for bed.

"Such beautiful balloons!" he thought, just as he was going to sleep. "Tomorrow I'll sell more than ever—"

And it seemed he would.

Because all the boys and girls, half-asleep in their beds, were thinking of balloons, too; red balloons, blue balloons, yellow, green, and purple ones.

And they all were thinking that the balloons they'd choose tomorrow would last much, much longer than the ones they'd had today.

Foxy's Secret

JULY 2

THE whole week before Bear's birthday, Foxy had been behaving very strangely indeed.

He wouldn't go fishing with Coony. He wouldn't go wading with Bear. He wouldn't even open his door, when Bear and Coony both came to remind him about Bear's party.

All he would do was to peep out the crack and say, "Shoo, you two! Shoo, and go away!"

"I don't think Foxy likes us any more," sighed Bear, on the morning of his birthday.

"I think he's just sick," said Coony. "Headache, maybe—or toothache, or some new sickness that makes him cranky—"

"Oh!" said Bear. "Well, in that case, we'd better do something nice for poor old sick Foxy."

So he ran home and got some red raspberry jam, which tastes delicious on toast. Coony picked a bouquet of flowers, all the kinds that look cheery in sick people's rooms. Then up the hill they went, and knocked on Foxy's door.

"Foxy," they said, "may we come in? Mrs. Foxy, please let us in to see poor old Foxy!"

Nobody answered. Nobody even said, "Shoo, and go away."

But suddenly, the door was flung open, and there stood Foxy himself—looking the picture of health.

"Come on in," he cried. "I can't wait to show you—"

Then he and Mrs. Foxy both pointed to the most beautiful fishing rod, all wound with red and yellow line—and a box of handmade fishing flies—both marked "Happy Birthday, Bear."

"Oh!" gasped Bear and Coony together. "So this is why you haven't had any time for us!"

"Yes sir," said Foxy. "Takes time to make these things, you know—and what a mess! With all the bits and scraps around, you'd have known in a minute what I was up to—"

"But now I really can clean up the place," smiled Mrs. Foxy, who was admiring the flowers and the jam. "That is, if you'll all go out."

"We will," said Foxy, reaching for his fishing rod, and one for Coony. "There should be time to land a trout or two before your party, shouldn't there, Bear?"

"There should be and there will!" cried Bear, hardly able to wait to try his beautiful new fishing things.

So away went all three friends, arm in arm and happy as larks—just as in the old days, before Foxy had begun acting so strangely.

Detective Donny

"OH, DONNY!" wailed Penny. "My baby's lost! I left her in the empty lot, and forgot I had— and now she's gone, carriage and all!"

Donny started to say, "What a silly thing to do, Penny!" But his little sister looked so worried that he didn't.

Instead, Donny said, "Come on, Penny— show me where you left her, and I'll be a detective and find her for you."

Penny showed him the very spot where her carriage had been, and he looked carefully for clues. Luckily, the ground was still damp after a shower, and the tracks were plain to see.

They led across the lot, along the sidewalk, and all the way to the driveway of the new house on the corner.

"This is mysterious," Donny said. "I thought nobody lived in this house—"

And nobody had, until today. But now the windows were open, and a car stood in the garage, and there were voices in the house, too. So up the driveway went Donny and Penny, and around to the back yard.

They looked over the fence, and there was a little girl just about Penny's size, rocking a doll baby in its carriage.

No, she was rocking two babies, in two carriages!

"And one's mine!" cried Penny. "Oh Donny, you are a good detective—you did find her!"

In a moment, Penny was in the yard, hugging her doll so hard that it was easy to see she would never forget her again. And the other little girl seemed so pleased to have just one baby to take care of—and a new playmate—that Donny turned toward home.

"No need for a detective around here now," he grinned. But just the same, he was glad he had been on the job when there had been some important detective work to be done.

July Fourth

JULY 4

All around the neighbors' yards
Quick firecrackers pop—
And pinwheels spin
Around and round—
I wish they'd never stop!

The sparklers shower fountains
Of silver, sparkling light,
And fireflies flash
Their little sparks
All through the sultry night.

Out in the park that's down the hill,
The rockets shoot up high,
And splinter and
Burst into stars
When they break on the sky!

A Perfect Spot for a Picnic

JULY 5

"IT'S a perfect day for a picnic," said Mr. Bear. "Do you s'pose you could pack us up a lunch?"

"I certainly do," said Mrs. Bear, and she and the two little bears bustled about finding more and more tasty and delicious-smelling things to eat. "Only this time, Mr. Bear, I do hope you won't be so choosy about a picnic spot that we'll end up eating in some silly place like a cow pasture—simply because we'll be too hungry to walk another step!"

"Well then, I won't," said Mr. Bear. "This time, you can choose the picnic spot. How does that suit you?"

"Perfectly!" smiled Mrs. Bear.

So that was settled. But once she and Mr. Bear and the two little bears were out in the summer woods, Mrs. Bear wasn't nearly so easily suited. One picnic spot struck her as shady, another was much too sunny and hot. A third had no wild flowers around it. And when at last they did find one with all those things, Mrs. Bear cried, "Oh, but here there's no brook to wade in! Surely we can find a better spot!"

By then it was lunchtime, and everyone was very hungry.

So on and on they went, till past lunchtime.

"We're starving dead!" cried the two little bears, at last. "Please hurry up and choose a picnic place!"

"Yes, please do," Mr. Bear groaned. "This basket's getting heavier and heavier—"

"All right," agreed Mrs. Bear with a sweet smile. "Let's just go around the next turn in the path—and there we will eat."

The Slide

JULY 6

The ladder's high—
And so I go
Up, step by step,
And very slow.

But when I'm at
The top at last,
I can slide down
Very fast!

Seven Little Sailors

JULY 7

Seven little sailors
Sail the summer seas,
Seven mice with sailor hats,
And sea chests full of cheese.

"We'll sail to some fair island,"
The seven sailors sing,
"Where cat has never set a foot,
And every mouse is king!"

They sail for lots of ages,
Their ship rocks to and fro,
They sight a seagull up above,
A turtle down below—

At last they sight an island,
But there upon the beach
Are seven cats with kingly crowns,
A greedy smile on each!

So seven little sailors
Sail home, full speed ahead,
To eat their cheese in seven holes,
And smoke their pipes in bed.

So around the turn they went, and there they were—Mr. Bear and Mrs. Bear and both little bears—right back home in their own back yard!

The little bears were too surprised to say anything, but Mr. Bear quickly put down his basket.

"I've never seen a more perfect spot for a picnic!" he cried briskly. "Chairs, and a table, and a wading pool—and a beautiful flower garden for looking at! Why, I think we should have lots and lots of picnics here all summer long!"

"We do, too," agreed the hungry little bears. "And oh, can we start having one right now?"

"We certainly can," said Mrs. Bear, still smiling to herself as she opened the picnic basket and began spreading out all those tasty and delicious-smelling things to eat.

The Middle One

BARBIE was the middle one.

She wasn't the biggest one like Janey, who could go to school, and cross the street to play with the children there, and read stories to herself—and stay up last of all.

Barbie wasn't the littlest, either.

Linda was. And Linda could cry for what she wanted, and get it. She could eat with her hands, and everyone just laughed with her. Linda sat on Mother's lap an awful lot, too. And Daddy tossed her up in the air, and let her ride up and down on his leg, ride-a-cock-horse.

But Barbie was the middle one, too big to do the things Linda did—too little to do the things Janey could do.

So Barbie did things like pushing the stroller when she and Mother took Linda for a walk. And digging in the sandbox. And giving the puppy his breakfast when Mother was too busy.

Barbie had things, too—things like being told she did a very good job dressing herself, and having stories read to her—sitting close to Mother. Barbie had rides on Daddy's back, when he acted like a bear, or a camel, or a pony.

Those weren't things for Linda.

She was too little.

They weren't for Janey. She was too big.

They were all things just for Barbie, no longer little like Linda, and not yet big like Janey.

Because they were all middle things.

And Barbie was the middle one.

The Mixed-Up Garden

IN APRIL, when Jimmy's daddy had planted his garden, he had made each row as straight as a string. Each one had had just one kind of seed in it, spaced just so. And at the end of each row, Daddy had stuck the seed envelope on a little stick, showing exactly how each plant should look.

Jimmy had watched his daddy, and he had tried to make his own little garden just as carefully. But, try as he did, Jimmy's rows got a little bit wobbly.

And the wind blew his seeds when he was planting them.

So there were radish seeds in the bean row, and carrots in with the onion sets—all helter-skelter. And the petunia and marigold seeds, that Jimmy had meant for a border, were all scattered about wherever they had landed.

What a mixed-up little garden that was! Jimmy wouldn't have known where to put his seed envelopes if he'd had any.

But all spring and summer, with Jimmy and his daddy taking good care of them, the seeds in both gardens had been growing. Now it was July, and the plants in Daddy's garden were big and strong, each row exactly like its seed envelope.

The plants in Jimmy's garden were big and strong, too.

And even without one single seed envelope, every one of them had grown to be exactly what it was supposed to be!

Cherry Time

High in the branches—
Look at me, perched like a bird
In the cherry tree—
With the big, black cherries
All around,
And the hard, little seeds
Down on the ground;
Enough for the squirrels—
All they please—
And more to grow to be cherry trees,
Full of black cherries,
Warm and sweet,
For the hungry birds
—and me—to eat.

That seemed like such a wonderful thing, that Jimmy was almost prouder of his little mixed-up garden than Daddy was of his big just-so one. And strangely enough, everyone who came to visit liked Jimmy's little mixed-up garden, too.

Lights in the Night

A LITTLE black cat went out in the night, all alone for the very first time. He sniffed the summer night smells. He listened to the summer night sounds.

And he peeped into a dark little puddle—and saw two round, bright lights, staring right back at him.

"What's that?" he cried, jumping back. Then that little black cat peeped in again, and saw that it was only his own round, bright eyes, shining out in the dark.

"Nothing but me!" he laughed, looking boldly around at the big, dark night.

And all around, in the dark grass and bushes, were dozens and dozens of tiny, tiny little lights that shone and flickered in the dark.

What were they? Bright little fireflies—though the little black cat didn't know that.

But he wasn't going to be fooled again. Not he!

So he told himself, "They're just nothing but lots of tiny little black kittens with shiny eyes, that's all—"

And now the little black cat felt so big and bold that he climbed up the nearest tree to see everything there was in the whole big night. From away up there, he could see a most enormous bright light, peeping over the mountain.

The round full moon it was—only the little black cat didn't know that.

He didn't wait to wonder about it, either.

"It's a big black cat!" he told himself. "A much-too-big black cat—and I don't like the way it's staring at me with its much-too-big bright eye!"

So down the tree he scrambled, across the dark grass, and up the damp path.

He fairly skidded across the wide front porch!

And the minute the door was opened, in streaked that little black cat—fur on end, tail like a brush. He came out of the big black night that was much too big for a little black cat, out all alone for the very first time.

The Music Lesson

1. " 'Scuse me, Bill—but may I try playing your other music things?" "Uh-uh. It's mine."

2. "Aw Bill, please? I watched you, and I bet we could play a duet." "Uh-uh. I don't."

3. "All right then, I'll just have to get some music things of my own!" "Go ahead. Good-by."

4. "There, Bill. How's that?" "Awful! Terrible! Stop! Oh, my poor music-tender ears! Here, play this—"

5. "All right, Bill, if you insist. You start, and I'll join in—" "Why, we even sound harmonious! I certainly am glad I talked the little fellow into this!"

I Like Water

I like water.
It's nice in tubs,
And nice for floors in need of scrubs.
It's nice on beaches, where small waves slide
Over your feet and out with the tide.
It's nice in puddles, and streams, and lakes,
And in waterfalls, where it glistens and breaks
Over rocky cliffs, into ferny places.
It's nice for washing hands and faces.
It's nice for gardens.
It makes them grow
With tasty plants in a sturdy row.
It's nice around islands—
It makes them be
Safe as a secret just known to me.
It's nice under bridges, shadowed there
Full of gliding fish that stop and stare
At watercress, and forget-me-nots
That fringe such shadowy, watery spots.
I like water. Water's nice.
It's nice when I'm hot—
And it's nice when it's ice!

Quick Change

Last week, whatever way we looked,
Wherever we were going,
The fields were bright with buttercups,
And big, white daisies blowing.
We picked such lots, for daisy chains,
And "who likes butter best?"
And still the fields were glowing with
The white and yellow rest.

This week, whatever way we look,
The fields are overgrown
With drifts of sky-blue chicory,
As if they'd never known
One shining, yellow buttercup,
Or lifted daisy face—
And not a one is anywhere,
Or growing any place!

Well, Why?

JULY 15

When I build a tower,
A house, or a town,
They always say, "Lovely!
Now please take it down,
And put all your blocks
Very neatly away—"

And I usually do,
But I didn't, today.
If Daddy has books
That are still staying out,
And Mother has sewing things
All strewn about—

I just don't see why
They should worry or frown,
Because, just for once,
My quite hard-to-build town
Is up—when I simply
Don't want it all down!

Too Little Tommy

JULY 16

WHENEVER Tommy went running out to play with the other boys and girls, he was smiling and happy. But when he came back home (which was never long after), he was always crying.

"They won't let me play, Mommie!" he sobbed. "They say I'm too little—and I'm not!"

"Now why do they say that, Tommy?" his mother asked. "You're as big as Andy and Jerry —and they seem to be in all the games—"

"I know it," said Tommy. "And I don't know why—but I wish I had somebody to play with!"

"I do, too," his mother said.

And one day, she said, "Why don't you play with Bobby? He's all alone today, too."

That seemed like a good idea to Tommy. So around to the sandbox he went, to play with his little brother. But it wasn't long until he was back on the porch—all by himself again.

"I can't play with Bobby, Mommie!" he explained. "He cried when I built him a good tunnel and it fell down, and he cried when I took his cars to show him the right way to run them. All he does is cry. Bobby's just too little to play with—and that's the whole crybaby reason!"

And right after Tommy said that—his eyes opened wide, and he looked most surprised. Then up he jumped—and away he ran, to play with the other boys and girls. This time, Tommy didn't come running right back, either.

He was gone all the rest of the morning.

"We had such a good time, Mommie!" he said when he came home for lunch. "We played cowboys, and robbers, and school—all the games the big kids made up. I played, too— and I never cried—not even when I fell down. And nobody said I was too little—not even once!"

"I'm glad, Tommy," smiled Mother. "Very glad."

"Oh, I am, too!" Tommy said. And he ran upstairs to wash, so he could eat and then go out and play with the other boys and girls all the whole afternoon.

Who Wants To Be a Rabbit?

JULY 17

"Hooo!" said a little tan rabbit, backing out of his house. "Down in a rabbit hole's too hot on a day like this!"

He felt too hot in the sunshiny meadow, too. And down at the brook, that little rabbit wanted to splash right in.

"But rabbits can't swim like frogs and fish," he told himself, as he hopped into the shady woods, where not a leaf was stirring.

Here the birds swooped about as if it were early spring. An old owl dozed in its cool tree home. A baby possum (with very thin fur) swung by its tail, making its own breeze. And a turtle trundled by, looking as cool as a cucumber in its dampish, spotted shell.

"I'm the only one too hot," panted the little tan rabbit. "Who wants to be a rabbit on a day like this, anyway?"

And there he sat, wishing he were anything else—even an old black spider with too many legs—until suddenly, the sky outside turned dark as night. A chilly wind came blowing the leaves inside out, and making the little rabbit's fur stand all on end.

Swish! came the big, cold raindrops, beating down.

Flash! came the sharp, brittle lightning.

And Boom-Boom-Boomty-Boom! came the thunder, making the little tan rabbit himself stand on end.

So down the nearest rabbit tunnel he scurried. And not a wish did he wish, and not a word did he say, until he was safe in his own snug rabbit hole.

Then, "Hooo!" said that little tan rabbit. "What a handy thing it is to be a rabbit—with a house down underground—when there's no place else in all the world fit for a little tan rabbit—or anyone else—to be!"

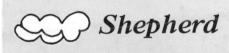 *Shepherd*

JULY 18

Up on the sunny hill I lie,
Tending the clouds in the close blue sky,
Just like a shepherd in a book,
With a willow branch
For my shepherd's crook.

I always keep my white flock going
Whichever way the wind is blowing,
By telling them, "Sheep, all go that way!"
And pointing my crook,
And they all obey.

The Cranky Crocodile

JULY 19

ONCE, in the hot, southern summer, a crocodile came to live in the river. Having a crocodile there was bad enough, but this was such a cranky crocodile!

He snapped up the dragonflies and fish as if they were peanuts, and if anyone dared come down for a swim, he tried to snap them up, too.

So of course, no one went swimming.

Hot as it was, that made all the animals feel cranky, and quarrel among themselves—until one day when old Mr. 'Coon decided that things had gone far enough, and would have to stop.

"By now, I guess I'm just about as cranky as any old crocodile," he said, picking up a stick.

And while all the other animals watched, down to the river he went—calm and collected.

"Ho, old Mr. Cranky Crocodile," he said. "I'm old Mr. Cranky 'Coon—and I've come down to take a swim."

At that, the crocodile swished forward, looking so dangerous with his big mouth open, that old Mr. 'Coon tried to back away. But before he could, his foot slipped. Then down he splashed—and up in the air went his stick.

"Poor old Mr. 'Coon!" wailed his friends. "This is surely the end of him!"

But just as they said that, down through the air came his stick, and it landed right in the crocodile's open jaws. And there it stuck, so that he couldn't close his mouth, or open it, either.

Crankier than ever he was, that old crocodile —but he was so embarrassed that he went swimming out of the river as fast as he could go.

But old Mr. 'Coon wasn't cranky at all.

"Come on in!" he called, grinning and trying to look as if he had planned the whole thing.

And his friends, joining him in the cool water, never once supposed Mr. 'Coon had not.

The Beach

JULY 20

When we go to the sandy beach
We have a pail and shovel each,
And lots of sand and crabs and shells,
And lots of at-the-seashore smells—
Of salty sea, and seaweed bunches,
And sunny sand, and picnic lunches,
And bathing suits and sun-baked wood,
And cool sea breezes, awfully good,
That smell, perhaps, of Spain and France,
And make the far-off whitecaps dance,

And make the seagulls turn and wheel.
I know exactly how they feel—
All light as air, and bare and free,
And warm as sun, and cool as sea,
And wild and lazy as the sound
Of all that ocean all around.
I guess there's no way you can know
Unless some day, you too can go
(With lunch and pail and shovel each)
Down to some wide and sandy beach.

Leo Comes Back

BEFORE his baby lion had come, Leo had been the fiercest, most exciting lion in the show.

But now everything was changed.

All Leo wanted to do was to cuddle his roly-poly baby, and play with it, and show it off.

"And when he is performing," sighed Leo's trainer, "he simply doesn't put his heart into the breath-taking fight between man and beast."

"Leo's famous roar isn't what it was, either," agreed the circus owner. "Sounds more like a lullaby."

And the ticket man reported that people just weren't buying tickets to see the trainer put his head into the jaws of a lion who kept purring.

Luckily, Tinker the clown heard all that—and he had an idea about what to do. So off he shuffled to see Leo.

"What's your nice baby lion going to be when he grows up?" Tinker asked. "A sort of tame, zoo lion, or a pet?"

"Neither one!" cried Leo. "He's going to be a circus lion. The greatest, just like me!"

"How's he going to learn?" asked Tinker.

"Why," said Leo, "Why, by watching me."

"When's he going to start?" Tinker asked. "Never too soon to learn to be a trouper, is it?"

"No," said Leo thoughtfully. "No, it's not."

So that very afternoon, Tinker came shuffling into the Big Top, pushing a baby carriage, with Leo's baby in it—smiling and waving to the delighted crowds.

But when Leo came out, the crowd quite forgot his baby.

How they shivered when that great lion fought with his trainer. How they held their breaths when he roared his famous, ferocious roar. And oh, how their eyes popped when the brave lion tamer put his head into Leo's fierce, growling, snarling jaws!

"What a lion!" they cried. "What a lion!"

The trainer and circus owner and ticket man were delighted at the change in Leo.

But Tinker was neither surprised nor amazed.

He just shuffled off, smiling his big, lopsided, painted-on smile, and wondering what was for supper that night.

Why, Mr. Pelican!

JULY 22

When Mr. Pelican came for lunch
On the rock by the deep blue sea,
The seagulls cried, "Just help yourself,
You're as welcome as you can be!"

"So kind of you," Mr. Pelican smiled.
"Just a mouthful, and no more—"
Then he opened his mouth, which looked,
Alas—like a cupboard without a door!

And when Mr. Pelican'd had his lunch,
The seagulls screamed—for he
Had stored away every lunch-sized fish
That there was in the deep blue sea!

So Mr. Pelican flapped away,
Barely glancing back to call,
"Such carryings-on—when all I had
Was a mouthful, and that's all!"

The Talking Whale

JULY 23

CAPTAIN McDermott was such a jolly man that his ship was a jolly ship. The sailors sang at their work. The cook jigged in his galley. And the captain himself went about his duties, parrot on his shoulder, laughing and joking between giving orders.

But one day, in a sudden gale, poor Poll the parrot was blown overboard—and after that, Captain McDermott was a changed man.

He quite forgot his duties. All he would do was to sail the sea, searching for his lost pet. And he looked so mournful and sad and downhearted that his crew, even to the cook, went about with tears in their eyes.

"Poor Poll was surely drowned the day of the storm," they told one another. "Our captain's daft to think he'll find her. Now how in the world can we cheer him up?"

What things they tried! Everything from catching a seagull, and trying to teach it to talk —to spinning him the wildest tales they could dream up.

"Aye," sighed the captain. "Strange things do be happening these days." But he just kept looking sadder and sadder, until one day, just off Labrador, they sighted a whaler after its catch.

"There she blows!" shouted the lookout.

And out went the ship's jolly boat.

But just as the jolly boat neared the whale— harpooner ready, not a sound anywhere—a great voice cried, "Avast, ye lubbers! Let a poor creature be!"

"The whale's talking!" cried the harpooner.

"A talking whale!" shouted the whaler's captain. "Back to the schooner lads, and we'll get out of these queer, bedeviled waters!"

"Nay, wait a bit!" called Captain McDermott, jumping to his feet and looking both calm and cheerful. With that, he let down a net, and drew up an old barrel that was floating nearby.

Into it he reached, and out of it he drew a damp, and thin, and bedraggled green bird.

"It's Poll!" cried his crew. "Poll herself—safe and sound. Our captain wasn't daft!"

"Daft I was, losing my pet," chuckled Captain McDermott. "But not daft enough to believe in a talking whale! Now, Poll my girl, tell the whalers you're sorry you scared them—"

"Aw," begged Poll, and she said, "Awk!"

Then she called, "Sorry, mateys—but a shipwrecked sailor has to have a bit o' fun—" in the very voice she had used for the whale, though not so loud outside the echoey barrel.

The whalers were most relieved to know they were after an ordinary whale after all. Captain McDermott was jollier than he had ever been, and his crew was even jollier.

As for Poll, hungrily eating sea-biscuits, she clung tightly to the captain's shoulder. It was easy to see that no wind would ever blow her overboard again.

Bouncy Bunny's House

JULY 24

"HELLO," said Bouncy Bunny to his cousin. "What are you building?"

"A playhouse," his cousin said. "Those are my plans, right there on the ground—"

"They're sort of plain plans, aren't they?" murmured Bouncy Bunny. "I think I'll build a house, too."

And presently, he was sawing and hammering, and working away—without any plans.

"Mine's going to be two stories high," he said. "With a chimney, and a fireplace, and shutters with trees cut in them—oops! my finger—and a front porch, and stairs for going up and down. It's going to a very fancy house, isn't it, Cousin?"

"Couldn't say," said his cousin. "Never saw the plans."

And just then, down tumbled Bouncy Bunny's house, because the parts hadn't fit right.

"Oh, my lovely, fancy house!" he wailed. "Now it's only a broken-up wreck!"

"Never mind, Bunny," said his cousin. "If you help me paint mine, it can be yours, too. And after we make some more plans, maybe we can fancy it up a bit."

"All right!" cried Bouncy Bunny, grabbing a brush. "How shall we paint it—pink, with butterflies? Green, with daisies?"

"Nope," said his cousin. "White, with a blue roof—exactly the way it is in the plans."

And Bouncy Bunny, looking sideways at his own wrecked house, just nodded his head, and dipped into the white paint.

Two Little Monkeys

ONCE there were two little monkeys who looked alike, did alike, and even thought alike. Which —since two heads are so much better than one —really was a shame.

When one little monkey thought he'd climb the banana tree and pick the one ripe banana there—the other little monkey thought the same. So up they both went.

But with two little monkeys reaching for the same banana, oops! out of their hands it slipped —right into the mouth of a hungry zebra below.

Off he raced, with the little monkeys after him. But not even two little monkeys can run as fast as one little zebra! So he was soon well hidden in the striped jungle shade, and chewing away, while they were just all out of breath.

"Whew!" panted one little monkey. "I think I want a drink!"

"Whew!" panted the other. "I do, too!"

Hand in hand, they ran down to the river bank. It was so wet and muddy that one little monkey began to slip. As he did, he pulled the other little monkey with him. And slip and splash! into the river they fell—almost into the mouth of a crocodile who was waiting there!

Both little monkeys scrambled out—but the one who had been pulled in got the tip of his tail sharply nipped.

And that made him so cross, that when the other little monkey said, "I don't think I like big biting crocodiles"—he would not say, "I don't think I do, either."

Instead, he said, "I don't think I like looking alike, doing alike, and 'specially thinking alike —'cause that's what keeps getting me into trouble!"

And away he went, scowly and sulky, to be all by himself behind a big rock. By and by, when his tail had stopped hurting, that little monkey began to feel very lonely.

He was glad when the other little monkey peeped at him.

So glad that he smiled and smiled.

But even then, when the other little monkey said, "I'm thinking of picking some wild strawberries for supper," he would not say, "I'm thinking the same thing."

"I'm thinking of getting some sugar and cream to put on the berries you're thinking of picking," he said instead. And he did.

"Mmmm, but berries taste good, all sweet and creamy," said the little monkey who had picked them. "I think they're twice as good as just berries—"

"Everything's going to be twice as good from now on," grinned the monkey who had made up his mind to think his own thoughts.

And since he did—and since two heads are so much better than one—that was exactly the way things turned out.

The New Little Man

JULY 26

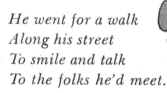

A new little man
Moved into town,
Very lonely he was—
But he didn't frown:

He went for a walk
Along his street
To smile and talk
To the folks he'd meet.

"Hello," he said,
"What a jolly dog!"
Or, "Here, I'll help
You chop that log!"

Or, "Madam, your garden
Is wonderfully gay!"
Then he went back home,
And that very same day—

That new little man
(Who didn't frown)
Had friends aplenty,
All over town!

Summer Ballet

JULY 27

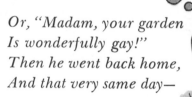

On the square of the screen door,
Shimmering and white,
There's a tiny ballet
Every summer night.

Little moths and big moths,
Dancing to the tune
Of the beetles buzzing
Underneath the moon;

Round about they flutter,
Bowing to their friends,
Till, screak! the door is opened,
And all the dancing ends.

Rainy-Day Way

JULY 28

I didn't know at all—
Did you?—
That squirrels have
Umbrellas, too.
They spread their tails
All wide and flat
Over their heads,
And fixed like that
It works just fine—
They never get
Their furry selves
The least bit wet.

The Toadstool

JULY 29

There it was
And nobody grew it,
Nobody I know
Even knew it
Was growing there
In a dampish spot,
That little white toadstool;
And I forgot
To ask how it got there,
Sudden and white,
When nothing at all
Was there last night.

Quiet, Please!

JULY 30

"QUIET, please!" called Grandmother Duck. "I need a nap, and all this noise makes my head all buzzy!"

The birds tried to keep quiet, but they kept forgetting. So did the merry frogs. And every now and then, plop! another little fish would leap out of the water and splash back in.

Pretty soon Grandmother Duck was very cross indeed.

"I said, 'Be quiet,' " she scolded. "Quiet, you birds—quiet, you frogs—quiet, you silly little fish. Quiet, please!"

She sounded so angry that suddenly everyone was as still and quiet as if there were no one in the whole wide world except Grandmother Duck herself.

"There now, this is better!" she murmured, settling down in the reeds and tucking her head under her wing. But somehow, she still couldn't sleep. That quiet seemed so big and wide and empty! It began to buzz in Grandmother Duck's head. And it made her feel strange and lonely inside.

Then, just as she was sure she could not stand one more bit of that lonesome quiet—quack! quack! quack! along swam a whole line of fuzzy new little ducklings, having the time of their lives.

"Hush!" whispered the birds.

"Shush!" whispered the frogs.

"Quiet!" whispered a little fish, leaping up. "Or Grandmother Duck will start scolding again!"

But Grandmother Duck sat on the bank, smiling and admiring her new little grandchildren.

"I won't at all!" she said, drowsily tucking her head under her wing. "Why, I never heard such a lovely, cozy sound in all my life!"

So the ducklings quacked to their hearts' content.

And the birds began to sing, and the frogs croaked, and the little fish leaped, and Grandmother Duck smiled in her sleep.

Strange Old Mr. Elias

JULY 31

Old Mr. Elias walked on the bias
Whenever he strolled through town—
Maybe because he never looked up,
But always kept looking straight down,
He found a quarter,
He found a nickel,
He found a dime and a penny;
But he never could spend them
In the stores—
For he never got into any.
Still he went on
As he always had, traveling on the bias,
And looking down, instead of up,
That strange old Mr. Elias!

A Bluejay for a Pet

ONE morning when Sally and Peter were drying dishes, they saw a baby bluejay out in the yard. Hop, hop, hop, it went—and it flapped its wings, but nothing happened.

That baby bluejay was too young to fly!

"You finish the dishes, Sally," Peter cried, "and I'll catch it for a pet—"

Then out the door he went, and around behind the flower bed where the baby bluejay had hopped. Sally could hardly wait for him to come back. And she hadn't very long to wait, either.

For suddenly, there was such a squawking and scolding outside that Mother and Daddy came to see what was going on. And around the flower bed and across the yard came Peter, with two big, angry bluejays after him.

Into the house he raced, with his hands empty, and a most surprised look on his face.

"I guess we aren't going to have a baby bluejay," gulped Sally.

"I guess not!" cried Daddy. "Peter's just lucky to have two eyes! You should have known that no big bluejays would ever let you get near their baby!

"Hurry up with those dishes," he added, "and we'll fix up a bird-feeding station. Then you can watch the wild birds and learn something about their ways—"

And Sally and Peter, sure that having lots of birds for sort-of-pets would be much nicer than one little lonesome indoor bluejay, started drying much faster than they had ever done before.

Grandma Oliver's Mistake

AUGUST 2

EVERY other year, when school closed, the Olivers all piled into their car and went to visit Grandma Oliver at her farm. And the year in between, Grandma Oliver hopped into her car, and came to visit them.

One way or the other, farm or city, it was always fun.

But one year, Grandma Oliver got things mixed up.

"This is my year for the city, I'm sure," said the forgetful old lady, carefully packing her bags.

At the very same time, Mrs. Oliver was packing bags, too. And while she did, she said that she wished they could go to the seashore—just this once, and just for a change.

"We do, too!" cried the little Olivers. "We could swim in the ocean, and dig in the sand, and—oh, Daddy, can't we go there this year?"

"Certainly not," said Mr. Oliver. "It's our year to visit Grandma, and disappointing her is out of the question."

Out of the question meant it was settled. So all the Olivers packed their things. And bright and early the next morning, they headed straight for Grandma's farm.

Along the hot highway they rode—still wishing they were off for the seashore—until everyone was so hot and thirsty that Mr. Oliver pulled in to the nearest drive-in.

"Look over there," said Mrs. Oliver. "There's a car that looks like Grandma's—"

"So it does," Mr. Oliver agreed.

"And so it is!" cried the little Olivers. "Because there's Grandma herself in it—having a lemonade!"

In a moment, all six Olivers (with lemonades of their own) were hugging Grandma, and asking what in the world she was doing there —halfway to their house.

"Going to your house, of course," said Grandma. "But if you've made other plans, you must go right ahead. Why, only last night I was thinking how much I'd like to go to the seashore—just this once, and just for a change—"

"You were?" cried Mrs. Oliver.

"So were we!" squealed the little Olivers.

Mr. Oliver, very busy with his road map, said, "Hmmm! At this very moment we're only nine miles from the seashore—so I suggest that we all spend our vacation right there—"

So off they started, Mr. and Mrs. Oliver chuckling over Grandma Oliver's mistake, and Grandma Oliver positive that *they* had gotten their years mixed up. But the little Olivers (all sniffing the air for the first, salty seashore smell) were sure that no one at all had made the littlest bit of a mistake.

A Different Place

AUGUST 3

Sometimes, on a summer day
When we need somewhere new to play,
Down to Miss Jones's yard we race—
It's such a lovely, different place.
Her hedge is taller than the rest,
With flowers in it, and a nest;
Her grass is deep, with lots of holes
Where rabbits live, and even moles,
And there's no other place we've found
Where dandelions grow big and round,
With seedy tops that you can blow
Up in the air. Just see them go
Over the hedge! When they come down,
They'll plant new plants
All over town!

Mrs. Crow's Song

AUGUST 4

"Please sing me a song," said the little crow. "The other mothers all sing to their sleepy children—and why don't you?"

Poor Mrs. Crow! She had a voice like a crow, not pretty at all. But she hated to tell that to her little crow. So she said, "Well, now—what kind of song? One about a little ripe blackberry, growing in the woods?"

"Yes, about that!" said her little crow, settling down.

But Mrs. Crow said, "No, wait! Perhaps a song about a crafty fox, stealing cheese from a silly young crow—"

"Oh, yes, that!" said the little crow. And his mother cleared her throat, sounding like an old, rusty gate.

"Dear me," she said. "I seem to have forgotten the words! Suppose I sing the song about a little black cloud blowing all around the world. Over mountains and valleys, over strange, lost places in Tibet, and tongue-twister places in Wales—very hard to say—and over the wide, dry prairies of the West, and the wider, rolling seas, dotted with ships—"

"Umm, about that," yawned her little crow.

"About a dark little cloud," his mother went on, "blowing everywhere to bring rainy weather. A tired little cloud, going on and on and on—across the bright world of daytime into the dark world of night. And then floating down and down through the night sky, soft as a soft black feather—and curling up on the moss of a mountainside, to sleep and rest and sleep. A dark, tired little cloud, sound asleep like a sleepy bird in his soft, dark nest—shall I sing you that song, my little crow?"

But this time, her little crow didn't answer. He didn't say yes, he didn't say no.

That little black crow was as sound asleep as a dark little cloud on the mountainside of the night.

"Well," sighed his mother, "that takes care of tonight. And if he asks for a song tomorrow, who knows? Perhaps I shall be in better voice—"

Then she fluffed her dark feathers, and closed her dark eyes, all ready to go to sleep in the dark night, too—like you, to sleep in the soft, dark night.

Rainy-Day Place

AUGUST 5

Under my porch is a dandy place
For rainy days. There's room to race,
And dig deep tunnels, and make a town,
When all outside is raining down.
You can hear the rain, and smell it, too—
And still stay dry. So come on, will you?
Come under my porch, where we can play
Outdoor games on this rainy day.

Too Big for the Game

THE LITTLE hippopotamus was much, much bigger than any of the other little animals.

When he tried to play with the little tigers —who were making a narrow, secret trail through the jungle—they called, "You're too big for the game! You'd make the trail so wide it wouldn't be secret, any more!"

The little giraffes, playing hide-and-seek behind the trees, called, "Too big for the game!" to the little hippopotamus, too.

"You couldn't hide behind the trees," they explained. You'd only show on both sides."

And the funny little monkeys, swinging merrily from the slender jungle vines, giggled, "Much, much too big for the game!" before that little hippopotamus even had time to say hello to them.

Very discouraged he was by now.

"There's just no game the right size for me," he sighed.

Sad as he was, he walked slowly back to the water hole. When he got there, all the others had come down for a nice, cool swim.

"But we can't go swimming!" they were saying. "After no rain, the water is too low even for wading!"

When the little hippopotamus heard that, he stopped being sad, and almost smiled. Then down the bank he went, into the shallow water. And as he did, his fat little body took up so much room, that the water rose up, and up, and up—almost to the rim of the water hole.

Now that little hippopotamus did smile.

"There!" he said. "Now you can all come in."

"Yes, we can!" the others cried, and in they splashed.

In a moment they were riding on the little hippopotamus' back, and playing all kinds of exciting water games.

What a good time they all had!

Such a good time that next time that little hippopotamus came to play with them, they didn't call, "Too big for the game!" Instead, they quickly started a new one—one that fit him just as well as he had made the too-low water hole fit them.

Signals

AUGUST 7

Last night, outside my window sill,
A light flashed on and off until
I simply had to go and see
Who could be signaling to me.

A firefly sat there, on the shelf,
Turning on his little self—
I guess for light enough to see
Who lived inside. He knows now—me!

Eight Little Polar Bears

AUGUST 8

Eight hot little polar bears
Said, "It's much too hot!"
But eight cool little swimming fish
Laughed and said, "It's not!"

Then eight cross little polar bears
Plunged into the pool—
Missed the fish, and clambered out,
And said, "Why, now it's cool!"

The eight tired little swimming fish
(Who'd raced to get away)
Thought, "Oh goodness! It is hot!"
But kept the peace all day.

146

The Wet Little Teddy Bear

AUGUST 9

DOWN the street went Kerry, going skip, skip, skip—with the rain on his umbrella going drip, drip, drip. The sidewalk was all shiny wet, and lying there—face down in a puddle—was a teddy bear.

A wet little teddy bear, a brown little teddy bear, such a sad little teddy bear—lying in the rain!

"I could take him home and dry him, so he'd feel fine," Kerry thought. Then Kerry said, "But he's not mine!"

So he picked up the teddy bear (wet as anything) and went from house to house to house.

Ring, ring, ring! Kerry rang the doorbells. But everyone said, "No, that's not my teddy bear—mine's upstairs in bed!"

Only one house was different. Inside there was a sighing, and a boo-hoo-hooing, such a very sad crying! It sounded just like someone who had lost a teddy bear. And when Kerry rang that doorbell—yes, the bear lived there!

So, away went Kerry with a skip, skip, skip, and the rain on his umbrella going drip, drip, drip. The sidewalk still was shiny wet, but in the puddle where the teddy had been lying, there was nothing to be seen.

Because that wet little teddy bear, that brown little teddy bear, that poor little teddy bear—who'd been lost in the rain—was snuggled in a warm towel, and safe at home again.

Berrying

AUGUST 10

Whenever we go to the berry patch,
And the berries are greenish white,
There's never a bird anywhere around—
There's never a bird in sight.
The branches hang in the quiet air
With their berries in the sun,
And we think what basketfuls we'll have
When the ripening is done!

But when we go down to the berry patch,
And the berries are sweet and red—
There's never a spot on branch or ground,
Or even up overhead,
That isn't full of the busy birds
All darting in the sun,
And we're lucky to have one basketful
When their berrying is done!

The New Camper

AUGUST 11

THE first time Kim went to camp, he was supposed to be there for two weeks. But when he had been there for two days, he wrote a letter home.

"Camp is very nice," he wrote. "We swim and play ball, and do interesting things. However, the food is not like at home. At night it is too quiet, too. Except for an owl that keeps me awake. Camp is very nice, but one week would be nicer than two. Do you think it could be arranged?"

Kim mailed his letter, and thought about Sunday, when his family would come to visit him. Right then, it seemed awfully far away.

But right after that, camp got to be more fun.

Kim's favorite counsellor, Jim Adams, chose him to help with the junior campers at the waterfront. That was after the watermelon race, of course, when Kim was the one who captured the big, bobbing melon—which he and his bunkmates ate for first prize.

And it turned out that Kim was very good at

148

August Storm

AUGUST 12

I smelled the storm
And heard it coming,
All thundery, like Indians drumming.
The smoky sky, as dark as night,
Flashed with a sudden, savage light,
And frightened leaves, turned inside-out,
Hung shivering at the wind's wild shout—
Till all at once there seemed to be
A lull—and then, all fearlessly,
The rain came sweeping, rushing down,
And drove the savage
Out of town.

archery. He practiced with his team whenever there was time. And it began to look as if they would get high score in the final contest.

So all at once it was Sunday, and Kim's family was there to visit him. His mother surprised him by very kindly not kissing him in front of all the other fellows. And his daddy amazed him by saying, "Well Kim, are all your things packed?"

"Packed?" asked Kim. "What for?"

"Why, so you can come home with us," his daddy said. "I thought you said that one week at camp would be enough—"

And then Kim remembered his letter.

"That's right, I did!" he said. "But that was only on Tuesday—now I think just the other way round. Can't I stay here an extra week?"

"It can be arranged," smiled Kim's daddy, pleased to see that Kim was a real camper now.

So away they went, Kim and his mother and daddy, so he could show them what a wonderful place camp really was.

The Sad-Looking Milkman

AUGUST 13

THERE was once a sad-looking milkman who simply hated going slowly. But clop-clop-clop he drove along the early morning streets, with his old horse clopping more slowly every day.

"Really," he said at last, "it's time she was retired!" And he looked so sad that his boss agreed with him.

"I'll tell you what," his boss said. "There's a horse auction down at the firehouse—so you go on down and bid for a retired firehorse to take her place."

So away went the milkman, his pocket full of dollars.

All the old firehorses were fine-looking—but the milkman saw one that was a real speedy-looking beauty.

"That's the horse for me!" he thought, bidding all the money his boss had given him, and all his own besides—until suddenly, that beautiful horse was his.

But just then, who should come along but the milkman's boss.

"Why, this is no horse for us!" he cried. "We can't have a milk wagon whizzing along the streets, with the milk bottles flying left, right, and every which way!"

And on top of that, the fire chief came running out of the firehouse.

"So *there's* my new lead-horse!" he cried, pointing at the horse the milkman had bought. "Who put her in the auction by mistake?"

Nobody answered him, but one fireman—a sad-looking one who hated racing to fires—quietly put down his fire hat.

"I did," he sighed. "And I resign—always did wish I'd been a milkman, anyway."

At that, the sad-looking milkman threw his hat in the air.

"I apply for the job he resigned from," he cried. "Because I guess what I've always wanted was to be a fireman!"

So all at once, everything was straightened out.

The milkman's boss was given back his money, and he soon hired the sad-looking fireman to be a merry milkman. The fire chief had his lead-horse back, and was so pleased that he clapped the ex-milkman's shoulder.

"If you really want that fireman job," he said, "you'd best get along upstairs to fireman's school—"

"I do, oh I do!" cried the ex-milkman.

And smiling the happiest smile you ever saw, he shook hands with his new boss, and went whizzing up the firehouse stairs.

Strategy

AUGUST 14

If I were a leopard in the zoo,
Pacing up and down, the way they do,
With spotted skin and eyes of green,
I'd pretend to be so fierce and mean
That nobody'd dare even clean my cage.
I'd snarl and claw in a terrible rage
Till they all agreed, with worried faces,
That I really belonged in other places—
Then I'd smile and wink at the people there
And trot along home, to my jungle lair.

The Wading Pool

AUGUST 15

When we are in the wading pool,
We can be giant fish,
Or ducks, in just a little pond;
And sometimes, when we wish—

We can get out, and have the pool
A sea, so deep and wide
That paper ships take half an hour
To sail from side to side.

Dog Days

AUGUST 16

Most of the year
My puppy's tail
Keeps beating like a drum.
But in the summer,
When the hot
And sultry Dog Days come,
He likes to go
To some dark place
(Like underneath my bed)
And wag his little panting tongue
To keep him cool, instead.

Something New To Do

ONE hot day it was so hot that the little bears didn't feel like doing just the usual things. And as for doing something new—they couldn't think of a thing they could do.

"If we had a sawhorse and a long board, we could make a seesaw and ride up and down on it," said one.

"Yes," said another. "And if we had a horse that wasn't a sawhorse, but a real one, we could ride him out to the seashore where it's lovely and cool—"

Then the third little bear said, "But we don't have a real horse, or a sawhorse, *or* a long board. All we have is a little short board, and a piece of rope—too thick for cowboy lassos—and what can we do with them?"

"Nothing I know of," said the first little bear.

"Nothing I know of, either," said the second.

But the third little bear had a sudden thought, and he jumped to his feet with a sudden thump.

"We can use the rope for a swing rope," he said. "We can use the little short board for a swing seat—and we can make ourselves a swing!"

So that was what those little bears did.

They made a swing under a shady tree, and took turns swinging high and low. That made a lovely, cool breeze. Besides, it was such fun that almost before the little bears knew it, the hot day was over, and their mother was calling them to come in for supper.

The Carnival

ALL week, Julie had been waiting for the carnival to come to town, and wondering what it would be like.

"It's hard to tell about," her mother had said.

And her daddy had said, "Guess you'd better wait till Friday, and see the carnival for yourself, Julie."

So Julie had waited and waited—and at last it was Friday—Friday morning, and Friday afternoon.

Now it was Friday evening, and Julie and her mother and daddy set out in the dusk. At the top of the hill they stopped and looked down, because the field below was all ablaze with carnival lights.

Some of the lights were strung like a necklace, some went round and round, and some went up and down. There was music, too, and people laughing, and people shouting.

The round-and-round lights were a merry-go-round where Julie could ride on a shiny black horse. The up-and-down lights were on the Ferris wheel. Julie rode on that, too—high in the air, her hand in Daddy's.

The music came from the merry-go-round, and from a pavilion—where people were dancing under the swaying lanterns.

And the shouting was from all the booths, where you won prizes by throwing rings or balls, or shooting clay ducks.

In one booth, a man sold real turtles with red or orange or yellow-painted backs. In another, the man sold big paper cones full of pink sugar fluff, and in still another there were balloons and pinwheels and birds on sticks.

And what things there were to see! A magician who took a silver dollar from behind Julie's pigtail, a fortune teller who knew everything that was going to happen—and told a little for a shiny coin.

There were clowns, too, and acrobats, and real Indians with dark, serious faces and bright clothes.

Julie had kept her eyes open for so long, that all at once they began to close themselves.

"Well," said Daddy. "Here's a young lady who needs a ride home!" And he swung his little girl, balloon, pinwheel, bird, turtle, prizes and all, up into his arms.

"The fireworks are starting," he said softly, stopping at the top of the hill. "Don't you want to see them, Julie?"

Julie tried to open her eyes, but she was too sleepy. She pushed her face into Daddy's collar, and went back to sleep. After all, she had seen the carnival at last. And next year, next year she would stay awake and see the fireworks, too.

Fishing

AUGUST 19

It seems to me it's very odd,
That when I go without my rod,
In the quiet pools there glide
Fish all spotted, fish all pied,
Fish of every kind and size,
Leaping up for passing flies.

But when I take my rod and bait—
There I sit, and there I wait,
There I watch, and there I wish,
And there I never see a fish!
Isn't it the oddest thing
How they know the things you bring?

Little Snake

AUGUST 20

Down where the shining waterfall
Tumbles over the stony wall
Into the other, lower lake,
There's a house
That belongs to a water snake.
Not a big one,
He's brown and small,
And he likes to sit on the stony wall
Flashing his tongue and turning his eyes
And watching the big, blue dragonflies;
But if you watch him,
He turns and goes swiftly gliding,
Slithery-sliding
Into his house in the stony wall,
And he doesn't come out again at all.

The Little Green Grapes

AUGUST 21

ON summer afternoons, the little foxes liked to take their naps in the grape arbor. It was so nice, with the cool, green leaves shading them from the sun, and the little green grapes hanging down in tempting clusters.

"Don't eat any," their mother always said before she dozed off. "Little green grapes taste awfully sour."

"We won't," said the little foxes.

But every day, those little green grapes looked more tempting and delicious! And one day, when their mother dozed off without saying, "Don't eat any—" both little foxes reached up, slyly and quickly, and snapped off one little green grape each, and bit into it.

"Ooof!" they both gasped, puckering up their mouths. "Oooh, ooof! but that was sour!"

After that, it looked as if those little foxes never would touch the grapes again.

Even when they had grown big and ripe and purple, and the little foxes' mother said, "Go ahead and have some—" both little foxes just puckered up their mouths and said, "Ooof!"

But one look at their faces, and their mother knew just what was the trouble.

So she quickly put one big, sweet purple grape into each little puckered-up mouth. And in a wink, both little foxes were smiling happy smiles and reaching for more of those delicious, sweet, ripe, purple grapes.

Spinner

SPINNER was a naughty little cat who liked to chase things—rabbits and chipmunks, moles and mice, butterflies and June bugs, and even her own little tail.

Round and round she went, spinning like a top—and that was how she got her name.

But one day, Spinner saw a baby bird on the lawn, and would have caught it, if her mistress had not caught her first.

"You naughty Spinner!" she cried angrily. "Don't ever, ever chase a bird again!"

Plainly enough, this meant nothing to the naughty little cat, who only glared at the bird and struggled to get free.

"I see I shall have to bell you," her mistress said, putting a row of silver bells on her cat's red collar. Very fine they looked, and very merry they sounded—but they did spoil all poor Spinner's fun.

Moles and chipmunks and rabbits, and especially birds, went streaking off when they heard her coming. And worst of all, the scurrying night mice soon had the run of the house.

They made such noises, gnawing and chewing away in the walls, that Spinner's mistress could not sleep a wink.

"Oh, Spinner," she sighed at last, "what are we to do?"

Spinner said, "Meow!" She meant, "Take off these bells, and I'll take care of the mice!" But it only sounded like, "Meow," to her mistress, who puzzled and thought for nights and nights and nights.

"I have it!" she cried at last, hopping out of bed. "Mice are creatures of the night, when baby birds—and big ones, too—are safely asleep high in the trees!"

With that, she took the collar from around Spinner's neck. Without the telltale bells, that little chasing cat quickly frightened all the mice out of the house, and out of the neighborhood as well.

Very proud of herself she was, was Spinner.

Her mistress—proud and happy, too, after a good night's sleep—saw to it that her collar was on in the daytime when the birds were hopping on the lawn. But at night, with no collar at all, Spinner was free to roam and prowl and chase —and to make sure that never a mouse ventured into their snug little house again.

The Garden Hose

AUGUST 23

If tomorrow is hot,
I'll take off my clothes
And play in the spray
Of the garden hose.
I'll sprinkle the grass
And all the plants,
I'll sprinkle the too-hot
Bugs and ants,
I'll sprinkle the path
And the windowpane
Till everything looks
Like we're having rain.
Then I'll sprinkle myself
All slickery wet—
'Cause nobody cares
How wet I get,
When I take off my shoes
And socks and clothes,
And play in the spray
Of the garden hose.

The Golden Pear

AUGUST 24

In our new pear tree
There was just one pear.
All golden and rosy
Hanging there,
It looked too pretty
To pick and eat,
So I only smelled it,
It did smell sweet,
And I only put out
My hand to see
If it really was ripe,
And then, suddenly—
There was our pear tree,
As bare as bare,
And I was eating
That golden pear!

One Cabbage Leaf Each

AUGUST 25

OH, BUT it was hot in the cabbage patch, where the little bunnies were helping their daddy!

Down the rows they went, shooing away the bugs that wanted to eat up the big, round cabbages—and stopping every few seconds to mop their foreheads and fan themselves.

"Daddy," they kept asking, "can't we each have just one leaf of cabbage each—just one?"

But their daddy kept saying, "Not till you're all finished working—then you may have all you want."

So the little rabbits worked and stopped, and fanned and mopped and asked, until their daddy—very hot, too—quite lost patience with them.

"You may not have a leaf each!" he cried. "You may not have even one tiny *bite* of cabbage till we're finished!"

"Bite?" asked the little bunnies. "We don't want our one leaf each to eat, Daddy. We want them to put under our hats to keep us cool, the same as Grandpa always does—"

"Oh yes, so he does—" said their daddy.

He gave each little bunny a big, cool leaf for under its hat, and put a bigger cool leaf under his own. And sure enough, all those bunnies were cool as cucumbers. They worked so fast, not having to stop, that almost in a wink all the cabbage bugs were gone.

"What a wise old bunny your grandpa is!" declared their daddy, cutting an especially big, beautiful cabbage for their supper—and an even bigger one for Grandpa, who was so fond of cabbage (and of putting a leaf under his hat) that he had already used up the last cabbage in his own patch.

All Kinds of Bugs

AUGUST 26

ONCE there was a funny little mouse who was specially quiet, even for a mouse.

In winter, he would sit quietly for hours on end, watching the snowflakes sift down. In spring, he sat so quietly that he could see the grass come up, and hear the seeds sprouting.

And in summer, he sat even more quietly. Because now there was a whole new world to watch. The world of bugs, little and big ones, flying ones and walking ones—bugs to watch, and bugs to watch out for.

"Like the stinging ones," thought that little mouse. "Buzzy mosquitoes, and fuzzy honeybees, and hornets and wasps, and the meaner kinds of flies."

So those he watched out for—not bothering them ever—but quietly getting out of their way. Quietly, he watched the caterpillars (fuzzy and smooth), and the big crickets and grasshoppers who hopped little hops, and the little leafhoppers—who hopped enormous big ones.

He learned their ways, and the ways of moths and butterflies. And he wondered at the wonder of fireflies, shining in the night.

Best of all, that quiet little mouse liked to watch the beetle bugs. There were so many kinds, so many colors—even stripes and polka dots, like circus clowns. And better than best of all, he liked to help the big, bumbling June bugs turn over when they fell pling! on their backs, and could not get up.

"There!" he would say, each time he had helped one. "If I didn't know lots about bugs, I wouldn't dare do that. What if that had been a bumblebee instead of a June bug? I'd have a sting instead of a thank you, that's what!"

Then back he'd go, that quiet little mouse, because—in spite of all he did know—he was sure there was much more to learn about that whole new world, that wonderful world of bugs.

Captain Nightshirt

AUGUST 27

Once there was a captain
Who sailed the seas all night
When the moon rode foamy billows,
And the curtains blew out white
As the mainsail on a schooner,
And the shiny, pinpoint stars
Looked like lanterns swung by sailors;
And the trees were masts and spars.
Then he went on wondrous journeys,
Though his family never knew—
They all thought he was upstairs in bed,
And he woke up there, too.

The Ice-Cream Man

AUGUST 28

The ice-cream man
Came by today.
"Popsicles!" he called,
And we said, "Hurray!"

He had lemon and lime,
And grape and cherry—
All kinds of kinds—
I chose strawberry.

Solution

AUGUST 29

A poodle in a puddle
Had a paddle all his own,
But he had no boat to paddle,
And he didn't have a bone.

So he went with his new paddle
To a hungry little cat
Who had a boat without a paddle—
Things were lovely after that!

Off they paddled on the puddle,
Fishing gaily up and down,
Till they caught five fish for supper—
Which they shared, fried crisp and brown.

And everything did. Everything stayed just that way until it was time to close up the lake cottage and go home.

"What a shame to leave with the weather like this!" Sandy thought at the last picnic supper.

He sighed, and looked sad, and went to bed.

But in the night, a change came. A cold wind blew across the lake, and Sandy shivered under his summer blankets. In the morning, all the clear, bright days were gone. The sun was lost behind low, gray clouds, and the lake was cold and sullen. So when the cottage was closed, and Sandy was riding back to the city with his family—he forgot the wonderful August for thinking how cozy it would be to sleep tonight in his own warm, soft bed at home.

The Perfect August

AUGUST 30

Once in August it was so beautiful that Sandy wished it would stay just as it was forever.

"Just like this," he wished. "With the sky clear and blue, and the clouds white and high—"

He wished the lake would stay as still and deep blue, too—with the sailboats skimming along in the fair little breeze that pushed against the sails—but never rippled the water—and the water so clear that he could see the tiny, water-clear minnows trying to nibble his toes. He wished the fields would stay full of scarlet paint-brush and black-eyed Susans, and that the woods would stay full of big, sweet blackberries for pie to eat after supper.

And he wished the thrush would stay right where he was in the cherry tree, singing the wonderful summer song he was pouring into the bright summer air.

The Magic Shell

AUGUST 31

At the beach I found
A magic shell,
So I brought it home
In my pail;
And I keep it up
On my top bookshelf—
Right under the picture whale.
And now, whenever I wish I were
Back there by the shining sea,
I hold the shell up close to my ear,
Till it brings the beach to me:
All the hushing sound,
And the rushing sound,
Of the seashore winds and waves
Are caught in my shell
That I brought home—
Like magical genie-slaves.

Changes

SEPTEMBER 1

When summer's sliding into fall,
You hardly notice it at all
Until one day, the meadows nod
With aster-stars and goldenrod;
And in the orchard, trees bow low
With burnished apples all aglow;
Until a starling flock screams by,
Like some dark shadow on the sky
That fills it full, and then moves on,
And when it goes—the summer's gone.

In the Meadow

SEPTEMBER 2

We sat in our nest in the meadow grass
And watched a baby rabbit pass,
Hippity-hop, through a little street
It had made for itself
With its hopping feet.
It sat up straight
And looked all around
When it stopped to take a rest,
But we kept so still that it never knew
We were there in our grassy nest.

Tonio, Tonio!

SEPTEMBER 3

"Tonio, Tonio!" called Tonio's father. "Help me carry the corn in from the fields!"

So away went Tonio, just as fast as his little brown legs could run.

Then, "Tonio, Tonio!" called his mother. "Quickly, get me more colored wool for my weaving."

And when Tonio had brought that, one of his three sisters was sure to call, "Tonio, Tonio!" and send him for more reeds for baskets, or more straw for sandals, or more clay for the beautiful bowls they made.

Sometimes it seemed that everyone was calling, "Tonio, Tonio, Tonio!" all day long. He was busy all the time, but on the night before market day, when his family was packing its wares to take to market, Tonio had nothing to pack.

"And with nothing to sell, I'll have no money to buy things with, either," he told himself sadly. Thinking of all the gay toys and delicious sweets one could buy at market, he went to bed feeling so sorry for himself that he thought he would not even go to market, that silly little Tonio.

But in the morning, the minute his mother called, "Tonio, Tonio! Time to get up—" up he hopped, eager to see the exciting market place, anyway.

He watched his mother take up her big bundle of rugs, and his father take up his great baskets of golden corn. Tonio watched his three sisters take up their wares, too. Then, with everyone loaded down, Tonio saw one bundle still on the ground.

In it was some corn, a rug, a pair of sandals, two baskets, and, carefully wrapped in corn husks, a beautiful clay bowl.

"Surely they don't mean to leave that bundle behind," he thought.

And just then, his whole family called, "Tonio, Tonio!"

"Pick up your bundle," they said, "your share of the wares you've helped us to make—and hurry now, Tonio—the sun is already coming up!"

So Tonio picked up his fine, proud bundle, and hurried to catch up. And big as his bundle was, and far as the market place was, he was sure his little brown legs wouldn't get tired of carrying it—or of doing his share of the work, ever again.

Bad Little Bears!

SEPTEMBER 4

ONCE there were two little bears.

And one took his daddy's gun without asking, and went out hunting. And the other took his daddy's bow and arrows without asking, and went out hunting. Away they went, those two little bears—one went left in a big circle, and one went right in a big circle.

And presently, each little bear came to a big rock, and heard the patter of feet behind it.

"Game to shoot with my gun!" whispered the bear with the gun, peeping out.

"Game to shoot with my bow and arrow!" thought the other little bear, tiptoeing up close to the rock and peeping around it.

And there were those two little bears, all ready to shoot, and looking right straight at each other.

"Oh help, don't shoot!" cried one bear.

"I should say not, and don't you, either!" cried the little bear with the bow and arrows.

And both together they went in a big circle back home to put their daddy's gun away, and their daddy's bow and arrows—and to play jacks on the back porch, because somehow neither little bear felt one bit like hunting, after all.

Poor Johnny New-Clothes

SEPTEMBER 5

"I CAN'T play this afternoon," Johnny told Mark. "After lunch, I have to go downtown for new school clothes—"

"Oh golly, and today's your turn to be pitcher!" said Mark. "Now you'll have to lose your turn."

"I guess so," Johnny agreed, trying hard to look not as disappointed as he felt.

And all through lunch, and all the way downtown, he was very quiet, thinking about his new curve ball, and wishing he were out there now—warming up.

Johnny even thought that if they hurried, he might get back in time to pitch the last few innings. But his mother was in no hurry. She took so long deciding on school trousers and shirts and shoes and socks! And when all those things were wrapped, she saw a rack of winter snow jackets, and stopped to look at them.

"Can't we come back tomorrow or sometime?" Johnny begged.

"No," said Mother. "These jackets are on sale today. Here Johnny, try this one on—"

So Johnny, the most discouraged pitcher in any league, began trying on those hot, bulky jackets. At last they chose one, and the shopping for school was over.

But it was half-past four.

"The game's over, too," thought Johnny, struggling with his packages. Then, just as he and Mother headed for the revolving door, Johnny saw Mark and his mother—loaded down with packages—and going out, too!

"Mark," he called. "Hey, Mark—did you have to miss playing ball, too?"

"No," said Mark. "Most of the kids had to go shopping for new school clothes today—so we're going to play ball tomorrow, instead."

"Tomorrow!" breathed Johnny, shifting his packages so he could stretch his pitching arm. "Oh golly, I'm glad we finished up today—"

And he smiled such a happy smile that even when his mother suggested going for chocolate sodas, his smile would not stretch one bit wider.

Cattails

SEPTEMBER 6

Big cattails
Stood around the pond
Waving at him to say,
"The bank is steep,
The water's deep,
Be careful, stay away!"
But little cat
Just laughed and said,
"I'm not afraid of slipping!"
Then splash! and he
Went running home,
His little cat tail
Dripping!

The Twins

SEPTEMBER 7

I have two friends
Named Peter and Paul,
And Paul's as tall as Peter is tall,
And Peter's as tall as Paul.
Each one has freckles on his nose,
And one tooth missing
In each of his rows;
You can't even tell them
By their clothes—
They're the same with Peter and Paul.
When you say, "Hi, Paul!" it's Peter you see,
When you say, "Hi, Peter!" it's never he—
It's Paul.
Paul and Peter, and Peter and Paul,
They look the same, and no one at all
Can tell Paul from Peter,
Or Peter from Paul,
Excepting Paul and Peter.

A Whole Dollar

SEPTEMBER 8

WHEN Skipper had been in second grade for a week, his father gave him an allowance.

"A whole dollar!" said Skip. "What will I do with all that?"

"That's up to you," his father smiled. "But you will have to buy your lunch milk out of it—eight cents a day, and put ten cents in the school bank, and ten cents in your Sunday School envelope. How much is that?"

Skip had to use a pencil and paper for all that arithmetic.

"Sixty cents," he said at last. "So I'll still have a whole forty cents for ice cream and candy—and I'm going to save part of it for equipment for my bike."

"That sounds like a good plan," said his father.

Skipper thought so, too. The next day, which was Saturday, he spent five cents for candy. Then, his pocket jingling with change, he looked at the bicycle things in Mr. Schmidt's showcase.

There was a fine assortment. Raccoon tails to blow in the wind, and headlights and tail-lights, a saddlebag with shiny studs, and a dandy chromium horn.

"May I see that horn?" Skipper asked.

Mr. Schmidt took it out of the case, and out of its box. He showed Skip the tricky way you just pushed a button to make a lovely, deep, warning *beep!*

"People will surely get out of the way when they hear that!" said Skip, trying it. He looked at the price tag, which said, "Special—sixty-nine cents," and blew the horn again. Then Skip forgot all about his allowance plans.

"I'll take it," he told Mr. Schmidt, and when Skip had paid for his horn, he certainly wasn't rich any more.

He had his ten cents for Sunday School, and his ten cents for the school bank. But after that, he had just six cents left—which wasn't enough for even one day's milk!

So all week, Skipper had just water with his lunch, and he never once had a popsicle or an ice-cream cone.

Proud as he was of his new bicycle horn, Skip got awfully tired of that! He got so tired of it that on Friday, when his friend Freddie wanted to stop at Mr. Schmidt's store for some sour balls, Skip said he guessed he wouldn't.

"Why not?" asked Freddie. "No money?"

"I have money," grinned Skipper, showing his six cents. "Only I'm saving it. I'm going to put it with part of my next week's allowance, toward a 'coon tail for my bike."

Then, very firmly, he put it back in his pocket —and for the first time in almost a whole, long week, Skipper was feeling rich again.

Nine Little Scholars

SEPTEMBER 9

Nine little scholars
Setting off for school:
Down the dusty cow-path,
Past the fishing pool,
Through the heavy orchard,
Down the slanting hill,
Straight across the millstream,
Right around the mill,
Past the church and steeple,
'Round the busy square,
Skip across the schoolyard,
And now they're there.
Nine little scholars,
Grinning happy grins,
Go into the schoolhouse—
And
    school
        begins!

New Shoes

SEPTEMBER 10

Here we go,
In ones and twos,
Down the street
In our new shoes:
Some are brown,
Some shiny black,
Some go fast—
And some turn back,
Some are red
And some are blue,
Some go squeaking
(Some shoes do),
Some go skip
And some go hop,
Here's the corner—
All shoes stop!
All the cars
Go by, and then
On our way
We go again,
Through the schoolyard,
All by twos—
And up the steps
In our new shoes.

So the little giraffe went to bed, too. What else could he do, all alone in the night? But lots of times he didn't go right to sleep. He kept wondering how he could ever find time in the day for playing—when all he ever had time to do was eat his meals. And one night, he thought he knew.

"I'll just stop eating!" that giddy little giraffe told himself. "Then I'll have lots of time to play—"

And the next morning, he didn't eat one single bite of breakfast. Instead, he played all morning with his friends—racing, and playing tag, and having the time of his life. By lunchtime, the little giraffe was as hungry as a bear.

"Oh dear," he said. "I'll have to eat after all!"

But with his fine big appetite, the little giraffe didn't finick, or dawdle, or fiddle around at all. He ate his whole lunch in a jiffy—and was ready to play even before his friends.

"Don't go away," they called. "Wait for us!"

"I will," smiled the little giraffe, feeling fine and full, and most awfully pleased to be the first one out to play.

The Giddy Little Giraffe

SEPTEMBER 11

THE little giraffe had such a silly way of eating!

He finicked over which leaf he should eat, and dawdled over every bite—and spent so much time looking around to see what his friends were doing that when he had finished breakfast, they were going in for their lunch.

Lunch took that giddy little giraffe until suppertime. And when he finally finished supper— all the other little animals were ready for bed.

"Ho hum," they were saying. "We're too sleepy to play any more today. Good night!"

Raincoats and Rubbers

SEPTEMBER 12

"Oh, Mommy! I'll be the *only* one wearing a raincoat and rubbers!"

The Cat Who Went to School

SEPTEMBER 13

LUCIUS was a big gray cat. He liked to play with Timmy, and when Timmy went to school, Lucius wished he could go, too. He wished that every day—that big gray Lucius. And one day, very slyly, very quietly, he followed Timmy down the hill—and he did go to school.

Being such a big cat, he thought he should go in eighth grade, or sixth grade, anyway. So up the stairs he went, and he peeped in those big classrooms.

But the eighth grade teacher closed her door before he'd had a good look. And the sixth grade teacher said, "Goodness, here's a cat in school. Well, the janitor will put him out." And she closed her door, too.

So Lucius, feeling very cross indeed, padded down the stairs. He walked along the hall till he came to the kindergarten room, where the door was still wide open.

In walked Lucius, tail high, and bold as brass.

"Whose cat is this?" smiled the teacher.

"He's mine," Timmy said, proudly but embarrassed, too. "I keep telling him cats can't come to school!"

"But he did," the teacher smiled. "And we're glad to have him—just this once."

Timmy was delighted, and so were the other children.

They gave Lucius some milk at recess time, and Lucius watched everything they did: painting, and clay work, and building with blocks. When they spelled cat, C-A-T—Lucius listened carefully, and learned to spell cat, too.

Then suddenly, *br-r-ring!* the school bell rang, and all the children put on their sweaters to go home.

Lucius didn't have to put a sweater on.

So he just padded along beside Timmy, tail held high, very pleased with himself—because he really had been to school (just like Timmy).

The Proud Little Indian

SEPTEMBER 14

ONCE there was a little Indian boy, going to school for the very first time. Proudly he put on his fine, new doeskin clothes, and his new beaded moccasins, and his beautiful, new feather headband.

He put his lunch in his new parfleche. Then away he went, sure that no little boy had finer school clothes than he.

But when that little Indian was in school, he didn't feel one bit proud. Because none of the other boys were wearing doeskin clothes, and beaded moccasins, and feather headbands.

Not even the other little Indians. They all wore bluejean trousers, and homespun shirts, and high-laced boots. All morning, the little Indian looked sideways at those other boys, and wished and wished his new school clothes were like theirs.

At lunchtime, he went around to the back of the schoolhouse, to eat his lunch all by himself. But before long, another little boy came and sat beside him.

That little boy looked at the little Indian's

fine, new doeskin clothes, and he sighed. He looked at his beaded moccasins, and sighed some more. Then he looked at the little Indian's feather headband, and he said, "Boy! I wish *I* had real Indian school clothes just like yours—"

"You really do?" asked the little Indian.

"Sure," the little boy said. "All the kids do."

"All the kids!" thought the little Indian, feeling proud again. But he didn't want to sound proud. So he just opened his new parfleche, and asked his new friend if he'd like to have some real Indian school lunch, too.

The Two Caterpillars

SEPTEMBER 15

"JIMMY!" said Jimmy's mother. "I will not have caterpillars in the house. You put them both outdoors right this minute!"

And Jimmy did. He caught the white one easily, and let him go without minding. Away went Whitey, down the porch steps, down the path, away on his own caterpillar business. The black one was harder to catch. He had climbed out of the box, and nearly up to the ceiling. He was harder to let go, too.

Jimmy stroked his soft, fluffy fur three times.

He said, "Good-by, Blackie," three times. Then he put Blackie down on the porch floor.

Blackie walked across the September sunshine, straight to the edge of the steps. But instead of going down them, he went up the post, all the way to the ledge at the top.

There the black caterpillar found a cozy place for spinning a cocoon—and there he began to spin. And Jimmy, who knew that Blackie would sleep in his cocoon all winter—and in spring, fly out as a beautiful butterfly—emptied the grass out of the caterpillar box and threw it away without minding one bit.

Moving Day

SEPTEMBER 16

ON MOVING day, Jeff looked so sad that the moving man asked him what was wrong.

"I like this house," Jeff said. "And the new one won't be the same, at all."

"No," agreed the moving man. "It won't. It will be different. Once I moved some people into a house with a nest of squirrels outside the window — and once there was a tree house already built—"

"What else?" asked Jeff.

"Oh, I forget," said the moving man, picking up Jeff's big chair. "But there are always new things to discover—new ways to fix rooms—"

Jeff thought about that. He thought he'd like putting all his things just where he wanted them. But then he thought of something else.

"In the new house," he said sadly, "I won't have my friends!"

"How many friends do you have?" asked the moving man.

"Nine," said Jeff. "Nine right near here."

"That's a lot of friends," the moving man said. "But one thing I do know—when a boy has lots of friends in one town, he always makes lots of friends in his new town, too. Don't know why—but it never fails."

Then he put Jeff's rolled-up rug on his shoulder, and the room was empty. The whole house was empty, and the big moving van was packed and ready to go. Mother and Daddy and Spot were in the car, ready to go, too.

And all Jeff's friends were sitting on the fence, to watch them go off.

"Good-by!" they called, as Jeff got into the back seat with Spot. Jeff tried to call good-by, but there was a big lump in his throat.

Then Mother waved and said, "It isn't really good-by, boys. We'll be coming back to see you!"

For a moment, Jeff just hugged Spot. Then he looked at the moving man who was grinning at him, and grinned back.

And then Jeff called, "See you soon, guys!"

And away went the moving van, and away went Daddy's car, and away went Jeff—toward all the new things and new friends—with his old friends still waving to him.

Forecast

SEPTEMBER 17

When geese fly over
In a wedge,
And grackles cry
In the willow hedge,
And sparrows fly
To the window ledge,
Looking for warmth
And scattered crumbs—
Harvest your corn,
And pick your plums,
For it won't be long
Until winter comes!

The Lopsided Bear

SEPTEMBER 18

OLD Mrs. McIntosh, who made teddy bears, was having a perfectly awful time with one particular teddy bear. He wriggled while she stuffed him, squirmed while she sewed him up—and wriggled and squirmed when she tried to sew his nose and mouth and eyes in place. No wonder that one bear ended up with a comical, lopsided look!

"I can't sell that one," said old Mr. McIntosh, taking all the other nice, neat, well-behaved teddies into his shop. "No one would want to buy him!"

Then he closed the door, and old Mrs. McIntosh, feeling most mortified, was just about to toss the leftover bear into the scrap heap—when a little boy popped his head in the back door.

"Please, Mrs. McIntosh," he said. "I need a bear very badly, but all I have to spend is sixty-eight cents. Do you happen to have any bears of the sixty-eight cent kind?"

"Why yes," smiled old Mrs. McIntosh. "Why yes, I do."

She held up the leftover bear, who was wriggling with excitement—and the little boy, wriggling for joy, took him and gave him a good, hard hug. Then he paid old Mrs. McIntosh and went running home with his new teddy bear, feeling sure as sure that it was much, much nicer than any neat, well-behaved, one-the-same-as-the-next bear in the McIntosh's whole tidy little shop.

The Walking Moon

SEPTEMBER 19

The moon goes walking.
This I know,
For every time I ever go
Outside when it is dark at night,
He soon slips out,
All round and bright,
From in behind some autumn tree,
And winks his light
And follows me.
The moon is lonesome.
This I know.
And I'd be, too, if I were he—
I'd wait out there
And watch for me,
And then go walking, two by two,
Which is a friendly way to do.

Good Morning!

SEPTEMBER 20

When we go walking down the street,
I speak to people that I meet;
Some I know
And some I don't,
But there's no one at all that won't
Say, "Good morning!" when I do—
So I know the ones
I don't know, too!

FALL

Angry Wind

SEPTEMBER 21

The angriest wind
Blew through today;
It banged the shutters
And tore away
Shingles and branches,
And with a whoop,
It blew off the roof
Of the chicken coop.
Then it slammed the gate,
And whirled down the lane,
And all that was left
Was the quiet rain.

Up in a Tree

SEPTEMBER 22

A FAT little boy was flying his kite, when it blew into a tree.

"Please throw me down my kite," he called to a fat little bear, who was sitting there, looking all around. But the little bear didn't understand. He didn't know people's language. So he just shook his head.

"All right, then," the little boy called. "I'll climb up and get my kite myself."

The little bear didn't understand that, either. And he didn't like to see that fat little boy climbing his tree.

"He may put a string on me, too," he growled, backing away. And as the boy climbed, he did, too. Higher and higher he went, that fat little bear, into the thin top. So, just as the boy reached his kite, swish! the tree bent right down to the ground. Because the fat little bear and the fat little boy were too heavy for it.

It was like a slide, that bent-over tree.

So down slid the little boy, kite and all. And down slid the little bear, glad to be on the ground.

Home he ran, as fast as his fat legs would go. "Goodness," said his mother (in bear talk), when he told her. "You do make up tall tales, little bear!"

That's what the little boy's mother said, too. "You do make up tall tales," she said, not believing her little boy, either.

But the little boy believed it, and the fat little bear did.

Because it was true.

The Rainy-Day Cookies

SEPTEMBER 23

IT WAS still raining when Jill walked home from school, but Jill didn't mind. Today was the day she and Mother were going to make cookies for the Brownie Scouts' party.

"And rainy days are nice when you're baking," Jill thought, as she slipped off her raincoat, and went to find Mother.

But when she saw Mother, propped up on the sofa with her eyes watery, and a sneeze ready to come out, Jill's face fell.

"Oh, it's hay fever again, isn't it?" she cried.

"I'm afraid so, Jill," Mother said, holding her sneeze back. "And I am sorry that we can't make cookies this time. But you can run down to the bakery and choose four dozen of any kind you'd like. That will be fun, won't it?"

"Yes, it will," Jill said doubtfully, though she did add, "And I'm sorry you have hay fever."

Then Mother tried to say, "Thank you, darling—" But she said "Achoo!" instead, and looked so watery and sad, that she and Jill both had to laugh. And while they were laughing, Jill had a wonderful idea.

"Mother," she said, "I always help with the cookies, and I always watch everything you do— so do you suppose that this time, I could make them myself?"

Mother thought for a minute, and sneezed for two minutes.

Then she said, "Why yes, Jill—if you'll just be careful about the stove, I'm sure you can."

Jill was careful. She was careful about measuring and sifting and mixing, too. She was especially careful to wear Mother's pot-holder mittens when she put her cookies in the oven.

And since Jill had made those cookies exactly as Mother did, they came out of the oven looking exactly like Mother's.

"They're delicious, Jill!" said Mother, when they had each sampled one.

"Yes, they are, aren't they?" said Jill, hurrying back to clean up in the kitchen.

"You know, Mother," she called back, " now that I can cook, you can have hay fever any time you want—"

That started Mother laughing and sneezing again. "Oh, Jill," she cried, "I don't want to have hay fever ever! But since I must—it certainly is wonderful to have a big girl who can take care of things for me!"

Jill thought it was, too. She thought she'd set the table for supper, when the dishes were done. But first, just for a moment, she stood very still listening to the rain drumming on the window pane, and smelling the proud, delicious smell of the cookies she had made for the Brownie Scouts' party.

The Racing Rabbit

SEPTEMBER 24

OLD Grandpa Tortoise looked wise, and more than anything else, he wanted folks to think he was wise.

So he was forever giving advice, which no one took—until one day, when he began advising a swift little rabbit who was practicing his racing.

"See here, Rabbit," old Grandpa Tortoise said, "the way you go at it, all swift and breathless, makes me think you've never heard that it's slow and steady that wins the race—"

"Slow and steady?" asked the rabbit, stopping short. "In that case, I'll never be a champion race-rabbit—unless I find some way to slow down my swift hind legs—"

Now while he was saying that, the little rabbit kept looking at Grandpa Tortoise's heavy-looking shell.

And all at once he blurted out, "Grandpa Tortoise—wise old Grandpa Tortoise—please lend me your big shell. That's the very thing to slow me down!"

Grandpa Tortoise was about to say no, he wouldn't lend his shell, when he noticed that the little rabbit had called him wise! Then he was so tickled that he quickly wriggled out of his shell. And the little rabbit squeezed into it.

A fine looking pair they were now! The little rabbit so weighed down that he couldn't go slow, steady, or at all. And old Grandpa Tortoise looking so bare and silly that the other creatures laughed themselves sick at the sight of him.

If Grandpa Tortoise was humiliated, he did not show it.

"Now you've learned your lesson, Rabbit," he said in a wise-sounding voice, "kindly hand me back my shell."

The little rabbit did, gladly enough—and Grandpa Tortoise more gladly wriggled back in. Then off he trundled, looking as if he'd done a great thing.

And the little rabbit was so glad to be out of that clumsy shell that he raced off, lickety-split, faster than he had ever run before.

He was so swift that he raced the champion, and won the race, and *he* became champion.

"My, oh my," whispered the other creatures, "Grandpa Tortoise must have taught him a very wise lesson!" And after they had stopped shouting, "Hurray for the new champion!" they all took a deep breath and shouted:

"Hurray for wise old Grandpa Tortoise!"

Which pleased the old tortoise so much that he stopped giving advice, and just smiled and looked wise, while things went along far better than they ever had before.

Where Are You Going, Little Pigs?

SEPTEMBER 25

THREE little pigs are out of their pen, going somewhere. Where are you going, little pigs? Down to the pond to roll in the mud, and to watch the ducks swim?

"No," says the first little pig. "Not there."

Where then, little pigs? Are you going to scratch your itchy little backs on the rough board fence? Is that where you're going? Or are you on your way to the kitchen garden, to root up the carrots and crunch and chew them in your droll little mouths?

"No," says the second little pig. "We scratched our backs on the milking stool first thing this morning—and last time we rooted in the garden, we all got spankings. No more of that, thank you!"

Where then, little pigs?

Up the hill to the orchard full of apple trees, where the ripe, warm apples, brushed by the breeze, fall from the branches to the ground, tangy, and tasty, and all around—is that where you three little pigs are going?

"Yes," says the third little pig. "That's where, that's where! That's the very place, and we're almost there! That's the place we're going!"

Admiral Bullfrog's Retreat

SEPTEMBER 26

ONE afternoon, a flock of wild geese settled on Admiral Bullfrog's pond. What a splashing and honking they set up! How they dived and searched for tasty young frogs to eat!

"We must make war on them!" cried the young frogs. "We will bite their feet, and pull their feathers, and chase them away with a great, loud croaking!"

"Har-umph!" said Admiral Bullfrog. "If we try any such tactics, they'll soon eat us all! I suggest that we just go below until tomorrow—"

"Admiral Bullfrog is afraid!" whispered the young frogs. "We must take away his hat, and choose a fearless leader!" But as it was late, and as the geese were very big, they went below for a bit of sleep before doing all this.

When morning came, the pond was deserted. High in the pink sky, a wedge of wild geese was flying south.

"The enemy has gone!" cried the amazed young frogs.

"Har-umph!" said Admiral Bullfrog. "So they have, and so they've done since I was a tadpole. It's simply a matter of hiding below till they've had a night's rest—"

And he looked so fearless, that instead of choosing a new leader, the young frogs sat about trying to learn to say, "Har-umph!" as wisely and calmly as he.

A House for Mrs. Fieldmouse

SEPTEMBER 27

"I THINK," said Mrs. Fieldmouse, putting down her knitting, "that we should move indoors for the winter."

"Indoors?" asked her husband. "Aren't we indoors now?"

"In a way," Mrs. Fieldmouse smiled. "We're indoors, of course, but our house isn't. Not like Cousin Theresa's house. Every time I think of it, in a nice, warm cellar, close to a furnace—I think we should have an indoors house."

Mr. Fieldmouse sighed. How he hated to leave the snug rooms they had furnished so cozily! "Couldn't we spend a few days with your cousin first?" he asked at last.

"We certainly could," his little wife agreed, so sure he would love living indoors—once he'd tried it—that she hurried to pack their bags.

And since Mr. Fieldmouse was equally sure that she'd soon tire of it, he helped and they set out. But their litle dispute never was settled.

For, just as they came to the edge of the field, whom did they meet but Cousin Theresa (almost in tears) with her entire family, and most of her household effects.

"Those people!" she cried. "You know, the ones in whose house we built our house? Well, they've seen fit to bring in a stray cat, and treat it as one of the family!"

"What a cruel thing!" said Mrs. Fieldmouse.

"So here we are," sighed Cousin Theresa, "tenants of how many years—without a roof over our heads!"

Here the little mice all whimpered so sadly that Mr. Fieldmouse was thoroughly touched.

"Look here!" he cried. "If you'd care to settle down next door to us, I'll dig you a house before nightfall!"

That he did, too, to Cousin Theresa's great joy—and Mrs. Fieldmouse's pride.

"It's going to be charming," said Cousin Theresa, as they all finished the good supper that Mrs. Fieldmouse had cooked.

"Indeed it will—once we've made curtains, and a few touches like that," little Mrs. Fieldmouse agreed.

And Mr. Fieldmouse, relieved to know that she would be far too busy to consider moving —at least until another winter had come and gone—lighted his pipe with an air of the greatest contentment.

All Kinds of Dogs

SEPTEMBER 28

All kinds of dogs—
Which kind is best?
The big buff one
With the neat white vest?

The very small one
With the quick, sharp bark,
The princely one
That you see in the park?

Or the funny little old
Waggly one,
All kinds of kinds,
And all kinds of fun?

All kinds of dogs,
And of all the rest,
The kind you have
Is the kind that's best.

About Butterflies

SEPTEMBER 29

My brother collects butterflies.
He keeps them in a case,
On cotton, with their wings spread out
Like scraps of silk and lace.
He likes to tell about them—
Their names and habitat—
And while I try to listen,
I'm so busy thinking that
They're much nicer in the meadow,
Dancing in the summer air,
That I never really hear him,
And I wriggle in my chair.

The Fair

SEPTEMBER 30

With his pennies and his pony,
And his, "Can't take you!"
Billy's riding to the Fair—
Wish that I were, too.

All the lovely things to see,
All the things to buy,
All the noise and music—
All the rides to try!

Everybody else is there—
When only I am not—
But someone's coming up the lane,
Coming at a trot!

It's Billy, and he's calling,
"Get your pennies, do—
All alone just wasn't fun,
So I've come back for you."

With our pennies and his pony,
And a loud, "Hallooo!"
Billy's riding to the Fair,
And look—I'm going, too!

Bothering Beetles

OCTOBER 1

ONE DAY, the little gray cat was out bothering beetles.

He batted a ladybug down to the ground after it had climbed up, up, up, all the way to the top of a goldenrod stem.

He kept putting his paw over a squash bug who was walking along. And when the poor squash bug went all crazy-wild trying to get away, and finally did, the little cat flipped a fat June bug over on its back.

"You're mean!" cried the June bug, wriggling its legs and trying to turn right-side up again. "We're little, and you're big—and you shouldn't be bothering us!"

"Should too," laughed the naughty little cat. "I like to bother beetles, and I will—"

He was just about to flip the June bug on its back again, when along came another beetle.

This was an enormous one, with shiny black eyes, and funny clawlike things that waved as it walked.

Now the little cat forgot all about the June bug. Nose to the ground, he stalked right up to the big, new beetle. But before he could reach out a paw, that beetle nipped his nose with its sharp, clawlike pincers.

"Let me go!" wailed the little cat.

"Will when I'm ready," the big bug replied.

And when he was ready and did, the little cat ran away as fast as he could go.

"Come back and bother me some more," laughed the big beetle. "You said you liked bothering beetles!"

"Not any more," said the little gray cat. "Not when beetles start bothering me!" And he rubbed his nose, turned his back, and went off to chase the bright, falling leaves instead.

The Drake at the Lake

OCTOBER 2

"Ha, ha, ha!" go the ducks at the lake,
They sound as if they're laughing at the drake—
Funny old drake who waddles past,
Flapping his wings to go extra-fast.

He doesn't mind, that funny old drake,
He's the first to get to my piece of cake.
When the ducks see that, they waddle fast,
But, "Ha, ha, ha!" laughs the drake at last.

The Artist

OCTOBER 3

1. "Now that I have my own paint things, I can use them any way I like—"

2. "—not like school, where you can't spill any, even if you happen to—"

3. "—not like school, where you have to wash your brush between colors—"

4. "—not like school, where you have to be so careful with your papers—"

5. "Not a bit like school! Now all my new colors are turned into muddy old brown—and my paper's all gone!"

My Sweater

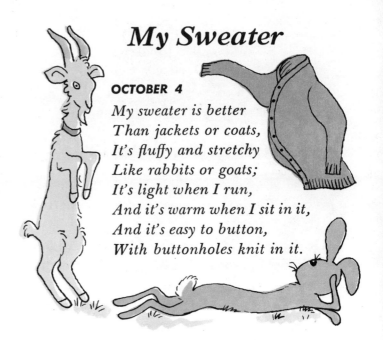

OCTOBER 4

*My sweater is better
Than jackets or coats,
It's fluffy and stretchy
Like rabbits or goats;
It's light when I run,
And it's warm when I sit in it,
And it's easy to button,
With buttonholes knit in it.*

The New Playmate

OCTOBER 5

EVERY DAY after school, Cindy and Bets played together. They rode their bikes, and drew pictures, and played with their dolls, and made clothes for them. One day, the two little girls

even made a fine playhouse out of the old chicken coop in Bets's back yard.

After that, they had lunch out there every Saturday.

And that was such fun that lots of times Cindy stayed at Bets's house all day, and never got home until she was almost late for supper.

Then, one day when Cindy went to play,

there was another little girl at Bets's house. Her name was Jeannie, and she had moved in next door. And that day, everything was different.

Jeannie asked to borrow Cindy's bike, and she and Bets went riding around the block while Cindy just waited.

When they played dolls, Bets was the mother and Jeannie was the nurse. Cindy had to be Daddy, and all he did was say, "Good-by, I'm off for the office," and "Hello, I am home again."

By lunchtime, Cindy was pretty tired of that.

"I guess I'll go home for lunch," she said. "I guess my mother wants me to be home."

So home she went, shuffling the leaves sadly on the way.

But right after lunch the telephone rang.

It was Bets.

"Can't you come over, Cindy?" she asked. "We want to play hide-and-seek—and we want the dolls to go to school, and we need a teacher. Besides, Cindy, we tried drawing pictures, and that's no fun without you to make up stories about what we're drawing. Can you come?"

"Yes," said Cindy. "Yes, I can!" Then she

hurried back to Bets's house as fast as she could.

And that afternoon was such fun—with all kinds of good games for three—that before Cindy knew it, it was suppertime.

Cindy didn't want to be late—so away she ran.

But she did turn back to wave to Bets.

"Good-by to you, too, Jeannie," she called. "I'll see you both tomorrow!"

Ripe Apples

OCTOBER 6

The orchard's
Like a fairyland,
With apples ripe
On every hand.

If they were rubies
Glowing there,
We'd pluck a fortune
From the air,

But have no apples
Left to eat:
And oh, they are
So crisp and sweet!

The Runaways

OCTOBER 7

A HORSE came galloping up the road, a beautiful, shining brown horse with a man riding on his back.

Laddie ran after him, barking and nipping at his heels. Kitty ran under the porch and hid herself. And all the children ran after the big, shining horse.

They ran all the way to the top of the hill, but when they got there, the horse was out of sight. Where had he gone?

Ginny said, "Perhaps down to the park. Maybe there's going to be a horse race, and he came to be in it—"

So everyone listened, and yes, there was shouting and cheering down there in the park where the duck ponds were.

"Let's go down and see!" said Ginny.

"Oh yes, let's!" cried Kathy, holding out her hand to Ann, who was only three. Then Colin took her hand, and Ginny took Colin's. And down the hill they ran—faster and faster—until they came to the busy street.

There they stopped, and crossed most carefully, and then there they were in the park.

Only the big, shining horse wasn't there, at all. There was no horse race, either. Just some big boys, playing baseball and shouting.

There were the swings, though, and the seesaws, and the rough, stone drinking-fountain, and the ponds where the white ducks swam. So everyone had lots of rides, and a good cold drink, and went and waded in the duck pond.

It was warm enough to wade. It was fine and warm, that bright October day. But Colin didn't wade. Suddenly, Colin wasn't feeling quite comfortable inside.

"We'd better go home," he said. "It might get to be night, you know. Besides, we shouldn't have come this far—"

The little girls, and Ginny, too, looked up at the sky, and quickly put on their socks and shoes. Back home seemed so far away that all four runaways were awfully glad to see Kathy's father coming, even though he did look stern.

Without a word, they all climbed into his car. And without a word, Kathy's father took them all back home.

Then, after all of them had been scolded for running away, and told they'd have to stay in their own yards for a whole week, the big, shining horse came trotting back down the hill.

Very proud and beautiful he looked, tossing his shining mane. Laddie ran after him, barking and nipping at his heels. Kitty ran under the porch and hid herself.

But Ginny and Colin and Kathy, and even Ann (who was only three), stayed right in their own yards and watched him go prancing down the hill to have his supper.

The Grumpy Camel

OCTOBER 8

A grumpy little camel
With a humpy little hump
Stumped across the sandy desert
With a grumpy, stumpy thump.
Said he hated carrying bundles
In a camel train like that,
Said the sunshine was too shiny,
Said he wished he had a hat;

Said his lunch had tasted awful
And had been too long ago,
Said the other camels made him
Walk too fast—or else too slow.
There was really nothing grumpy
That he didn't snort and say,
But his mother didn't scold him—
For all camels talk that way.

Afraid of What?

OCTOBER 9

"COME for a walk," said the rhinoceros to a shy little jerboa who was peeping out of its hole.

"Not me," the jerboa replied. "I'm afraid!"

That made the rhinoceros laugh.

"Afraid of what?" he asked. "I don't see anything to be afraid of!"

"Neither would I, if I had your tough skin and your big, sharp horn," said the jerboa. "But I don't, and I am—"

And he would not budge.

The lion said it was the silliest thing he had ever heard.

"Why, I go for walks every day," he said, roaring with laughter. "And I'm never the least bit afraid!"

"If I had your big sharp teeth and your loud, ferocious roar, I wouldn't be, either," said the jerboa. "But I don't, and I am afraid, and here I stay."

And there he did stay, until one day when a wee little mouse peeped into his hole just as he was peeping out.

"Oh help!" squeaked the mouse, backing away and shaking with fright. "What a terrible scare you gave me!"

"Did I?" the jerboa asked. "Did I really?"

"Oh my, yes," the mouse replied, "my heart's still pounding! But I'm not afraid now, so come on, let's go for a walk—"

The jerboa looked very thoughtfully at that wee, soft little mouse. He didn't have a tough skin and a sharp horn like the rhinoceros, and he didn't have big, sharp teeth and a loud, ferocious roar like the lion. He was even smaller than the jerboa himself. And yet, there he was, smiling and waiting, and not too afraid to go for a walk.

"And neither am I," thought the jerboa.

Then he laughed, "Here I come!"

And he hopped right out of his hole.

And he and his friend the wee gray mouse set bravely and adventurously off for a walk.

Ten Little Owls

OCTOBER 10

Ten little owls
In the bare, autumn trees,
Took out their hankies
And started to sneeze.
"The nights are quite chilly!"
They sniffled and said,
And they put on warm jackets
With hoods for the head.

They put on warm mittens
And tied them on tight,
So their feet would be warm
Through the long chilly night.
Then they put back their hankies,
Moved out of the breeze,
And hooted till morning
With never a sneeze!

The Digging Place

OCTOBER 11

"THERE!" said Kenny one Saturday morning. "Now I have no digging place again!"

"What do you mean?" his father asked.

"Whenever I find a place to dig, it turns out to be for something else," Kenny explained. "When I dug around the side of the house, that was the place for the lawn. When I dug in front of the garage, that was the place where the driveway was going. When I dug beside the porch, it turned out to be the place for the new rosebushes—"

Then he exploded.

"And now, when I've been digging here in back of the porch, Mother's put in little plants with names on sticks!"

"Hollyhocks, delphinium, and Shasta dai-sies," Daddy read. "Pretty. Don't you want our new house to look nice, Kenny?"

"Yes, I do," Kenny admitted. "But I want our new house to have some place for making tunnels and mountains, and running cars."

"It certainly should," his father agreed.

So together they found a place that was well out of the way. It was right behind the garage, and Daddy built a fence around it.

"We'll paint the fence," he said that afternoon, so he and Kenny did.

"And next spring," Daddy said then, "we'll plant some kind of viney flowers around the outside—just to please your mother. But nothing inside. Inside is all yours to dig in—"

So it really did look as if Kenny had his digging place, safe and sure, at last.

184

Christopher's Discovery

OCTOBER 12

"I WISH," said Christopher on Columbus Day, "that there were still some places in the world to discover—"

"Well, there is outer space, you know," his mother said.

And just as he was deciding to be an outer-space explorer when he grew up, she added, "I'm going to start cleaning the attic today. That's sort of exploring. Want to come?"

"Sure," said Christopher, taking the brushes and dust cloths his mother held out. And upstairs they both went.

The attic did look mysterious, with dust and cobwebs everywhere. When most of that was cleared away, Christopher and his mother began opening the boxes and trunks.

They found, looking over the woolens, that he had outgrown all his winter things, and would need new ones. Christopher liked discovering that he had grown that much. He liked it, too, when his mother opened an old trunk, and brought out pictures of his great-grandparents, and his great-great-grandparents.

It made him feel important. As if he'd been coming for an awful lot of years.

"Almost since America was discovered," he told himself.

And then Christopher made a most wonderful discovery.

Up on a shelf was a large box wrapped in old newspaper. Christopher had wondered about it when they were dusting. Now he wondered again, so he took it down.

He carefully unwrapped the paper.

And he opened the lid, and looked inside.

Inside, with tissue paper all around, was the most beautiful ship model he had ever seen. It was painted a dull red, and touched with gold. It had many tiny sails, and on the bow was lettered *Santa Maria!*

"Columbus's ship!" Christopher cried. "Where did it come from?"

"Oh," said Mother, turning around. "It must have come with Grandmother Gilbert's things. Her father was a sea captain, and good at ship models—"

Then Mother said, "This one's so beautiful that it should be downstairs where we can all enjoy looking at it."

Christopher said, "Could it be in my room?"

"Why yes," said Mother. "Yes, I think it should. After all, it was your discovery, Chris."

So down the stairs went Christopher, to put the *Santa Maria* on top of the highboy in his room. And there it stands, to this very day. Except on Columbus Day of each year.

Then it sails the center of the dining-room table—on a mirror like a calm sea—in honor of Christopher Columbus, and his discovery. And in honor of young Chris, and his discovery, too.

Being Twins

OCTOBER 13

Two of us, two of us climb the stairs,
Two of us, two of us say our prayers·

We get into bed, then, two by two,
And sing and tell stories—that's fun to do!

And we whisper secrets, and laugh, until
Somebody calls, "You two be still!"

Then we close our eyes (all four shut tight)
And wonder why in the day we fight,
When we like being two by two
At night.

Hasty Bear

OCTOBER 14

"HASTY BEAR," said his mother one day, "will you please hurry out and pick some pretty, colored leaves for me?"

"Yes, ma'am, I will," said Hasty Bear. And off he went, in such a hurry that he never heard his mother saying, "Only don't pick the shiny, red, three-leaved kind with berries—"

So, by the time she was saying, "—because they're poison ivy, and they make you itch—" he was well into the woods, looking for the brightest leaves he could find.

The sycamore leaves were a beautiful yellow.

Hasty Bear thought they'd be nice, until he saw how red and bright the maple leaves were.

"I'll get a big bunch of those," he thought. But just then, he saw a patch of still redder leaves, shiny ones, three together on a stem, with beautiful dark berries besides.

So he picked and picked till he had a most enormous red bunch, and started back home.

But halfway, Hasty Bear rubbed his nose.

And it began to itch. His paws felt itchy, too. So did his toes, and the edges of his ears. By the

time that little bear got home, and held the leaves out to his mother, he was itching all over.

What was worse, his mother backed away from the leaves.

"Oh, Hasty Bear!" she cried. "After all I said—you've picked poison ivy leaves!"

"Have I?" asked Hasty Bear. "And what did you say?"

"I said, 'Don't-pick-the-shiny-three-leaved-kind-with-berries, because-they're-poison-ivy-and-make-you-itch,'" said his mother. "And now let me scrub you, and put lotion on you for the itching—"

"Oh, yes," said Hasty Bear, dropping the leaves in one spot, and his clothes in another, "please do!"

So pretty soon Hasty Bear was much more comfortable, itching just a little, and all dressed in clean clothes.

"I'll get you some maple leaves," he said.

"Fine," smiled his mother, who was busily sweeping the poison ivy ones out the door. "Maple leaves are lovely."

And this time, before he went running out, Hasty Bear waited a whole minute to be sure he had heard everything his mother had to say.

School Lunch

OCTOBER 15

"Jimmy, you've asked for peanut-butter sandwiches all week. Today let's change to a different kind—"

"OK, Mom. What else do we have?"

"Sliced ham, minced ham, spiced ham, egg salad, cream cheese and jelly, tuna fish, bologna—"

"—roast beef, corned beef, chicken, tomato and lettuce—anything you'd like. Which shall it be?"

"Um—gosh—golly—so many kinds! Well, guess I'll take peanut butter!"

Down Goes Chris!

OCTOBER 16

"Bill," said Chris one morning, "will you teach me how to skate on my new skates?"

"Not now," his big brother told him. "Pete and I are going down to the playground—maybe tomorrow, Chris."

So Chris asked Sally, who lived next door, and Jane and Robert and Skip. But everyone on the whole street was going to the playground to go skating, and Chris thought he just could not wait until tomorrow to start learning.

"I'm going to teach myself!" he said, buckling on his skates, and tightening the clamps.

Then, very cautiously, Chris stood up.

But when he tried to glide one foot— thump! down he went.

Chris got up, and rubbed himself, and tried again. And three times, down he went again. By then he felt so sore, and so discouraged, that he thought he would have to wait until tomorrow.

But just then, Chris noticed the iron fence along the driveway. It had a smooth railing, and it was strong, too.

So he inched himself over to that fence. Holding on, he got up on his feet. And by holding on, Chris could glide along without falling. He did that—left foot, right foot—until his feet got used to skating.

Then, brave as could be, Chris let go of the railing, and—left foot, right foot—he was skating all by himself!

What a wonderful feeling! Chris thought he could just go on skating forever. But after a while he needed a rest, so he sat down on the steps. And while he was resting, along came Bill and Pete, and Sally and Jane, and Robert and Skip.

They felt very sorry for Chris—just sitting there in his shiny new skates!

"Come on, Chris," said Bill. "I'll teach you a little about skating right now. Can you stand up by yourself?"

That made Chris smile inside.

"Yes, I can," he said. Then up he got, and when he skated up and down the sidewalk all by himself, too—the others watched him with round eyes and open mouths.

"Why, Chris," they cried. "You can skate!"

"You sure can!" said Bill. "You're even good enough to go skating down at the playground. So come on, we'll go have lunch—and all meet here right after!"

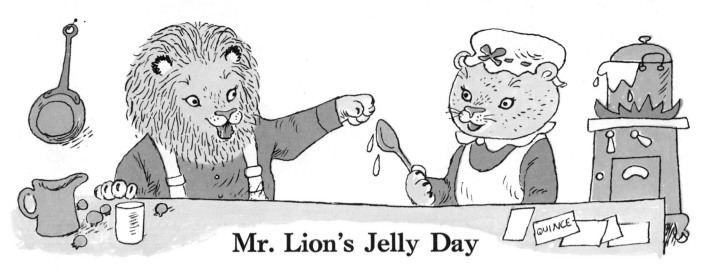

Mr. Lion's Jelly Day

ALL WEEK Mr. Lion had been longing to take Mrs. Lion on a ride through the bright autumn countryside. But all week Mrs. Lion had been making jelly—a new kind each day—and on Thursday she still was at it.

"How many more kinds?" asked Mr. Lion.

"Four," said Mrs. Lion, carefully printing stickers that said QUINCE, KUMQUAT, GOOSE-BERRY, and MINT. "I should be finished by Saturday, around suppertime—"

"Saturday indeed!" cried Mr. Lion. "Look here, you clear out of the kitchen, and I'll finish the jelly – in time for a ride before sunset!"

So out of the kitchen went Mrs. Lion, wondering how on earth he'd do that. And the moment she was gone, Mr. Lion took an enormous pot, into which he put quinces, kumquats, gooseberries, and mint, with some apples and plenty of sugar.

While that was cooking, he rocked in the rocking chair and read his road map. When the fruit had cooked, he quickly strained it through cheesecloth into the sparkling jelly glasses.

"Wax over the top," he murmured.

"Stickers on the outsides," he said, putting on the stickers at random. QUINCE, KUMQUAT, GOOSEBERRY, and MINT—all on the one kind of jelly.

Then Mr. Lion put on his hat, did up the dishes, and drove his car around to the front of the house.

Honk! Honk! went his horn, and out came Mrs. Lion, hardly able to believe they were setting out so soon. The car purred along as smoothly as a kitten. The countryside was magnificent, a blaze of colored leaves and bright sky. And promptly at sunset, Mr. Lion pulled up at his own front door.

"A lovely ride," smiled Mrs. Lion, "now I'll fix tea."

That she did, with buttered toast and a jar of Mr. Lion's jelly—one that was marked QUINCE.

"Quince," read Mrs. Lion, dipping in her spoon. She tasted it, and added, "Most delicious quince jelly! Why, I've never tasted jelly that seemed so quince-y!"

"Good," smiled Mr. Lion. "I'm glad." And he hoped that when Mrs. Lion read KUMQUAT, GOOSEBERRY, or MINT—and then tasted those kinds—she would think each one tasted exactly like what it was supposed to be, too!

The Old-Fashioned Day

OCTOBER 18

ANN WAS sure her mother had forgotten all about what it was like to be a little girl.

"Such a stormy day," she thought. "No electricity—so there's no television *or* radio—and when I asked what I could do, Mother said, 'Why not make up the beds!'"

Just the same, Ann did make the beds as neatly as she could.

"Here, Ann," Mother said then. "You can shell the peas now."

"Shell peas?" asked Ann. "I didn't know they had shells."

"Fresh ones do," Mother explained, showing Ann how to open the pods with her thumbs, and push out the green rows. It was fun shelling those peas. Pop-pop-pop! they went into the pan, while Mother made gingerbread, and put it in the oven.

"Is it nearly lunchtime?" Ann asked.

"No," said Mother, "we have time to play hearts first—"

So she and Ann sat at the kitchen table and played four games, and Ann won the last two. By then, the storm made everything as dark as evening. Mother lighted candles for lunch. She and Ann did the dishes by candlelight, too.

"Now," said Mother, "will you read to me, while I make applesauce, and put the chicken on to cook?"

Ann chose *Uncle Remus,* because it was so funny. And she had read only three stories— because of the strange words, and because of laughing so much—when Daddy came home.

"I'm early," he said, "because of the storm. What a day! But it certainly looks and smells and sounds cozy in here. What have you two been doing?"

"Lots of things," said Ann. "Why, we did a whole week of things today. Mother, how did we get so much time?"

"I'm not sure," laughed Mother. "But today was just like days when I was a little girl. Maybe we had more time together because we had fewer modern conveniences—"

Ann thought about that, and she thought she understood.

Without radio, and television, and the dishwasher, and all that, they had done everything two by two.

Maybe that was what Mother meant. Ann wasn't sure.

But she was sure—very sure—that her mother had not forgotten what it was like to be a little girl, after all.

Autumn Leaves

OCTOBER 19

How bright they were
When they first came down!
Blazing colors.
But now they're brown,
So we raked them up
In a big, dry pile

That's fun to jump in;
And after a while
They'll all be burning,
And then, oh then,
How bright they'll be
All over again!

The Old Stone Wall

OCTOBER 20

INDIAN SUMMER had come and gone. The wind was cold, and the pond was cold. It was cold everywhere except in the bright sunshine on the old stone wall.

There a fly sat sunning himself, and a bee.

A little green lizard lay with his arrow head raised. A little red snake panted, with his forked little tongue darting in and out. A turtle, who had just climbed up, up, up the broken place, stretched his head and legs and tail out to the warm sunshine.

Nobody talked, nobody moved. But a cloud came along, moving slowly across the sky until it covered the sun. There it stayed, and in its shadow the old stone wall was cold.

The fly found a tiny crevice to winter in; the bee blew off to the drowsily buzzing hive.

The lizard slipped into the wall. The snake slid down it, and slithered into his winter house. The turtle, slowest to notice, slowest to move, slowly clicked his way down the broken place. Slowly he made his way down to the pond, to burrow his way under the mud.

Now the last of the summer creatures had gone to bed.

And up on the old stone wall at the end of the garden, sat two little red squirrels. Snug in their warm fur coats, they scolded the wind for being so slow in shaking down acorns for their supper—and for them to store away.

Nutting

OCTOBER 21

Deep in the woods
The ripe nuts lie,
Brown as the leaves
And hard to spy.
Who'll find them first,
The boys and girls,
Or the hurrying,
Scurrying, bright-eyed
Squirrels?

Harvest Time

OCTOBER 22

USUALLY, when Billy and Joan visited their grandparents, all they did was play and have fun. But this time they had come to work. It was harvest time, and everyone on the farm was working, bringing in the crops that had been growing all summer.

"This is fun, too," Billy and Joan had agreed at first.

The grapes and apples and pears were so beautiful to touch and to look at. The big, ripe berries filled up their baskets in almost no time. They were easy to find, too—the bushes were heavy with them.

It was fun to pull up carrots and beets, to strip the yellowing vines of full bean pods.

Picking the corn was best of all. Snap! went the big ears as they broke from the stalks, and thud! they went into the big bushel baskets.

But after a while, it seemed that the more things they picked—the more there was to be picked. As the sun moved slowly up the sky, getting hotter and hotter, Joan's arms began to ache from all that picking. Billy's back hurt, from helping to carry basket after full basket.

"You know," Joan said at last, "I think Grandpa grows just too many kinds of things on his farm!"

"You know," said Billy, from behind a heaping basket of corn, "I think he grows too many things of each kind—"

"You know," smiled Grandpa, who had just come up, "I think it's time we had dinner—"

Just then Grandma's bell began to ring. So into the house they went, along with the neighbors' boys and girls, who had been helping, too.

The big table seemed set for a feast. And what a feast it was!

"Some of everything we've picked and canned so far," Grandma said. "With jelly, and chicken, and chocolate cake besides—"

Halfway through that wonderful meal, Grandpa turned to Joan and asked, "Do you still think I grow too many kinds of things?"

"No," Joan sighed happily. "Just enough kinds."

And no one had to ask Billy if he still thought Grandpa grew too much of each kind. Because he was eyeing the last few ears of corn on the big platter, and saying, "Oh well. We can have more tomorrow. There's lots more—just waiting to be picked and cooked and eaten!"

Indian Summer

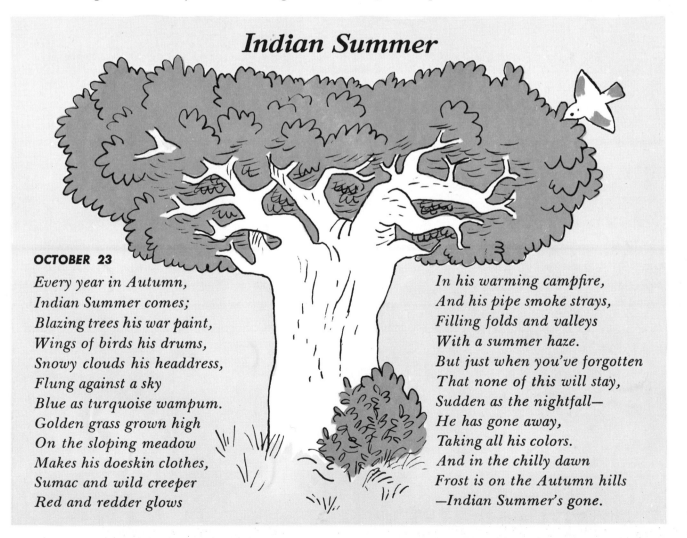

OCTOBER 23

Every year in Autumn,
Indian Summer comes;
Blazing trees his war paint,
Wings of birds his drums,
Snowy clouds his headdress,
Flung against a sky
Blue as turquoise wampum.
Golden grass grown high
On the sloping meadow
Makes his doeskin clothes,
Sumac and wild creeper
Red and redder glows

In his warming campfire,
And his pipe smoke strays,
Filling folds and valleys
With a summer haze.
But just when you've forgotten
That none of this will stay,
Sudden as the nightfall—
He has gone away,
Taking all his colors.
And in the chilly dawn
Frost is on the Autumn hills
—Indian Summer's gone.

Autumn Garden

OCTOBER 24

Out there in the garden
Now that nights are cold,

Only white petunia,
Burnished marigold.

Saucy they, as ever—
How they love to tease

With their autumn fragrance,
Summer's last few bees!

Every Man for Himself

OCTOBER 25

CHATTERBOX SQUIRREL had the brightest eyes. He was always first to see the brown nuts fall.

"Nuts, nuts, nuts!" he would call.

Then off he would run to gather them up. But he didn't have the quickest legs!

No, indeed. The bigger squirrels could run so much faster that they were first to get to the nuts he had spied. Then, their cheeks full, they scampered past him again and hid their hoard.

"What nice, full cupboards they must have," thought Chatterbox Squirrel one day, as he peeped into his empty one.

Then he said, "Maybe, since I spied all the nuts, each of the other squirrels will give me one to put away—"

That was a good idea. That way, he would have a nice, full cupboard, too. But when Chatterbox Squirrel asked the others, they threw up their paws and shook their heads.

"No, indeed!" they said. "Not that you aren't a nice, bright-eyed, friendly little chap. One of the best. But when it comes to nuts to hoard for winter, it's every man for himself!"

Then they all sat around, waiting for him to call, "Nuts, nuts, nuts! I see nuts!" again.

But that, Chatterbox Squirrel did not do.

Instead, whenever he saw a brown nut fall, he kept quite still about it, until it was safely in his own bulging cupboard. And the other squirrels, every man for himself, wondered what in the world had come over Chatterbox Squirrel.

Long Live the King!

OCTOBER 26

ONE DAY, while all the young chimpanzees were arguing over who should be the next king, an explorer came into the jungle.

Very handsome he looked, dressed in a white sun hat, spanking white riding-pants, high-laced boots, and the most elegant plaid shirt besides. But he was tired, too, because of the big bundle he was carrying.

"If only someone would carry my equipment for me!" he said, mopping his brow.

Each of the chimpanzees thought about that. And each of them (except one) thought, "If I go away now, I never will argue myself into being king!"

So they all sat staring. But one chimpanzee stepped forward without a single thought.

"Let me carry it!" he cried, and off he went with the grateful explorer.

That young chimpanzee was a very good helper. Besides carrying things, he learned to put up the explorer's tent, to make excellent pancakes, and to play the explorer's mandolin most beautifully and mournfully on quiet African nights.

What's more, he stood guard to protect his new friend from cannibals or tigers if any should come near. And while none ever did, the explorer thought it extremely brave.

"My friend," he said, when at last the two came to the seaport, "I hate to part from you."

"And I from you," the young chimpanzee admitted. "Still and all, everything comes to an end sometime—"

"True," agreed the explorer. "But now you must accept something for all your help—and to remember me by—"

With that, he presented the young chimpanzee with his big white sun hat, his spanking white riding-pants, his high-laced boots, and his most elegant plaid shirt.

How proud he looked, strolling into the jungle where all the other chimpanzees were still arguing over who should be the next king!

After one look at him in his fine new clothes, they all cried, "Long live the King!" and led that young chimpanzee straight to the throne.

And there he sits to this day, ruling wisely and well, and being very careful never to spill coconut milk on his most elegant plaid shirt.

Jolly Jack

OCTOBER 27

I'll make a jack-o'-lantern
Of this pumpkin, round and big;
With a carrot for a nose, and
Lots of parsley for a wig;

He'll have acorn squash for ears,
And a cut-out, jolly grin,
To say to folks on Halloween,
"Hello there! Come on in!"

South for the Winter

OCTOBER 28

ALL WEEK, Poll had seemed quiet and worried, sitting close to the window and watching the birds fly by.

"They're all going south for the winter," she explained to her friend Mitty. "That's what they keep saying—'Hurry, hurry, hurry! It's going to be cold up here.'"

"Oh, Poll," purred Mitty, "I wouldn't worry about that if I were you—"

"You would so," Poll snapped. "If you were me, you wouldn't have your warm fur coat. All you'd have would be a handful of feathers—not nearly enough to keep you warm in winter."

With that, Poll shivered.

"It's getting pretty chilly right now," she complained. "Please, Mitty, open my cage so I can fly south, too."

But Mitty refused.

"You couldn't fly three blocks, Poll," she said. "Anyway, what would our mistress say?"

"And besides, you don't care if I freeze dead!" squawked Poll angrily. "I may as well start right now!"

Then she stretched out on the bottom of her cage, feet up and looking so forlorn that Mitty let out an alarmed little cry.

"Mitty, what's wrong?" asked their mistress, hurrying in.

When she saw poor Poll, her heart gave a frightened thump.

"Why Poll! Poll, dear," she said. "I do think this room is too cold for you—"

So she quickly put Poll's cage in a sunny

window. And she quickly turned on the heat.

In almost no time, Polly was as warm as toast.

"Well, what do you know?" she cried.

"Well, what do you think?" she laughed, swinging merrily on her perch. "I didn't have to go south for the winter—south came right here to me!"

The Real Little Ghost

OCTOBER 29

"You're Jack!" said a cat to a pirate bold.
"You're Jill!" said Captain Jack.
Then everyone guessed who everyone was—
Except one little ghost in back.
One little ghost who trailed along
As friendly as he could be,
But very hard to guess about—
He was often so hard to see.
He wouldn't talk, that one little ghost,
All he said was, "Oooo! Oooo! Oooo!"
And he didn't eat any kind of treat,
Which was most unusual, too.
And when all the others took off their masks,
All that little ghost did, was steal
Up the hill toward the haunted house—
So maybe—he—really—was—real!

The Barn Dance

OCTOBER 30

"Did you hear?" cried Cat, waving his hat. "There's going to be a barn dance!"

"There is?" asked Bear. "Do tell us where!"

"In the barn, I'd think," clucked Mrs. Hen. "The question I'd like to ask is—when?"

"Not now," said Cow, adding with a smile, "it's probably going to be after a while—"

"We'll need some music, of course," said Horse.

"And jack-o'-lanterns, I surmise," said Owl, flying off for that surprise.

"And doughnuts and cider'd be very nice," said two little always-hungry mice.

"We'd best get busy," buzzed busy Bee. "I'll get wax for the floor—"

"Count on me for plenty of cider," cried the pig. "I'll fill a whole pitcher I have. It's big!"

"I'll bring the doughnuts," said the hen with a smile. "Good-by! I'll see you after a while—"

Then they all ran off till after a while. And after a while, it was after a while and everything was ready. Cat brought his fiddle and made it hum. Rabbit brought his accordion. Bear brought his drum. When all three were playing a tune, the rooster stood on his toes to call:

"A dance in the barn! Come one, come all!"

And everyone hurried in, of course.

"What a lovely party it is!" cried Horse. "Let's drink a toast to the one who's giving it! Who's our host?"

But nobody said, "I am, it's me!"

"Aha!" laughed Owl. "I think I see—we're *all* of us giving it! But how did it start?"

And Cat admitted he'd done that part. But when everyone shouted, "Hurray for Cat!" he modestly said there'd been nothing to that.

Said he, in the greatest of great good humor:

"It's no trouble at all—to start a rumor!"

Trick or Treat

OCTOBER 31

Isn't it fun
To be looking so scary
That you shiver and shake
In your boots—
To be dressed up as witches
Or scarecrows or ghosts
Or in terrible
Skeleton suits?

Isn't it fun
With the dark trees all bare,
And the frightened moon
Staring between,
To be out in the night,
And to be such a sight,
When it's shivery
Dark Halloween?

Meeting

NOVEMBER 1

This morning, while it still was dawn,
I saw—right there, out on our lawn—
A little, spotted, long-legged fawn.
But when I waved to say that he
Should stay right there, and wait for me,
Up went his tail. And in a wink—
Away he went. And now I'd think
I'd only dreamed that little fawn,
Except for hoofprints on the lawn.

The Rudiments

NOVEMBER 2

EVERY day, when Joe was coming home from school, there were two boys waiting for him at the bottom of the hill.

"Wanta fight, kid?" they always asked.

"No, I don't," Joe said. One day, he even said he'd much rather be friends.

But that only made those boys laugh.

"Friends!" they said. "You're *afraid!*"

After that, besides waiting for him and trying to get him to fight, they called, "fraidy-friendly," every time they saw Joe. And that got so bad that one day Joe just had to tell his mother and daddy about it.

"I think fighting is silly," his mother said.

But his father said, "Well, I don't believe in starting fights, Joey. But there are times when a man has to stand up for himself. Come on downstairs, and I'll teach you the rudiments of the manly art of self-defense—"

All that week end, Joe and his daddy practiced those rudiments, and Joe learned quickly. By Sunday night, Daddy couldn't land so many punches—and Joe was landing quite a few. And on Monday—he was hoping those boys would be waiting for him after school.

They were. And this time, when they said, "Wanta fight?" he said, "I don't start fights—"

"Then I'll start—" laughed one of them.

He jabbed at Joe's nose—but up came Joe's arm, and that boy was so surprised that he forgot to protect himself—and thump! Joe punched him just above the belt!

"Ouch!" he yelled, doubling up. Then he stared at Joe.

"Where did you learn to fight?" he asked.

"I don't really know how—all I know is the rudiments," said Joe. "My dad's teaching me—"

"He must be a champ!" the boy said. "Wish he'd teach me!"

"Maybe he will," Joe said. "I'll ask him tonight, and let you know tomorrow."

Then he started up the hill. And this time both those boys waved to Joe, and called, "So long, Joey—we'll see you tomorrow!"

A Home for a Puppy

NOVEMBER 3

A STRAY little puppy was trying to find a home for himself, so he peeped into a big doghouse, a middle-sized doghouse, and a little doghouse.

The big doghouse was roomy and handsome. In it there was a big soft bed, and a juicy bone, and a fine big bowl full of milk.

But there was a fine big dog in that doghouse.

When he saw the stray little puppy peeping in, he growled such a loud, warning growl that the puppy raced away.

"That was no house for me, anyway," he told himself. "It was much too big!" And he went to peep in the middle-sized doghouse. It was snug and roomy, too, with a bowl full of meat scraps and another of milk. But in it there was a mother dog with five puppies of her own.

They filled the middle-sized doghouse full, and were so busily gobbling the meat and lapping the milk that it was gone in a wink.

"There's certainly no place for me there," the stray little puppy told himself. "I'd just be one puppy too many!"

Off he went to peep into the little doghouse.

It was brand new, so new that when he sniffed it, it still smelled of paint. The inside was small, but very cozy, with a soft little pillow for a puppy to sleep on.

And there was no puppy in it at all.

"Maybe this is the home for me!" thought the stray little puppy, wagging his tail like a little signal flag. And the little boy who had just painted that little doghouse saw the signal from his window.

"Oh, Mommie, look!" he cried. "A puppy has come to live in my doghouse. A real puppy really has!"

Then out he hurried, with a tasty little meat-bone and a small bowl full of warm milk—and the stray little puppy ran to meet him, sure as sure that he had found his own home, at last.

A Very Small Dragon

NOVEMBER 4

I asked and they said,
"No, there never were dragons—
Dragons are only pretend."
So I guess there's no use,
Any more, in pretending
I have a small one
For a friend.
But it would be pleasant,
I think, don't you—
On stormy nights,
When the wind goes woooo!
To have a dragon, a very small one,
Nodding his sleepy head
(But there, just the same,
And brave as a lion)
Curled up on the foot of your bed?

The Firemen's Parade

NOVEMBER 5

TOBY LIVED in a town where there was a Firemen's Parade every year. It was supposed to begin at two o'clock in the afternoon, but the excitement started long before that!

Extra policemen buzzed through town on their motorcycles, going to direct traffic, and to welcome the visiting fire companies. Big, shining engines were seen here, there, and everywhere. And buses carrying firemen and many different bands came streaming into town.

At first, it always seemed to Toby that two o'clock would never come. Then it was two o'clock, and he and his mother were down at the Square—and it seemed the parade would never start.

"Back, there! Off the Square!" shouted the smiling policemen, blowing their whistles and re-directing the cars.

"Balloons! Firemen's hats! Souvenir buttons!" called the vendors. And car horns blew, and the crowd talked and laughed, and flags

waved, and runaway balloons went sailing up, up, up through the bright air.

Toby's balloon didn't run away. He held it tightly as he sat on the curb for a while, and watched the excitement.

And just as he was sure that this year something had gone wrong—that they were standing in the wrong place, or that the parade had taken a wrong turning—he heard the sound of horns and drums, and saw the first color guard across the Square.

Here came the parade at last—and what a parade it was!

High-stepping drum majors, bands in gorgeous uniforms, whole armies of firemen (all wearing white gloves, and waving as they marched) and more fire chiefs' cars, and emergency cars, and engines of every kind, than most people see in their whole lives.

There was even a clown's fire engine—with a funny, clumsy clown-fireman who squirted himself and the crowd with a thin, tickly stream of water, and laughed himself sick.

As for the real firemen on the engines, when Toby and the other children called, "Blow your siren!" they blew away to a fare-thee-well.

So *who-ooo-ooo!* went the sirens, band after band played merrily, the fire dogs barked for joy, and the crowd cheered until it seemed as if the parade was all there was in the world.

Then the last band came marching by.

Around the corner it went, squarely and smartly, horns and drums silent as it made the turn. Then the music started up again, and moved farther and farther away.

"The parade's over, Toby," said Mother, squeezing his hand. "Time to go home for supper now—"

"Yes," sighed Toby, suddenly glad to remember home and supper, and even more glad that his home was in a town that had a Firemen's Parade every single year.

Time To Go to Bed

NOVEMBER 6

THE NOVEMBER sun was so warm that six young frogs popped out of the pond and sat themselves on a log.

"Garum-garum-garum!" they sang, in their new voices that were much deeper than they had been in the spring.

"Garum-garum-garum!" over and over, there in the warm November sunshine.

"Oh, there you are!" cried their mother, popping her head up. "Come along now, time for bed—time for our winter sleeping under the deep, cozy mud."

But the young frogs didn't come along.

"Garum," they said. "It's too nice and warm for sleeping. We'll stay right here in the sun."

"You'll not!" said their mother.

"Garum!" sang the young frogs, all looking very stubborn, until a cloud scudded along.

Then how cold it was on the old log, and how gray and cold the whole world seemed! All six young frogs shivered a shiver each, and dived into the water with their mother.

Down through the chilly water they swam.

Down through the mud they wriggled, down where everything was dark and cozy and sleepy.

And most obediently, they all went to sleep.

So not another garum! was heard again, until autumn and winter had passed, and the warm spring sunshine was strong and bright on the young frogs' log again.

The Shiny Car

NOVEMBER 7

I told my mother, and told my dad
That I wanted it
Terribly, awfully bad—
That shiny car
With a horn that blew,
And pushing pedals
To drive it, too.
But they said a boy as big as I
Was too big to have it,
And wouldn't I try
A bike instead?
The bike was red,
And they bought me
The new red bike instead.
I like my bike, it goes fast and far,
It's better than any shiny car;
If they'd bought me one
(As I wished they had)
I'd be wanting my bike
Most awfully bad.

Sly Little Bear

THERE WAS a little bear who didn't like to take a bath.

When his mother said, "It's Saturday, Little Bear, so go on in and take your bath," he didn't.

He ran the water and took off his clothes.

He sat down on the floor and flipped one paw in the water, back and forth, back and forth—as if he were washing all nice and clean.

Then he dried his paw and got dressed in his clean clothes, and came out. He thought he was pretty smart, that sly little bear!

But one day his mother took a good look at him at inspection time. She even put on her glasses and took a better look.

Then she said, "Little Bear, you look pretty dirty for a little bear who takes a bath every Saturday. It seems to me that you'd better take one every day of the week."

And after that, he did.

Because his mother stood in the doorway, tapping her foot and watching to see that he used lots of soap.

In a week, that little bear was all clean and glossy and smooth, and he sort of liked it, too.

His mother noticed and said, "You look clean even before you take your daily bath—which is a lot for a little bear to take—so I guess you can go back to having just a Saturday one."

So after that, the little bear had to take only one bath a week. And when his mother said, "Little Bear, go on in and take your bath—" he went right on in and did.

Snow Flurry

NOVEMBER 9

What do you think?
It snowed today,
A swift, white flurry
That went away
As quick as the flick
Of a bunny's tail.
But I was out there
Getting the mail,
I was there for
The whole, white minute—
All by myself—and
Standing in it!

Timothy's Tails

NOVEMBER 10

LOTS OF times Timothy liked to be something different from just a little boy. And he could, very easily, with only some pieces of rope.

When he had a short piece tucked into the back of his belt, that meant he was a puppy dog, and the rope was his tail.

With a longer piece for a tail, Timothy was a pussycat. If the end of the rope was fringed, he was a camel—or a lion. Lots of people couldn't tell which, but Timothy always knew.

And with a very short fringed tail, just a puff of a tail, Timothy could be a bunny. Best of all, though, he liked a long, long tail, because then Timothy was a mouse.

Creep, creep, creep into the kitchen he went, looking for something tasty to nibble. One rainy day he went outdoors, with his long mouse's tail dragging behind his raincoat.

That mouse's tail of Timothy's got all wet and muddy.

"Please take off your tail before you come in the house," said his mother, when Timothy was ready to come in again.

And Timothy did.

He took off his muddy, draggled tail and left it outside, which was much better even than being a real mouse—who could never change tails and be something else—and never leave his muddy tail outdoors to get dry, either.

Eleven Fat Pumpkins

NOVEMBER 11

Eleven fat pumpkins, all still on the vine,
Looked as frosty and round as big moons in a line
Till the farmer's wife took them, and used them for pies.
The farmer soon saw them, and said in surprise,
"Eleven fat pumpkins, all golden and tasty,
Seem twice as delicious when baked in a pasty!"
He straightway ate two, with one more for a snack,
And one before milking—and two coming back—

Little Rabbit's Surprise

ONE COLD day, a fat little rabbit felt very cold.

"I'll chop some wood and make me a fire," he said, setting out with his ax and wheelbarrow.

But that was hard work for a fat little rabbit.

He had chopped only a few sticks when along came Mr. Bear, his nose quite blue with the cold.

"Please lend me your ax, little rabbit," he said, "so I can chop some wood for my stove."

The little rabbit hated to give up his ax. He would never get a nice, warm fire that way! But poor Mr. Bear promised to give it back in a jiffy. Besides, he did look so cold and shivery that the little rabbit said, "All right. Here, take the ax."

Then whack! whack! whack! went Mr. Bear, swinging it with his great, strong arms. He soon had a fine big pile of firewood, and gratefully returned the ax.

"You *were* only a jiffy!" said the little rabbit. "Chopping my wood will take me much, much longer—"

And he was just about to start again, when Mr. Bear said, "Why chop wood, little rabbit? Without your ax, I wouldn't have any—so, the way I figure it, some of these logs are yours."

"About half," he added, putting all the smaller logs in the fat little rabbit's green wheelbarrow. Then, smiling and happy, Mr. Bear took up his armload of big logs and hurried home to build a fine warm fire.

And the fat little rabbit, still shaking his head in surprise, and murmuring, "Oh my, thank you, Mr. Bear!" was soon all toasty and warm beside his own little log fire, too.

And two for his dinner. For supper, two more,
And one while he latched up the latch on the door!
Then he rolled up the stairs,
And he rolled into bed,
Quite as round and as fat as the moon overhead—
As round as a pumpkin, and feeling so fine
That he dreamed of ripe pumpkins, all still on the vine.

Lots of Acorns

NOVEMBER 13

Lots of acorns were falling down.

Plop! went one on the ground. Then one fell on the roof. It went plop! rattle-rattle-rattle, and plop! again as it landed on the ground.

All the children ran about, gathering the acorns as they fell.

Debbie had a boxful. Penny had a bagful, and Ricky had a whole wagonful.

Debbie took two of her acorns, and with toothpicks for arms and legs, made a little doll. She painted a face on it, and its acorn cap made a fine beret.

Penny took some of her acorn caps and used them for doll dishes. Some were saucers, too, with acorns for cups.

Then Penny made a doll like Debbie's.

And the dolls had a party, which the two girls shared.

But Ricky didn't come. He was too busy planting acorns to grow into oak trees.

He planted three, then it was lunchtime.

He went in, and so did Debbie and Penny.

And three little squirrels came whisking out of their house.

"Lots of acorns! Plenty of acorns!" they chattered, reaching into Debbie's box, and Penny's bag, and Ricky's wagon, and helping themselves.

Back and forth they ran, storing away enough acorns to last them all winter. Debbie saw them. So did Penny and Ricky. But nobody minded. There were still lots of acorns, and the two little dolls still sat under the tree. The squirrels had never even gone near them.

So there they sat, having their party over and over again, while the acorns fell plop! on the ground, or plop! rattle-rattle-rattle, plop! on the roof.

Rainy-Day Fun

NOVEMBER 14

We don't mind when it rains, do you?
With paper and crayons and scissors and glue
There is no end to the things we can do—
We can make farms and Noah's Arks,
Trees and fences, and zoos in parks,
Indian villages, soldier camps,
Doll-house furniture, rugs, and lamps,
Ships at sea, or aeroplanes,
Pictures to paste on the window panes
That seem to laugh at the splashy drops—
We don't care if it never stops!
With paper and crayons and scissors and glue,
We don't mind when it rains—do you?

Mr. Perkins

NOVEMBER 15

MR. PERKINS was a good old rooster.

Early every morning, he hopped up on the barnyard fence and crowed his fine, loud cock-a-doodle-doo until everyone was up and about their business.

But these crisp fall mornings no one wanted to get up.

Everyone mumbled, "Quiet, please!" and "Let us be!" and turned over for another forty winks. Especially the farmer. One morning he even said, "Drat that pesky rooster! I wish he'd stop crowing and never crow again!"

Mr. Perkins heard him, and it made him so angry. Up went his comb. His yellow eyes flashed. "All right then," he thought. "I will let them sleep!"

So the next morning, Mr. Perkins didn't crow. He didn't even peep like a brand-new baby chick just out of its shell.

Everyone slept and slept until the whole morning was gone.

And what a to-do there was then!

The cows mooed to be milked. The sheep bleated to be let out to pasture. The pigs squealed and grunted for their mash. The hens set about laying eggs with such a cackling that this, added to the other noises, had everyone mixed up.

The farmer's family tumbled over themselves, milking the cows into the egg baskets, dropping eggs as fast as they gathered them, letting the pigs out into the sheep pasture, and giving the sheep pig mash—which didn't suit them at all.

As for the farmer's children, they just howled because they had missed the school bus and would have to walk all the way—besides being kept in for a whole hour. It was a topsy-turvy day!

That evening, when everyone had had supper (or was it lunch? no one was quite sure) they all went to see Mr. Perkins.

"See that you wake us up on time tomorrow!" they said.

"I will not," sulked Mr. Perkins. "Not to be mumbled and grumbled at, and called a pesky rooster!"

"Oh, we won't do that!" everyone promised.

"Well, I won't crow anyway," said Mr. Perkins. "Especially not without a please."

"Please, Mr. Perkins!" begged everyone.

"If I do, will you cheer for me?" Mr. Perkins asked.

"We certainly will," everyone promised. To prove it, they all cheered such a loud, hearty "Hurray for Mr. Perkins!" that he forgot he had ever been angry.

So the next morning he was back on the fence again, crowing as loudly and cheerfully as ever.

Mr. Perkins really was a good old rooster.

A Little Girl Named Sarah

NOVEMBER 16

ONCE THERE was a little girl named Sarah, and she did not like her name. She wished it could be Judy or Ann or Jill, or Karen or Betsy—anything except Sarah.

"Why *is* my name Sarah?" she asked her mother one day.

And her mother, busily cleaning closets, said, "Because we named you for your great-aunt Sarah, who never had a little girl of her own. Wasn't that a good reason?"

"Yes," said Sarah thoughtfully. "Yes, it was."

But even with that good reason, Sarah didn't think Sarah was a good name to have. So another day, she asked her great-aunt Sarah, "Why were you named Sarah, Aunt Sarah?"

That made Great-Aunt Sarah smile.

"Oh," she said. "I was named for my grandmother, Sarah Chapin. And, oh my—when I was just about your age, I wished she had been named something else. I just thought Sarah was the worst name any little girl could have!"

"Did you really?" asked Sarah. "And do you still?"

"Oh no," smiled Aunt Sarah. "No indeed.

Because one day I asked my grandmother why she had been named Sarah—and she told me what the name Sarah means—"

"What does it mean?" asked the little girl named Sarah.

"It means Princess," her great-aunt said, sitting up even straighter and more proudly than usual. "And once I knew that, I was glad every time I heard my name. What do you think of that, young Sarah?"

"Why," said the little girl named Sarah, suddenly standing up very straight and proud and tall. "Why, Aunt Sarah, I just seem to feel exactly the very same way!"

Wise Little Owl!

NOVEMBER 17

"Come live with me
In a hollow tree,
Little owl,"
Said a big brown bear,
"Though it's cold as ice,
We'll be warm and nice
With the two of us
Living there!"

But the owl said
As he shook his head,
"Mister Bear,
That would never do.
If I know my name,
When the springtime came,
There'd be nobody
There but you!"

The Merry Tinker

LONG, LONG ago, there was a merry tinker who went from place to place mending pots, and telling tales, and sometimes selling a few trinkets—such as ribbons and lace, and pictures of faraway places.

In those days, the houses were few and far between, and people longed for visitors to come, bringing a bit of news. So, whenever that little tinker came whistling along the road, they were very happy.

They brought him in to their hearths, and spread out the finest of meals.

They watched round-eyed while he deftly mended old pots and pans, and listened spellbound while he told his tales. They chose most carefully which trinkets they wanted most, and when it came to the pictures of faraway places— why, they couldn't make enough of a man who had traveled so widely!

Then perhaps the merry tinker would teach them all a song to sing. And while they were singing it, over and over, he would take up his pack, and start on his way.

Down the road he would go, whistling the selfsame merry tune, with the people looking after him and wishing they might all be traveling tinkers, too.

"Ah," they thought. "What a merry life he lives!"

But often, just after the tinker turned the bend in the road, he would stop and look back toward some snug house, and think how gladly he would give up all the faraway places, just to live in such a cozy place as that.

Then he'd shoulder his pack and go on his way, that merry tinker, whistling a new little tune—one that he had learned from the kettle, singing back there on the warm, snug hearth.

The Fat Little Pig

NOVEMBER 19

ONCE THERE were five little pigs, all squealing and pink. And four of them were such finicking little pigs that they never did eat a full meal.

They said that corn was too hard to chew, and that mash was too soft. And when the farmer gave them nice crisp vegetables for dinner, those four little pigs just poked about, picking out the bits and morsels they liked best of all.

But the fifth little pig liked everything. He gobbled away, almost climbing into the trough to get the last bit of mash.

"Good little pig!" smiled his mother.

"Greedy little pig!" sniffed his brothers and sisters, picking daintily away. So of course they stayed thin and small, while the fifth little pig grew so rosy and plump that the farmer washed and groomed him, and drove him off to the Fair in town.

"Where's he going?" asked the other pigs.

"You'll learn, when he comes back," their mother smiled.

And learn they did. Because when the fat little pig came riding home again, both he and the farmer were smiling proudly, and waving the fine blue ribbon he had won for being the best young pig in seven counties.

"We want to go to the Fair, too!" squealed his brothers and sisters.

"And maybe you will some day," said the fat little pig. Then he said, "When's supper? Isn't it past suppertime?"

It was at that, because the farmer had been so busy showing the blue ribbon to all his neighbors. But when at last he did bring their supper of corn and mash, and all kinds of vegetables, all five young pigs rushed to the trough—squealing and pushing and eager to eat—just as greedy and hungry as young little pigs are always supposed to be.

Big Eyes

NOVEMBER 20

The turkey keeps on growing,
He really is a prize—
The pumpkins each are big enough
To make two pumpkin pies,
The corn is tall and full and sweet,
The grapes, all smoky blue,
Are bigger than they've ever been.
I'm glad I'm bigger, too—
'Cause always at Thanksgiving time,
There's much more on the table
Than I can even taste and try—
And this year, I'll be able!

The Brave Little Army

NOVEMBER 21

ONE DAY, a brave little army rode forth to battle.

First came the brave little horsemen on their shining steeds. Next, the brave little cannoneers with their rattling cannons. Then the brave little foot soldiers, with their sharp little swords.

They encountered a dragon, and were about to slay him, when he ran under a rock, the way quick little lizards always do.

They encountered a giant, who looked exactly like a chipmunk, and he ran into a stone wall at the very sight of them.

They even surrounded a castle, and shouted, "Come out, varlets, and perish at our hands!"

But the castle happened to be a sand castle, solid with sand, and nobody was in it—so nobody came out. Just the same, the brave little army would have routed them if they had.

"We have defeated our enemies!" they cried.

And back they went to their encampment, blowing their little bugles, flying their little flags, looking braver than ever, and very proud and important.

Especially when the little boy who owned them said, "You have served your country faithfully and well!" and brushed the dirt off their little feet and hoofs and wheels, and put them in their box for a good long night's rest.

The Barberry Bush

NOVEMBER 22

ROUND and round the barberry bush ran three little gray squirrels.

"What pretty berries!" they all cried. "Let's pick some and use them for something useful!"

So all three filled their pockets full.

"I'm going to use mine for cinnamon candy drops!" said the first little squirrel, popping one into her mouth.

But, ugh! that berry wasn't good for cinnamon candy at all. It was so bitter that she spat it out again.

"I'll use my berries for currant jelly!" said the second little squirrel. But even cooked with lots of sugar, her barberry berries did not make good currant jelly.

"It tastes awful!" she wailed, looking most surprised and disappointed.

Meantime, the third little squirrel had watched the others, and found out what barberry berries weren't good for. So she thought about what they *would* be good for.

And presently she began to string hers on a string, making herself a most beautiful red bead necklace. My, but the other little squirrels thought she was clever!

"Why!" they cried. "That's exactly the thing to do with pretty red barberry berries!"

Then back to the barberry bush ran all three little squirrels. And round and round it they went, picking berries enough for a red bead necklace each, and barberry bracelets, besides.

In Bed at Night

NOVEMBER 23

I like to be in bed at night.
Under my door, a strip of light
Creeps in. And voices from below
Come wandering up. I never know
Exactly what it is they're saying—
But pretty soon I find I'm playing
That I'm not here, but there instead,
And all my children are in bed,
While I am up extremely late
(Perhaps a quarter after *eight)*
And murmuring the way they do,
And laughing some, well, wouldn't you?
To think how secret it must sound
To all my children, tucked around
In puffy quilts—and watching light
Creep under their closed doors at night!

The Little Spoons

NOVEMBER 24

LAURIE lived in a big house that was two houses, really. She and her mother and daddy and baby brother lived in the downstairs part, and her grandmother lived in the upstairs part.

And one day, Laurie's grandmother was going on a trip.

"Laurie," she asked. "Do you think you can take care of my plants while I'm away?"

"Yes, I do," said Laurie, watching Grandmother water the plants. "I know how to feel them to see if they're dry, and how to water them without spilling any—"

Then she stood on a footstool, and carefully watered the plants in the little wall rack that also held six shiny little silver spoons. Laurie loved those spoons. She had always wished that Grandmother would let her use them.

And when she was all alone in Grandmother's house, watering the plants, she wanted more than ever to touch them.

After all, who would ever know she had?

"Nobody at all," thought Laurie.

But every time her hand almost went out to touch the spoons, Laurie remembered that Grandmother had told her how old and thin and delicate they were, and how much Grandmother loved them, too.

So she sighed, and pulled back her hand, and just took good care of the plants.

Grandmother was very pleased to see how healthy they looked when she came home again.

She polished her little silver spoons, too. And she got out six tiny chocolate cups with roses on them, and a tall, thin pot made just for holding hot chocolate. Then she made chocolate and cinnamon toast, and set up a small table with all those things on it.

"Laurie," she called downstairs. "Laurie, I'm having a coming-home party—can you and four of your dolls come on up?"

"Oh yes," called Laurie. "Yes, we'd love to—"

So up the stairs she started, two dolls in each arm—smelling the delicious smells from Grandmother's house—but never even guessing that she really was going to have a tea party with the beautiful, shiny little spoons at last.

The Very First Thanksgiving

NOVEMBER 25

JEREMY liked almost everything about his new home.

Helping to clear the wilderness of trees—to make room for houses and farmlands—seemed to him high adventure.

He had helped to build his own log house, and the meeting house. Jeremy had cheerfully helped to turn the soil and plant the crops, too.

And because he worked so well and said so little, he was always treated as one of the menfolk. That alone was enough to make a boy take pride in himself and in his big, new country!

The only thing Jeremy minded was being hungry all the time. For although the friendly Indians had shown the pilgrims new, native vegetables to plant, and the best places to hunt and fish, their food was scarce enough. And the little band was so careful to keep stores for tomorrow, that it seemed to Jeremy that he hadn't had a full stomach in a whole year.

But now it was November, and the harvest was bountiful. Tonight, in the firelight, the men agreed that they would have a feast.

"We will hunt for wild turkeys tomorrow," they said.

"We will make cornbread and sweet squash pies, and elderberry jelly," the women said. They spoke of other foods, too, potatoes and beans and delicious Indian corn, until Jeremy's mouth was watering.

"Will everyone get all he wants to eat?" he asked, so eager that for once he forgot to be silent.

"All he wants," smiled his father. "The Lord has blessed us with plenty, and we will give Him thanks—"

That very night in bed, Jeremy forgot the hunger inside him, and pictured the big table spread for a feast instead.

So, when he said his prayers, with his hands folded on his flat little stomach, it was Jeremy who made the very first Thanksgiving in that great, exciting new country across the seas from his old home.

The Wide-Awake Bear

WHEN ALL the other little bears were taking their winter naps, one little bear was still wide awake.

He tried playing hopping games with some merry little rabbits. But hopping isn't a bear's way to play. He soon got tired of that, and looked for someone different to play with.

Foxes there were, two young red foxes, playing follow-the-leader on a stone wall. The little bear played, too—along the wall, across the fields, through the woods. There the young foxes hid in a bush until the little bear went by, and doubled back on their tracks, laughing to themselves.

Doubling back isn't a bear's way, so hunt and search as he did, the little bear could not find them.

He did find some squirrels though, busily eating their lunch of acorns.

"You have some," they chattered. "Have some, too!"

But even though they kindly cracked acorns for him, the meat was much too hard and sharp-tasting for a little bear. Not that the little bear cared.

He didn't like acorns.

Besides, all at once he felt so sleepy that he yawned.

That made the squirrels yawn, too. And the rabbits, and the young red foxes.

"Let's take our naps," they all called to each other.

And nap they did, short afternoon naps. But the little bear went home so sleepy that he napped till springtime.

And when he woke up, all the other little bears were calling him to come and and play real bear games with them.

Silly Puppy

NOVEMBER 27

*Although he hates
To have his bath,
He seems to think
It's fun
To dip his paws
Into the tub,
When I am
Having one.*

Remembering

NOVEMBER 28

SOMETIMES at night, when Jimmy couldn't go right to sleep, he wished the nighttime weren't so dark.

He wished the sounds and shadows didn't seem so scarey when he was all alone. And oh, how he wished everything didn't seem so big and black.

But one night, when Jimmy was wishing all that especially hard, he remembered last summer when he and his father had gone camping in the woods.

The night had been big and dark then, too. His woods bed, made of springy pine boughs, hadn't been as soft and cozy as his bed at home. There had been strange shadows in the woods,

too, and eerie noises, such as an owl calling, "Who-oo, who-oo, who-oo!"

Jimmy remembered that he had been pretty scared that night, too. Maybe he had even shivered under his blanket.

Then his daddy had murmured, "Jimmy, don't the trees look as if they were bending over to watch over us?"

Jimmy had looked up. Up and up at the tall trees with the stars twinkling above their black tops. And yes, that was just the way those trees had looked. A little wind in their tops had been singing a quiet, sleepy-sounding song. And the bright, friendly stars had seemed to be watching over Jimmy, too.

"Yes," he had murmured back. "And, Daddy, do you hear that owl? I think he's sleepy, and saying goodnight—"

So after that, it had been easy to go to sleep in the big, dark, friendly woods. And tonight, after remembering the outdoors night, Jimmy remembered that there were friendly stars shining over his house, too. And friendly trees bending over and singing soft, sleepy-sounding songs all around it.

When he listened very hard, he could even hear a little owl calling, "Who-oo, who-oo!"

So he whispered goodnight to the sleepy owl, and went right to sleep in the friendly night.

New Friends

NOVEMBER 29

The birds, so shy in summer,
So high among the leaves,
Are coming so much closer;
They sleep up in the eaves
And gather on the porch rail,
And cluster all about

To see if I have bread crumbs
Whenever I go out.
The birds, so shy in summer,
And all so far away,
Are getting to be friendly now—
I hope they stay that way.

Winter Quarters

NOVEMBER 30

We went to the zoo,
But no one was there
Except some seals
And a polar bear.

He showed us a door,
And opened it, too.
And there, inside,
Was the inside-zoo—

So we asked the keeper,
"Where are the rest?
The elephants, sir,
Are what we liked best—"

With lions and monkeys
And all the rest,
And the elephants, too—
Which we liked the best.

Danny's Dilemma

DECEMBER 1

DANNY was worried. He just didn't know what to do about the little stray kitten he was carrying in his pocket.

"I can't take it home," he thought. "Chipper hates cats, and he'd only chase it and bark at it all day long."

But he couldn't put that poor little kitten back on the cold sidewalk, either. So Danny stopped right where he was to do some hard thinking about what he could do.

He had stopped right in front of old Mrs. McAllister's house. And while he was standing there, she came to her door.

"Hello, Danny," she called. "Just peep in my mailbox and see if there's anything for me, will you? Not that there will be, of course. There never is. Deary me, it's a lonely life for me—no chick or child, no kith or kin—not even a pet to love and pat, which would be a comfort—"

Then she smiled wistfully and said, "Oh well —you go look, Danny, and tell me."

So Danny ran to her mailbox, and when he opened it, it was empty. But when he closed it again, it wasn't empty at all. Because quickly and gently, he had taken the little stray kitten out of his pocket and slipped it into the box.

"There *is* something for you today, Mrs. McAllister," Danny said. "Shall I take it up to you?"

"Oh no, thank you, Danny," the old lady said proudly. "I'll come down and get it myself."

So home went Danny, his pocket empty and his heart light. And down her steps came old Mrs. McAllister, wearing a happy, expectant smile. But that smile was only a sample of the one she wore, when—with the sleepy little kitten tucked under her soft, warm shawl—she started up her steps again.

The Gingerbread Man

DECEMBER 2

EVEN when he was just cut out, the big gingerbread man looked much livelier and merrier than any of the little ones.

Then came his currant buttons, and mouth and nose, and his eyes—which seemed to twinkle with mischief.

"He might be the kind that runs away!" thought Trina.

And when Mother and Trina and Tony peeped into the oven and saw him rising, puffing up plumper than any of the others, Tony thought the same thing and asked his mother about it.

"Do you think he may run away when we set him out to cool?" he asked. "Do you think he will?"

"Oh no," said Mother. "Things like that happen only in stories, you know." Then she took the gingerbread man out of the oven to cool, and he didn't run away.

She even made him a gay little hat of pink frosting, and a jacket, and fat little shoes.

And he still didn't run away.

He just stayed on the plate with the other gingerbread men, all smelling so spicy and good that Trina and Tony and Mother each had to try one.

But they didn't try that one special gingerbread man.

"Let's put him in the middle of the supper table, for a decoration," said Mother.

Trina and Tony cried, "Yes, let's!"

So that's what they did. He made a fine decoration, that merry gingerbread man, for three nights in a row.

And then he disappeared!

Mother didn't think he had run away. She thought Daddy had gobbled him up at bedtime. Daddy didn't think the gingerbread man had run away, either.

"Things like that happen only in stories!" he laughed.

But Trina and Tony were sure as sure that he had.

They could almost see him, running along on his little pink shoes, and laughing, and calling out, "You can't catch me—I'm the Gingerbread Man!"

And who can be sure? Maybe that's exactly what he was doing.

Snow in the Night

DECEMBER 3

When it snows in the night
You can tell by the sound;
Everything's silent all around,
So muffled-still
That you almost know,
Before you look,
That there must be snow.

The Unlucky Little Store

THERE WAS once a frowning man who kept a little store.

But hardly anyone ever came in to buy the ice cream and candy and popcorn and newspapers he had to sell.

"It's because not enough children live around here," he told himself. "Or because not enough people pass by and see my wares. Or else it's because everyone who does pass, is on his way to the big store on the avenue—

"Or maybe," he went on, one particularly dull day, "it's because this is an unlucky store."

With that, he frowned such a frown as he'd never frowned before.

"Goodness!" thought a customer in a black overcoat. "I don't want to go in there, after all."

And he turned around and started off. But as he did, his black coat made the glass door into a sort of mirror. The frowning man, who was just inside, caught sight of his reflected frown.

"There, that proves it," he growled. "When my unlucky little store gets a customer—it's the awful, frowning kind!"

And then, suddenly that frowning man saw that it wasn't a customer at all, but his own face frowning that way.

What a surprise that was! Why, the man

himself began to laugh. "No wonder hardly anyone comes into my store," he cried. "Who would want to buy from a frown like that?"

He laughed so hard that the customer in the black coat heard him, and came back and bought three whole gallons of ice cream. And the children down the street heard him and came to buy candy and popcorn. And the mothers and fathers came to buy newspapers.

In and out they streamed, all afternoon, and ever after. Because, busy as he was, the store man never did frown again, and he always had time for a jolly smile, and word, and nod.

"How do you manage to keep smiling day in and day out, early morning and late night, *and* rain or shine?" a customer asked him.

"That's simple," said the jolly store man. "It's because my little store is so lucky—it's in a neighborhood just full of children, and with plenty of passers-by to see my wares. And no one at all who passes by ever seems to be on his way to the much bigger store over on the avenue."

When it snows in the night
You can tell by the feel;
The passing air's as sharp as steel,
It nips your nose
And makes it glow,
And you know at once
That there must be snow.

I Know a Man

DECEMBER 5

I know a man, and when it snows,
He goes outdoors in his rainy-day clothes;
Umbrella and raincoat, and all of that,
So he never gets snowflakes on his hat.
He always stays all dry and trim,
But he has a sad sort of look to him—
As if he'd like very much to know
The difference there is
Between rain and snow.

Packages

DECEMBER 6

The milkman brings the clinking milk,
The breadman brings the bread,
The laundryman brings fluffy towels
And clean sheets for my bed.
The cleaner brings clean clothes to wear
And leaves them in the hall,
And when I go to say hello,
I always see them all.

But when it's close to Christmas
And the world's as white as chalk,
The mailman brings us packages—
He trudges up the walk
And rings the bell, and I run out,
But when I reach the hall—
There's someone running up the stairs,
And nothing else at all!

The Christmas Star

DECEMBER 7

"THIS YEAR," said Mr. Merriweather one morning at breakfast, "we can have a really enormous, gorgeous Christmas tree."

"Yes, we can," smiled Mrs. Merriweather, looking up at the high ceilings of their big, new house. "The biggest ever—"

All five little Merriweathers thought that sounded wonderful. And that night, when Mr. Merriweather brought home boxes and boxes of big, new ornaments—they admired every one of them.

What gorgeous things they were, too! Big shining balls that would have dwarfed their old trees, and fruits made of blown glass, and shiny bells that really rang, and flying birds in rainbow colors. And a most beautiful, shiny golden angel.

"For the top of the tree," said Mr. Merriweather proudly. "We've used our star a long time, and I thought something new would be nice."

But at that, Mrs. Merriweather's face fell. So did the faces of all five little Merriweathers.

"Why, that star was on my tree when I was a little girl!" thought Mrs. Merriweather.

"That star is the thing we think of when we think of Christmas!" thought the two biggest little Merriweathers.

Presents

DECEMBER 8

With all my presents
Wrapped and tied,
I've quite forgotten
What's inside.

Suspense

DECEMBER 9

I'd like a train for Christmas,
And a lot of other things:
My stocking full of presents,
And a music box that sings,
And a pair of cowboy pistols—
And a belt with holsters, too—
And one thing I didn't think up;
But I hardly think, do you,
That Santa'd ever bring one boy
All that? I'll have to wait and see,
When it's really Christmas morning,
What he brings to me.

Molly and Mickey, the second two, thought they must have the star. And Martha, the smallest Merriweather, said, "No star, Daddy? I want a star!"

At that, Mr. Merriweather got an idea.

Very carefully, he put the angel on the mantelpiece.

"That's the place for it," he said. "It looks lovely here, doesn't it? I guess we don't want our tree to be so gorgeous that it doesn't even look like *our* tree, at that—"

And all the Merriweathers sighed with relief, and went in to supper with eyes so bright that it almost seemed as if their old, familiar, bright star were shining in every single pair.

Sentinels

DECEMBER 10

The big house is a castle,
Guarded all around
By giants, darkly towering
Above the snowy ground—
Giant elms and poplars,
Bare and gaunt and tall—

But down beside the gatehouse
(The garden there is small)
There isn't room for giants,
So its guard has to be
A green-and-scarlet elfman—
One little holly tree.

When people open them,
They'll be
No more surprised,
I guess, than me!

Last Year's Toys

DECEMBER 11

WHEN CHRISTMAS was coming, Tommy and his mother always cleaned out his toy box, and all his toy shelves.

Tommy picked out the toys that he didn't play with any more, and the broken ones, and the books he didn't need.

Then Mother scrubbed the shelves and the toy box.

And Tommy put back all the things he still did need—which left room enough for all the things he wanted for Christmas.

"There!" he always said. "If Santa Claus is looking through his spyglass—he must be smiling and nodding!"

And one year, Santa Claus was. He thought Tommy's shelves were in fine order for Christmas. But when he saw what Tommy did next, he fairly beamed.

Because next, Tommy and his daddy fixed and mended all the broken toys. They painted all the ones that needed paint.

And when all the old toys were fixed and bright as new, they put them in the car and took them to Friendship House. In a big house like that, where two-hundred-and-twelve boys and girls lived—with no mothers and fathers—it was a big job for Santa Claus to manage one present all around.

Now, with Tommy's toys and books, there was an extra present for each of the little boys the age Tommy had been last year at Christmas.

"Just look at that!" said Santa Claus, smiling his happiest smile. "Why, I guess I just never did know that Tommy is one of my best helpers!" He was very happy. And Tommy, riding back home through the snowy dusk, was feeling almost as pleased and happy as Santa Claus himself.

Twelve Little Christmas Trees

DECEMBER 12

Twelve little Christmas trees
Growing in a line,
Growing straight and spicy-green,
Growing tall and fine.
Twelve little Christmas trees
Riding through the snow
In a red and rumbling truck,
Wondering where they'll go.

Twelve little Christmas trees
Think they're sure to freeze,
When all at once, they all are sold
To twelve gay families!
Twelve little Christmas trees
Sparkling with light,
In twelve snug and happy homes
On Christmas Eve, at night.

222

Snow Sliding

DECEMBER 13

I don't need skates
For sliding in,
I can choose any spot
Where the snow is thin—

And run along,
Then sort of glide,
And have a lovely,
Slickery slide!

The Right Doll

DECEMBER 14

Of all the dolls in the toy shop, there was just one that Linnie wanted for Christmas. It was a doll exactly the right size, with just the right kind of brown curls, and a smile that made Linnie smile back.

Besides, that one particular doll had a look in her eyes that said she wanted to be Linnie's doll, too.

So Linnie told Santa Claus about it.

But after she had told him, a bit timidly (because it was so exciting and magic to talk to Santa himself), she wasn't sure she had told him plainly enough.

"Santa Claus might think I meant a doll *like* that one," she thought, riding down in the elevator.

What a terrible thought that was! Linnie was sure that if she couldn't have that one doll whom she loved already, she would always be lonesome for it.

She asked her mother if they could go back to see Santa—just for a minute. And she looked so worried that Mother said yes, they might.

Then up again they went, to the toy-shop floor, and Linnie headed straight for Santa Claus. There was a long line of boys and girls waiting to talk to him—so Linnie took just a second to go and visit her doll first.

But the doll was gone, curls and smile and loving brown eyes and all! Another doll was sitting where she had been.

"Oh!" said Linnie to the toy clerk. "Oh, please, where is the doll that was right here only a minute ago?"

"Wrapped up and put away," said the clerk. "She's reserved."

"Are you sure?" asked Linnie with tears in her eyes.

"Of course I'm sure," said the clerk, picking up a box with a sign on it. "See for yourself—"

Reserved, the sign said. Linnie could read that. She could read the rest, too.

"For Linnie Peters, a Good Girl," she read out loud. Then she sighed a deep, happy sigh, and took her mother's hand, and started back to the elevator.

"Why, Linnie," her mother said, "didn't you want to see Santa Claus again—didn't you have something to tell him?"

"I did," smiled Linnie. "But I don't have to now—I guess Santa just knows everything there is to know."

The Escalator

DECEMBER 15

Up we go, and then down we go,
On the gliding, sliding stair,
Looking at all the Christmas things
All over and everywhere.
We can choose the presents we want to buy
As easy as Christmas pie,
But there's just one thing
We never can do, no matter how hard we try.
We never remember to just get off,
We keep riding up and down,
Till it's time for the Christmas store to close—
And for us to go home from town!

Plan

DECEMBER 16

This Christmas Eve
When I go to bed,
I won't stay awake;
I've planned instead
To close my eyes
Up very tight,
And pretend it's
Any other night.
Then I'll go to sleep
In my any-night-way
And wake up to find
That it's Christmas Day!

The Wonderful Present

DECEMBER 17

ONCE, before Christmas, there was a mother who was making a present for her little boy.

She was making it of wool, and the little boy knew that, because sometimes he found bits of wool outside the room where his mother did her Christmas work.

He found a piece of red wool, and he thought, "Oh, I know what she's making. She's making me a red wool cap."

Then he found some bits of green wool. Dark green and light green bits, and he thought, "No, it must be mittens she's making me—green ones with red and dark green stripes."

But after that, the little boy found white wool, blue wool, tan wool, and black wool.

Then he thought his mother must be making him a sweater with a design on it in many colors. And he was sure he'd like that sweater very much, even though it was something to wear—and not something to play with.

That's what that little boy thought, but his mother wasn't making him a sweater at all.

She was making a rug for her little boy, and it was a wonderful rug. The light green wool places were grass, and the dark green wool made trees. The blue wool made lakes and rivers. The tan wool made roads and highways. The white wool made houses, and the red wool made roofs and shutters, and flowers growing, and apples on the apple trees.

"When this rug is finished and down on the floor," she thought as she worked away, "my little boy can use it for a whole make-believe town. He can run cars on the roads, and sail ships on the water, and build houses, and put all his little barnyard animals out in the green country grass—"

Then she smiled, thinking what a wonderful present she had thought up for her little boy.

Better than a cap. Better than mittens.

Better even than a sweater with all kinds of designs in it.

And she looked at her calendar and her clock, and worked faster than ever so that the wonderful rug would be ready for a present for her little boy on Christmas Day.

The Little Tree

DECEMBER 18

ONCE THERE WAS a big snow with a little tree in it.

And the little tree was cold.

"Go away!" it said to the snow.

But the snow stayed. It kept right on being there, coming down deeper and deeper around the little tree.

The birds said, and the people said, and the big trees in the forest said, "What a nice snow! Everything is going to look white and Christmasy for Christmas!"

But the little tree, all by itself in the snow said, "It's a bad snow—it's going to cover me all up, and I'll be lost!"

And just then, with a jingling of bells, along came a little sleigh in the snow.

There was a little boy in it. And he said, "Look! There's a little tree—just the kind I want."

Down he jumped into the snow, too.

He dug the little tree up out of the snow and out of the ground, roots and all.

He put it in his sleigh.

And he took it home to be his Christmas tree.

And the snow stayed, coming down and down, and making everything deep and white and quiet for Christmas, with no little tree in it at all.

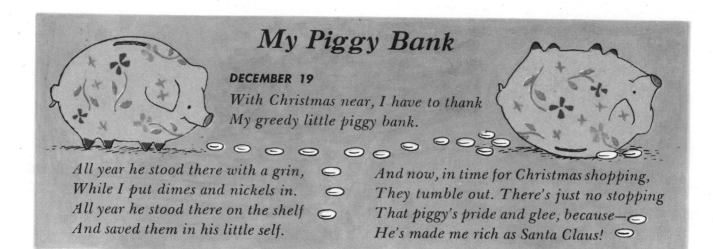

My Piggy Bank

DECEMBER 19

With Christmas near, I have to thank
My greedy little piggy bank.

All year he stood there with a grin,
While I put dimes and nickels in.
All year he stood there on the shelf
And saved them in his little self.

And now, in time for Christmas shopping,
They tumble out. There's just no stopping
That piggy's pride and glee, because—
He's made me rich as Santa Claus!

Mr. Lion's Christmas Boxes

DECEMBER 20

"MR. LION," said Mrs. Lion, "this year, do please be sure you buy Christmas presents that will fit into boxes, won't you? Remember what a time we had wrapping last year?"

"Yes, I do," laughed Mr. Lion. "That toy giraffe, for instance, that we finally had to bend double! Oh yes, this year I'll see that we get into no such pickles—"

So this year, when Mr. Lion got down to the busy Christmas town, he went straight to the ten cent store. Once there, he went straight to the box counter, and bought boxes and boxes and boxes—in every possible shape and size.

What an enormous package that made!

It heaped right up to Mr. Lion's hat, and he had to peep through a little hole even to see where he was going. As for choosing presents to put in the boxes, that was impossible.

Mr. Lion couldn't put his boxes down, for fear the busy crowds would step on them and squash them. And with such a load, he couldn't get near enough to any counter to say, "Here, miss, let me hear how that music box sounds."

There wasn't a thing to do, except climb into a taxi, and go right back home.

"How quick you were!" marveled Mrs. Lion, as he eased himself through the door. "Are you sure you've gotten a present for everyone on our list?"

"No," said Mr. Lion, looking rather sheepish. "I'm sure I haven't a present for *anybody*."

"However," he added, sampling one of the cookies Mrs. Lion had been making, and brightening up, "there *are* four more shopping days before Christmas, and this year—no matter what shape presents I happen to choose—we're absolutely and surely sure to have exactly the right-shaped box to put them in."

WINTER

Sally's First Snow

DECEMBER 21

THERE was once a little girl named Sally who had lived all her five years down in the warm, green South. And then, not long before Christmas, Sally and her mother and father moved up to the North.

What a change that was! Sally wore a snowsuit for the first time. The frosty air nipped her nose, and the ponds froze over. And while Sally liked learning to ice-skate, she wasn't sure she liked the bare, brown look of the North.

Often she thought of her friends, out digging in the bright sand down South where it was always warm and green.

"They may even be in swimming right now," she thought on the dark, cold afternoon of Christmas Eve.

But just as she thought that, a wonderful thing happened.

Big white flakes came swirling down from the gray sky, covering everything that was brown and dull. They frosted the roofs, and heaped on the bare tree branches, and glistened and shimmered on the evergreen tree that Sally's father had strung with Christmas lights.

Soon the lights came on all over town, and then Sally knew she had never seen anything so beautiful in all her life. And the quiet snow kept falling while she had supper, and listened to some Christmas stories, and helped wrap packages. All those things Sally had done other years down in the South.

But never with snow coming down outside! So, when she took one last peep out the window, and then hopped into bed, Sally wasn't missing her old home any more. She was just smiling and thinking that her first Northern Christmas was going to be the most beautiful one she had ever known.

Don't Look!

DECEMBER 22

Don't look in the closets,
Or under the beds,
Or in any mysterious nook
Where things may be hidden—
It's simply forbidden
When Christmas is coming—
Don't look!

Don't take up a package
That comes in the mail,
And give it a squeeze or a shake,
To guess what's inside it
Before they can hide it—
It's really a Christmas
Mistake.

Don't listen at bedtime
To hear what they're saying,
Or peep in when doors are ajar.
Hold your ears, shut your eyes,
For a Christmas surprise
Is better on Christmas,
By far!

Last-Minute Shopping

DECEMBER 23

Holly and mistletoe,
Green boughs of pine,

Ribbons and wrappings,
And candles to shine;

Last-minute shopping's
The best kind of fun—

And it almost is Christmas
When all of it's done!

The Waiting Reindeer

DECEMBER 24

ONCE THERE was one little reindeer who wanted to grow up to be one of Santa Claus's reindeer.

So all through the year he was good as gold, eating such big meals—and going to bed so early —that he grew at a great rate.

"I'm plenty big enough to do some speedy pulling right now," he told himself as Christmas drew near. And every day he asked his mother if Santa Claus had sent for him.

"Why no, dear," his mother always said. "Not today."

Even on Christmas Eve at bedtime, Santa Claus had not sent for that eager little reindeer.

So up to bed he went, good as gold. But he could not go right to sleep. No, indeed. He sat bolt upright, looking out his window—and still hoping that Santa would stop by to get him.

He waited and waited and waited, his eyes wide open, and his heart thumping. And of course Santa Claus was waiting, too. He couldn't very well start out with that little reindeer awake and watching for him.

"It's way past starting time," Santa said at last. "And that little chap hasn't even nodded. I just don't know what to do!"

"I do," smiled Mrs. Santa Claus.

Then she whispered in Santa's ear.

"Why, yes," said Santa Claus thoughtfully. "He certainly is a good little reindeer—and he is growing big and strong. And yes, I do start out while my *own* reindeer are still awake—"

Then he picked up his telephone and called the little reindeer's house.

"Please send your little reindeer over to my place," he said to the little reindeer's mother. "He's still too little to help pull my sleigh, of course—but then he's just the size to ride along with me to get an idea of how we do things."

"I will, Santa Claus," said the little reindeer's mother. "I'll wake him up right away—"

But that, of course, she never had to do. Because that wide-awake, waiting little reindeer had heard the telephone ring, too. So, at that very moment he was on his way downstairs —his little hoofs tapping like reindeer hoofs on a roof—and the bells on his best collar jingling as merrily as the ones on Santa's sleigh.

The Second Christmas

DECEMBER 25

POLLY and David were twice as lucky as most boys and girls, because they had two Christmases every single year.

First they had the wonderful one at their own house, and then, just as they had settled down enough to eat a good, big breakfast—it was time to go to Grandfather's house.

There was a beautiful, shining tree there, too, and more presents and packages. There was Christmas dinner—with aunts and uncles and cousins all around the big, merry table—and Grandfather carving the enormous, steaming turkey, and Grandmother serving everything that goes with turkey.

What fun that second Christmas always was! Polly and David thought it was almost better than the one at home.

But one Christmas morning when they hopped out of bed, the world was so deep in snow that their daddy said he couldn't possibly get the car out of the garage—let alone drive out to the country.

"We can have fun right here," said Mother. "But first I'd better call Grandmother and tell her that we can't come today—"

"Oh!" whispered Polly. "I wish we hadn't wished for snow!"

"So do I," agreed David.

And they both stood sadly at the big front window, watching the snow and sleet, when suddenly—with the merry sound of sleighbells—a big sleigh came driving up to their door.

It was a bright red sleigh that looked very much like the one that Santa Claus drives, but it was pulled by two horses that looked exactly like Grandfather's Dobbin and Gray.

And when the driver hopped out, all lively and quick, who should he be—but Grandfather himself!

"I started at dawn," he chuckled. "The minute I remembered the old sleigh out in the carriage house. So come along now, we'll have to hurry to get back there in time for dinner—"

In a wink, everyone was bundled up and out in that big red sleigh. Polly held her new doll in her arms. David held his best new car. Mother and Daddy held armfuls of presents. And Grandfather held the reins, as away they went—bells jingling and snow flying—to their wonderful second Christmas, after all.

Imagine That!

DECEMBER 26

It's the day after Christmas,
And all through the house
New toys by the dozen!
But still as a mouse,

Tommy is napping—
As little boys do—
With a Teddy that's sheddy,
And not at all new.

Sir Mortimer Burt

DECEMBER 27

In olden days, when knights rode forth,
To keep from getting hurt
They all wore armor, all except
The bold Sir Mortimer Burt.

Said Sir Mortimer Burt
(Also known as The Fearless),
"Armor? I cannot abide it.
I'd rather be bruised
By a blow from without—
Than from bumping around
*   when inside it!"*

Why, Mr. Skunk!

DECEMBER 28

ONE COLD, dark, blustery afternoon when Mr. Skunk went out for his evening paper, he found a little lost baby. It was out in the snow with no hat or coat, and so little that it couldn't even tell where it lived.

"Never mind," said kind Mr. Skunk. "I'll just bundle you up in my warm muffler and find your house for you—"

But before he could even undo his muffler, all the doors on the street were flung open, and all his neighbors began scolding him!

"Why, Mr. Skunk!" cried Mrs. Squirrel. "Your poor baby will freeze! Here, put this warm coat on it at once!"

"Why, Mr. Skunk!" scolded Mrs. Chipmunk. "You know your baby shouldn't be out in the snow with no boots! Catch these and put them on it!"

"Why, Mr. Skunk!" called Mrs. Possum. "Hurry and put this warm cap on your baby, and these mittens. You must have taken leave of your senses to bring it out like that!"

What a hubbub! Poor Mr. Skunk never even had a chance to explain that it wasn't his baby.

He just stood there bundling it up, and saying, "But it's—but it's—but it's—" over and over, until Mrs. Cat opened her door.

"Why, Mr. Skunk!" she cried. "Do you know it's two below zero today? This is no day to take your baby out walking!"

Then, just by chance, Mrs. Cat took a better look at the baby that Mr. Skunk had found.

"Muffy!" she squealed. "Why, it's my own little Muffy! I left her safely asleep on the sofa when I went in the kitchen to make our supper!"

And down the steps she ran, to pick up her baby and carry it into her warm house.

"Thank you very much for bringing Muffy home, Mr. Skunk," she called back. "You were just wonderful to find her."

"Yes, you were, Mr. Skunk," the neighbors all agreed. "You are a hero! But why, oh why, didn't you tell us it wasn't even your baby?"

"You never gave me a chance to explain," said Mr. Skunk. And down the blustery street he went for his paper, secretly thinking that perhaps tomorrow night his picture would be in it—as the brave, modest hero who had found Mrs. Cat's little lost baby in the snow.

Pretend

DECEMBER 29

I wish there were people
As small as a mouse,
To live like a family
In my new dolls' house:
To open the cupboards,
And walk on the stairs,
And sit down for supper
In these little chairs.
They'd have tiny voices,
But maybe some day,
If I stayed so quiet,
I might hear them say,
"Isn't this cozy—
And weren't we wise—
To find us a house
That's exactly our size!"

The New Tool Box

DECEMBER 30

JIMMY's best present was a fine, new tool box, with all kinds of tools in it. But he had no wood to saw and hammer nails into, and all that

"I wish I had some wood, Daddy," Jimmy said on Christmas afternoon. And his daddy said, "Yes, we'll have to get you some, Jimmy— but not today, of course."

The next day, when Daddy was reading his paper, Jimmy said he wished he had some wood again—and again Daddy said, "Yes, but not now, Jimmy."

He said the same thing the next day.

And the day after that, when Jimmy said he wished he had some wood, his daddy said, "I have a wish, too. I wish you'd put your Christmas toys away. On the shelves in your room, or somewhere. It's getting so that a man can't walk in the living room."

"I know it, Daddy," Jimmy said. "And your wish and mine go right together—because what I want some wood for is to make some more shelves. Then I will have room in my room for all my toys—"

"Oh," said Daddy. "Oh, I see."

Then he laughed and said, "Well, come on, Jimmy—we'll go down to the lumberyard *now!*"

So away they went.

And after that, Daddy didn't mind having the Christmas toys in the living room a little while longer.

Because he and Jimmy were both down in the cellar.

And Daddy was just as busy showing Jimmy how to make toy shelves, as Jimmy was, sawing and hammering away with the tools from his fine, new tool box.

New Year's Eve

DECEMBER 31

This is New Year's Eve,
A magical time.
While we're asleep in bed,
The whole old year will disappear—
And there will come, instead,
A whole new year of winter days,
And spring, and summer, and fall,
And we'll wake up and start right in
And have fun in them all.

INDEX

FFGGHHII

Tonight, when I looked under the bed for my monster, I found this note instead.

So long, kid.
Gotta go.
Someone needs me
more than you do.

-Gabe

What?! Gabe was MY monster!
Nobody needed him more than me!

But someone sure DID need a monster – my little sister Emma.

Now that Emma slept
in a toddler bed,
she liked to…

…climb out,

roam the
house,

and play noisy games at night.

I knew a monster would keep her
in bed so she could fall asleep.

But not MY monster!
I *had* to get Gabe back.

I tiptoed across the hall to Emma's room.

She wasn't even there.

But Gabe was!
I gulped, zoomed across
the carpet, and leaped
onto Emma's bed before
Gabe could grab my toes.

"Gabe," I whispered.
"Please go back to our room.
I'll get Emma to sleep."

"You?!" he snorted.
"You're gonna
get her to sleep?
Ha! That's a good one!
But you know what?
I like you, kid, so I'll give you
three chances. If she's not
asleep, I'll be back!"

And Gabe
was gone.

Just then Emma toddled into the room.
She clearly needed a monster.

Maybe she didn't know how to get one.

But *I* did.

"Hey, Emma," I said.
"Let's play. Can you
knock on the floor?"

Emma knocked –
with a dinosaur.

It worked.
I heard some creaking
under Emma's bed.
Then something
sniffled.
It squelched
and dripped.

So far so good, I thought.
This monster sounds
scary enough for Emma.

But Emma kept on playing.

A slime-covered monster slid out.
It oozed toward Emma.

"Icky!" she laughed, wiping
one of the monster's noses.
"Icky! Wipe!"

Emma wasn't scared at all!

"Excuse me," I said to the mucus monster. "I didn't catch your name."

"By dabe is Agatha," she said through stuffed noses. "Tibe for bed, Ebba."

Emma giggled and wiped some more.

I knew this wouldn't work. "Thanks, Agatha. Nice try. But I think we need a monster with claws."

Agatha snuffled, and then she was gone.

"Emma," I coaxed again,
"knock, knock."

She knocked on the floor –
with a teapot this time –
and I heard more creaking.

Then a slippery tail
slithered out from
under the bed.

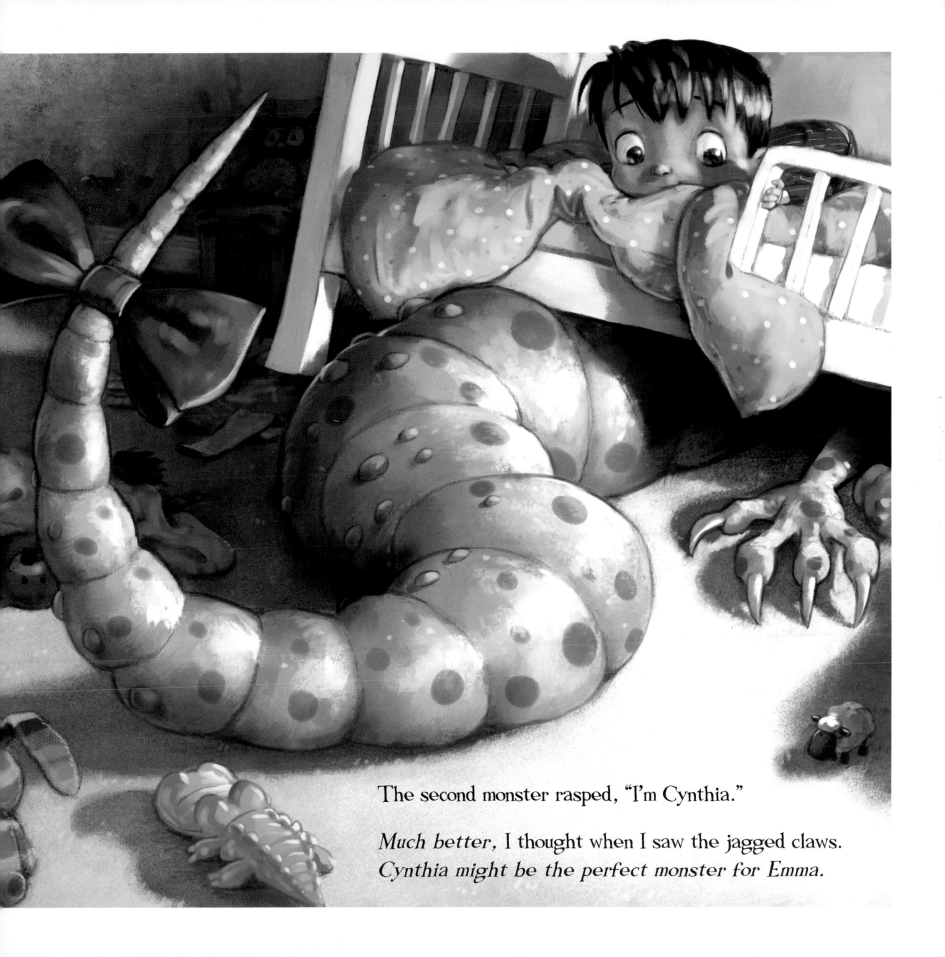

The second monster rasped, "I'm Cynthia."

Much better, I thought when I saw the jagged claws. *Cynthia might be the perfect monster for Emma.*

But Emma blinked and said, "Pretty!"

Then she decorated Cynthia's tail
with bracelets.

"Ugh," Cynthia snarled. "I'm not here to play dress up! I'm here to scare you into bed!" Cynthia rattled loudly, but Emma danced to the beat.

"I'm sorry, Cynthia," I said. "This isn't going to work."

"Well, I never!" she sniffed, and then she was gone.

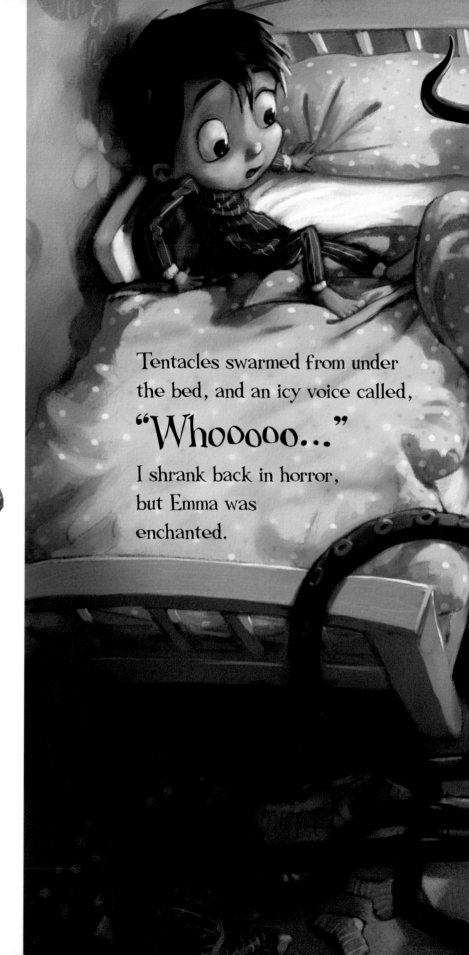

"Cymfia, come back!" Emma demanded, stomping on the floor.

Excellent, I thought.
Maybe **that** *would summon the perfect monster for Emma.*

Tentacles swarmed from under the bed, and an icy voice called,

"Whooooo..."

I shrank back in horror, but Emma was enchanted.

"Whooooo's out of bed?" the monster continued. "Come to Vla-a-adimir...."

Emma high-fived one of the tentacles, and the third monster emerged.

I already had doubts about this one, but he was my last chance.
"Vladimir," I asked, "can you get Emma to sleep?"

"Yes-s-s-s," he hissed, reaching for Emma. "I can GET her!"

Emma giggled and hopped over the tentacles like jump ropes.

"Oh, no!" I blurted. "She's not supposed to be having fun! This'll never work!"

Vlad's tentacles drooped, he slunk under the bed, and he was gone.

"Sorry, Vlad..." I called.

Boy, was I sorry. I was about to lose Gabe – forever.

Now Emma
was coloring.
And singing.
"Blabamir, bla, bla,
Cymfia, ya, ya,
Agafa, fa, fa...."

Gabe must have heard her,
because he was back.
"That's it, kid," he grunted.
"You had your three tries.
Now it's MY turn."

Gabe's green ooze sizzled across
the floor as he growled,

"Put. The crayon. Down."

Emma peered at my hulking, sharp-clawed monster and said, "Fuzzy."

"Hey, Gabe!" I cheered. "Emma isn't afraid of you!"

"*WHAT?!!*" Gabe burst out from under the bed and loomed over Emma. Steam spurted from his ears.

"Get.
Into.
Bed!"

Gabe thundered.

Emma hopped up. But she kept singing,
"Fuzzy, fuzzy monster."

"Gabe," I said, "Emma's not scared
enough to fall asleep. Please, let's
go back to our room."

"No can do, kid," Gabe growled. "I may not be the perfect monster for Emma, but I'm
the best so far. At least she's in bed now. I gotta stay here. You're on your own."

I knew Emma needed Gabe, but he was MY monster.
How was I ever going to get to sleep without him?

Just then, we heard a tiny noise.

hic.

hic.

hic.

Emma froze. Gabe and I peered
under the bed.

"Stella, what are *you* doing here?" Gabe asked.

"Hi, Gabe," Stella said, tugging on her tutu. "You forgot –*hic*– your snack. Mama thought –*hic*– you'd be hungry, so she –*hic*– sent this."

Who knew? Gabe had a little sister too!

I thought Stella's hiccups were cute, but Emma obviously didn't.

Stella sure noticed. She tiptoed closer, hiccupping with every step.

hic. hic. hic.

From under her covers, Emma squeaked, "SHOO!"

"Shoo?" Stella repeated.
"Oh! Shoe! That's where
toes go. I *loooove* toes."
Stella crept toward
Emma's feet.

Emma squealed,
scrunched in her feet,
and giggled,
"No toes,
no toes!"

Gabe laughed. "Stella, it looks like you're the perfect monster for Emma. Now, if you don't mind, *you* can get her to sleep while *I* get back to what *I* do best."

Stella nodded. *"Hic!"*